WHATEVER IT TAKES

MICHAEL PRESTON

PRESTON MEDIA

First edition 2025

ISBN: 979-8-9927285-0-7 Digital

ISBN: 979-8-9927285-1-4 Paperback

Published in the United States of America

This book is dedicated to Dora Chavez, who at the age of one hundred and one, is an inspiration to us all.

ACKNOWLEDGEMENTS

The author would like to gratefully acknowledge the contribution of Brandi Badgett as a beta reader and editor of this novel. Without her suggestions, this novel would be nowhere near as polished. Also, beta readers Debbie Frank and Rodney McWilliams for their valuable suggestions. And the advice of so many in the chat groups who have helped me navigate the treacherous waters of self publishing.

Contents

CHAPTER 1

The enemy might be anywhere and everywhere. If you wanted to survive, the rule was to stay out of sight in one of the many bombed-out buildings lining the street. However, that wasn't an option when Abu Osama al-Tunisi, the commander defending the city of Raqqa, Syria, wanted to see you.

Kaina al-Badawi hurried down a rubble-strewn street towards the ruined city center, the air catching in her throat as she cursed the long black skirt that threatened to trip her as she ran. Despite her small stature, slightly over five feet tall, she moved with a cat-like grace, gliding over the rough terrain. Physical training was required at the camps, resulting in her body being all muscle under her clothing. Her abilities outshone most men's—she ran faster, jumped higher, and fought better.

At nineteen, she possessed natural beauty, without makeup. High cheekbones framed a slender nose, while her dark eyes and olive skin complemented her long black hair. Even though she was at a suitable age for marriage, the thought disgusted her. After what she had been through, she couldn't imagine falling in love with anyone. That would require an amount of trust she was incapable of providing. Besides that, during the five years she had lived with al-Tunisi, he repeatedly pounded into her head that outside of the camps, she should do nothing to draw attention to herself. The mission depended on it.

Despite the early hour, the relentless sun's heat made her sweat under her black niqab. She hated wearing it. In her opinion, it was just one more way men oppressed women. Her veil covered everything except her eyes, making breathing difficult while she ran. But she adjusted it to keep it from falling below her chin as she pressed on. Even a minor infraction of the strict dress code imposed by ISIS could result in a flogging.

She followed a street that was once a primary artery into the old city. Faded posters praising the leaders of ISIS dotted once-grand buildings full of history. The city was their capital, the last stronghold of a once extensive empire. At present, the street resembled a war zone, with the scent of smoke and gunpowder overpowering amid two feet of debris. She hugged the walls of the destroyed buildings while moving, using them as cover against snipers the Syrian Democratic Forces (SDF) had deployed in the area. The snipers would shoot anyone, regardless of gender or age. In the distance, she could hear automatic weapons and the occasional thump of an incoming mortar round.

The Battle of Raqqa started two months earlier, on June 6th. Abu Osama al-Tunisi, the ISIS fundamentalist commander, arrogantly taunted the ragtag coalition forces of the SDF, claiming that the city was unconquerable. Over four thousand fighters had been preparing for months, digging deep trenches and tunnels connecting major strong points. His troops were battle-hardened fanatics, ready to die for Allah. They would make quick work of any SDF attack.

Despite his personnel advantage, Kaina felt he underestimated the powerful and precise firepower of the U.S. Special Forces, who hammered his positions with artillery and aerial bombing campaigns. Each day, they faced an endless supply of death raining down upon them without mercy. With no air force or long-range artillery, his men had no power to prevent it.

There was nowhere safe for Kaina to hide. The coalition forces systematically destroyed al-Tunisi's once-impregnable positions, reducing them to nothing more than rubble, and forcing his remaining troops to retreat towards the city center. Today, ISIS controlled forty-five percent of the city, tomorrow it would be less.

Near the Uwais al-Qarni Mosque, a bunker provided shelter for Kaina and ten other women after intense fighting the previous day demolished their previous hiding spot. An hour prior, a mujahideen soldier had appeared at the bunker, announcing his orders were to bring her to the headquarters of al-Tunisi.

Kaina recognized the mujahideen. She had seen him with the commander several times. Gathering up her few remaining belongings, she meekly followed him out of the bunker into the danger outside. A small cloth bag, slung over her shoulder, carried all her possessions: a change of clothing, a copy of the Qur'an, a comb, a pistol, a rudimentary first aid kit, and a chunk of bread, all the food she had left to eat.

She wondered about al-Tunisi's sudden desire to meet, but refrained from asking questions. It wasn't her place to do so, and it might infuriate the mujahideen. The soldiers viewed women as property, and they had no rights.

During their last meeting, al-Tunisi had ordered her to stay out of harm's way once the fighting started. Losing her to a stray bullet after all the time and resources invested in her training was unthinkable. So she had hidden in bunkers with the other women when she could have been fighting alongside the soldiers. But what did that matter now? The SDF surrounded the city, backed up by the American infidels. The fool should have let her leave months ago when it was easy to disappear without a trace. Her options now were death or surrender. It only remained a question of when.

Emerging from the bunker, the mujahideen scanned the buildings ahead, watching for any sign of movement or the glint of sunlight reflecting off metal. Either would indicate the presence of a sniper. The front lines were only a few blocks away, and the enemy could have easily infiltrated down one of the many narrow alleyways that honeycombed the area.

Kaina stood by, waiting for instructions, even though she knew what to do. She had spent years at hidden ISIS training centers scattered throughout Syria and Iraq, learning how to shoot weapons, infiltrate camps, and follow people without being seen. If granted a two-minute advantage, she could vanish without a trace amidst the rubble of Raqqa, leaving the mujahideen clueless. *Do nothing to draw attention to yourself.*

Because they didn't understand why they should train a woman, the instructors at the training centers treated the only female with disdain. Survival depended on determination and outperforming the men. The training came naturally to her. She grew up as a foster child in situations where the less you were noticed, the better off you were. The instructors couldn't ignore her skills, and a grudging respect eventually replaced the disdain.

She felt a great satisfaction in earning their respect. It was the first time anyone had shown her that in her entire life. She was part of a noble cause to restore Islam to its rightful place, ruling the Middle East through ISIS. Allah would guide and protect her.

The mujahideen turned to her and frowned. "Do you know the way to the National Hospital?"

"Yes, of course. I've been there many times."

He looked annoyed at her answer. "If so, you were there solely to assist the jihad, as per the commander's orders. Do not pretend otherwise. We're going there now. Stay behind me. There are areas we must pass through that aren't secure. If I'm killed or wounded, continue without me. Show this to anyone who challenges you." He removed a piece of paper from his pocket and pressed it into her hand. "This will give you safe passage."

Turning his back to her, he scanned the street one more time. Satisfied there was no immediate danger, he started ahead. His gaze lingered on the broken windows, searching for any enemy who might be lurking. Loose stones rattled away as he stepped on them. She trailed behind, knowing that any snipers in the area would hear them coming.

Chapter 2

The alley made her nervous. The narrow, lengthy space felt claustrophobic. Tall, two-story buildings lined each side, with no windows on the first floors. If snipers were ahead, set up to shoot down the alley, they were sitting ducks, with nowhere to hide.

Sweeping her eyes side to side, she watched the blown-out windows on the second floors for movement. One grenade dropped out of a window would kill them both. The sun hovered near its zenith, scorching Kaina in her black niqab as she trailed her guide through the alley toward the National Hospital.

The alley emptied into a quiet neighborhood square, once bustling with merchants selling goods at the market. Except for a thin stray dog that barked at them and vanished into a building, the square appeared deserted. From their position in the shadows, the mujahideen surveyed the terrain ahead. Kaina crowded up behind him and studied the square.

In the recent past, someone had subjected it to heavy shelling. Bomb craters littered a plaza surrounded by small houses. Four streets ran off north/south and east/west. A burned-out tank occupied the middle of the road heading north; its cannon pointed up at the sky. All the houses suffered some damage, and several had received direct hits, reducing them to rubble. The smell of charred wood and burned flesh hung in the air.

"The Americans forced us back by bombing the square last night," he said. "When I passed through this morning, nobody was here. That may no longer be true. If the enemy has come, that dog gave away our position. To reach the hospital, we need to use that street." He pointed to the road on his right. Kaina now understood why the mujahideen had chosen the alley. It afforded the closest access to the street.

She stretched her neck out to view the terrain they would have to cross. Several destroyed homes sat lined up along the plaza between them and the street. In a pinch, they could duck inside the ruins for cover. If someone didn't shoot them the moment they left the alley. Every sniper hidden around the square could have his gun trained on it, just waiting for them to make a move.

The mujahideen made his decision. "I will go first. When I reach the street, I'll signal and provide cover while you run to me as fast as possible. If I am wounded or killed, seek an alternative path to the hospital. Allah will take care of me. You must reach the commander."

Kaina nodded her understanding. Willing to sacrifice himself to carry out his orders, he was acting as bait to determine the enemy's presence and protect her. He stood, stretching his legs. Then he was gone, zig-zagging down the sidewalk toward the street. She watched the square's distant edge for any signs of movement.

The mujahideen reached the building next to the street without difficulty and disappeared inside. She gathered up her belongings and got ready to run on his signal. Suddenly, out of the corner of her eye, she detected movement near the other side of the plaza, along the street running west. As she watched, soldiers approached in a skirmish line, taking advantage of the available cover. A flash of light reflected off a metal object above them in the sky. *It's a drone.*

There was no time to waste. She bolted out of the alley, hugging the ruined buildings while running, trying to stay invisible to the drone. In a few moments, she reached the surprised mujahideen.

"Why did you not wait for my signal?" he growled.

"No time," she gasped, out of breath. "Soldiers are at the entrance to the square on the west street. We must leave quickly. They have a drone."

Drones were a feared weapon of the SDF. They went anywhere, flying high enough to be invisible to someone on the ground. Operators launched missiles from most of them when they found a target. In seconds, you would be dead without even knowing what was coming. The best defense against them was to stay out of sight.

Eyes narrowing, the mujahideen scowled, cursing the drone. "We must run now. Don't worry about snipers. Try to stay hidden from the drone."

As they moved up the street, hugging the buildings, she had a thought. *Would the enemy waste a missile on only two soldiers?* She didn't want to find out.

After another hour of zig-zag traveling, they arrived at the al-Naim roundabout in the city center. Burned-out cars lined the sides of the street, bomb craters were everywhere, and no building remained undamaged. Despite the destruction, the statue of a long-forgotten patriot stood untouched amidst it all. The area looked deserted, but Kaina knew better. Many men were hiding in the ruined buildings.

The mujahideen slowed his pace, perhaps feeling safe from snipers. Kaina, her body covered in sweat from her hot garments, was grateful for the break. Their destination lay a short distance ahead.

CHAPTER 3

Women weren't welcome here. She felt the soldier's eyes upon her as she moved toward the hospital. But since she traveled with the mujahideen, they let her pass. Everyone knew he reported to the commander.

The National Hospital stood on the opposite side of the round-about. The building was a compact two-story structure with a basement, serving as the headquarters for the ISIS command staff. Artillery fire had damaged the second floor, leaving gaping holes in the roof. Shrapnel pockmarked the walls. Al-Tunisi's most loyal soldiers guarded the sandbagged entrance.

The pair cleared the last checkpoint and entered the hospital. Weak sunlight filtered through broken windows, struggling to reach inside. Dark shadows filled the room's corners as they made their way to the stairs leading down to the basement. The mujahideen stopped and whispered to a soldier who stood guard there. The soldier nodded and disappeared down the stairway.

Kaina knew the floor plan well. Its basement offered unique protection against enemy shelling. Al-Tunisi's office and living quarters were located to the right of the stairs. A communications center, filled with radios, stood to the left, followed by a large room stacked with ammunition. If the American shells ever reached it, the resulting explosion would kill everyone within fifty yards of the hospital. It made her nervous, knowing that every time she visited was a gamble with her life. The rest of the basement was a barracks where soldiers would huddle during bombardments. Lit with flickering kerosene lamps, it reeked of sweat and mold. It also housed a large population of rats, who tormented anyone working there.

The soldier returned and beckoned the mujahideen to follow him. The smell grew progressively worse as they descended the stairs, turning right at the bottom. Kaina choked down the bile rising in her throat. She had forgotten how bad it was. After a quick knock, they heard a muffled order to enter. The soldier pushed the door open, gesturing for the mujahideen and Kaina to enter. He did not follow, letting the door slam shut behind them with a dull thud.

A flickering lamp cast eerie shadows throughout the room. A few tattered chairs, their once-vibrant upholstery now dull and threadbare, sat near a desk at the rear of the room. The black flag of ISIS hung on the dingy wall behind it. Someone had tacked a city map to a side wall, with pins designating the front lines. A military cot, covered with a ragged blanket, occupied a corner. No one could determine the original color of the neglected, dusty brown linoleum floor. An AK-47, its barrel glinting in the light, rested against the edge of the desk.

A middle-aged man with piercing eyes stared at them from behind the desk. The deep lines on his face spoke of a life spent battling the relentless desert sun. A scraggly white beard covered his chin and crept up the sides of his cheeks. His once jet-black hair was now white and thinning. On his head was a black turban, stained with sweat and dust. A faint odor of tobacco hung in the surrounding air.

As they approached, the man stood up to greet them. He was thin, of average height, and his uniform gave no indication of his rank. Despite this, he had an unmistakable commanding presence, leaving no doubt of his importance.

The mujahideen placed his hand over his heart and gave a slight bow. "Abu Osama al-Tunisi, I've brought the woman here as you commanded. Thanks be to Allah. How else may this humble servant be of service?"

The commander stepped from behind his desk and shook the mujahideen's calloused hand. "Brother, you've done a great service to the cause. I feared that you wouldn't find her in all the chaos. Please wait outside while I talk with her."

The mujahideen's face remained impassive. After a quick appraising glance at Kaina, he bowed again and left the room.

Al-Tunisi gestured to a chair and returned to sit behind his desk. Fatigued from the long march, Kaina sat down and observed the commander. She recalled arriving with him when the supreme commander gave him command of Raqqa after he led his victorious troops into Mosul. Raqqa was the capital of the caliphate and needed to be held at all costs. In those days, the enemy was far away, giving him time to build up the city's defenses. He appeared to have aged twenty years since then. Kaina guessed his age as forty-five, but he looked closer to sixty. The last seven months hadn't been kind to him.

She realized she sat across the table from a tired and humbled man. Most of his adult life he spent fighting for ISIS, moving up the ranks as he proved himself in battle. Overconfident in his abilities, he had failed to anticipate the Americans' impact on the battle. There was nothing he could do now but watch helplessly as, block by block, they reduced Raqqa to rubble. The most sophisticated weapons his troops had left were rocket-propelled grenades and armored suicide vehicles packed with explosives, which volunteers would attempt to drive into enemy lines and detonate. Rarely did they achieve success.

She had witnessed the bravery of his men when the SDF attacked their positions with tanks, but the truth was they were about to face a massacre. Years from now, people will remember the battle as ISIS' last stand, led by a scorned commander unable to fulfill his promises. She was desperate to get out of Raqqa before that happened.

Al-Tunisi cleared his throat, drawing her attention. "Kaina al-Badawi, thanks be to Allah that you are in good health. These days are hard for us, and many of my best soldiers have fallen. The time when our faith prevailed, and we governed over many, is gone."

He paused, and a smile flickered across his face. Perhaps he thought of those happier times. "I had hoped for more time to prepare you for the mission, but there isn't any. I've kept an eye on your development, and you've exceeded my expectations with each passing day. Many doubted your ability to become what you are, but that is no longer true. Very few men could have done better."

Bowing his head, a look of sadness crossed his face. "Keeping you here longer will serve no purpose. Allah has chosen you to strike a mighty blow against the infidels. It's time for you to leave the city and complete the mission."

How could she leave when the SDF surrounded the city? She kept her face a mask to hide her despair, saying nothing so as not to betray herself. *Had the strain of battle caused him to lose touch with reality?*

As though reading her thoughts, al-Tunisi continued. "The challenge lies in ensuring your safe exit from the city. The SDF has snipers everywhere, and I cannot risk losing you before your mission has even begun."

He lifted his head to gaze at her, and in that moment, she glimpsed his cunning. His eyes narrowed, and the ghost of a smile crossed his face. "However, an opportunity has presented itself. Tomorrow morning, we'll evacuate women and children from the city and hand them over to the infidels. They are using valuable resources better reserved for my men, and if they stay here any longer, the American bombs will kill them."

As if to emphasize his point, a muffled explosion shook the ground. Dust and debris fell from the ceiling, limiting visibility. Kaina thought of the ammunition stored nearby and held her breath. When nothing happened, she heard soldiers shouting outside the door, but no one entered. The dust cleared, and Kaina saw al-Tunisi still sitting in his chair, unperturbed by the near miss. He pointed his index finger at her.

"You'll be among them. Thousands will be leaving, so you will blend in with the crowd. Make sure the Americans question you and repeat exactly what you've been trained to say. Speak to no one else, for your safety. Once they verify your identity, they'll arrange for you to fly to the United States, where they will subject you to a more detailed interrogation. When that ends, your mission will begin, God willing. A man named Mohammad Mustafa will contact you with instructions."

"How will I find this man?"

"Do not try to find him. He will find you."

Kaina nodded, concealing her excitement. She was getting out of this hellhole, but would it be in time to accomplish her goals?

CHAPTER 4

Rising at dawn the following morning, Kaina kneeled on a prayer rug in the room al-Tunisi had provided. Closing her eyes, she bowed towards Mecca, experiencing the warmth of Allah's presence as she asked for His blessing for her safety and that of the women and children about to be delivered into enemy hands.

Upon arriving in this part of the world six years ago, Islam was a foreign concept to her, but she soon realized its importance to her survival. Non-believers were infidels, disciples of Satan, and never to be trusted. At first, she memorized the prayers to satisfy her captors. Later, she spent many hours studying passages of the Holy Qur'an and became a true believer. Outwardly, she showed qualities of a devout believer in Allah and the ISIS lifestyle. The first part was true, the second was not.

Although ISIS professed to fight for the oppressed, the way they treated women was appalling. Their men regarded women as property, subject to their whims. Despite being reminded daily of her worthlessness, her spirit remained uncrushed. No one was a piece of property. Six years of slavery had taught her that. During those years, she had endured more than she thought possible and kept herself going by thoughts of revenge. These thoughts she kept to herself. Any show of defiance would have cast suspicion upon her and pierced the facade that she was a true believer in ISIS. *Do nothing to draw attention to yourself.*

After waiting years for an opportunity to escape, she was so close to it happening. A frightened thirteen-year-old with a poor attitude six years ago versus a confident nineteen-year-old killing machine now. She was one last step away from freedom, assisted, ironically, by those she most despised.

The rumble of engines grew loud outside her window as the convoy formed. She heard snatches of nervous conversations mixed with the slamming of car doors. Outside the window, she saw a convoy of cars, trucks, and buses stretching for miles. Al-Tunisi was emptying the city of civilians. Those left behind were expected to fight to the death.

A soft knock on her door interrupted her thoughts. The mujahideen stood there, his face expressionless. The moment to depart had arrived. She followed three steps behind him, her bag slung over her shoulder, down the stairs to the ground floor. When they reached it, he stopped and turned to face her. "Go to the fifth car in line. Talk to no one. May the blessings of Allah be upon you."

Kaina nodded to signify she understood, adjusted her veil to cover all but her eyes, and walked out the front door. Al-Tunisi remained out of sight. She understood why. She had to avoid attracting attention from fellow travelers and enemy spies. They would notice if al-Tunisi singled her out to say farewell. They might mention it to the SDF to curry favor. She existed as just another refugee, her presence marked only by the faint smell of sweat and desperation.

She was on her own now. No one could rescue her if the Kurds detained her, or if she said the wrong thing to the Americans. She felt a strange mixture of joy at being free, and fear of the future.

A tense silence fell over the soldiers as women and children boarded the vehicles. Despite the temporary ceasefire agreement, a sense of unease flowed among them. Both sides had broken similar agreements before. The convoy contained three thousand civilians, and it stretched for miles—a prime target for the American artillery.

The moment Kaina reached the fifth car in line, the driver, smoking a vile-smelling Turkish cigarette, approached.

"Who are you?" he asked.

"Kaina al-Badawi."

"I was told to expect you. Get in."

She placed her bag in the trunk and wedged herself into the sedan's backseat amid icy stares from the other three women in the car. The cramped space forced her to sit sideways between two women, their knees touching. No one spoke. The city was so quiet it seemed like a ghost town, a stark difference from the usual sounds of explosions and gunfire. An hour later, a flare arched overhead, and the caravan started a slow journey toward enemy lines.

The burning mid-day heat radiating from the ground was causing the desert air to shimmer in the distance when the convoy slowed to a stop a few miles outside of Raqqa. The journey to leave the city seemed like an endless maze, taking hours to escape its grasp. Navigating through rubble-filled streets required frequent stops to clear a path or find detours around bomb craters.

For Kaina, the trip was torture. She was shoe-horned between two women in a hot car with no air conditioning. The woman on her left was about her age. Tears ran down the corners of her eyes above her veil. Kaina guessed she was leaving someone important behind, perhaps her husband, whom she might never see again. The other woman appeared old from the look of her gnarled hands and the deep wrinkles around her eyes. She sat stoically without saying a word.

Scowling Kurdish fighters belonging to the SDF surrounded the convoy. "Get out of the car," shouted a uniformed soldier with a bullhorn.

When the women heard the shouted orders to exit the cars, they flung open the doors and scrambled out. Gratitude overwhelmed Kaina as she stretched her cramped legs to recover from the numbness and savored the sensation of a gentle breeze cooling her sweaty skin. In front of her, hundreds of burlap tents and Quonset huts were scattered about, creating a small city. A barbed wire fence surrounded the entire camp, connected to guard towers in each corner. No other buildings were within sight, just a parched, desolate landscape of sand devoid of life. *Even if you escaped, there was nowhere to go.*

CHAPTER 5

The soldiers herded the refugees inside the fence towards several tables and told them to form lines. Nothing in Kaina's training had prepared her for this. Behind the tables sat soldiers from the Kurdish Women's Protection Units, known as the YPJ, made up entirely of women. The Kurds allowed them to fight, and the YPJ had a reputation for ruthlessness. Many were widows, their husbands killed battling ISIS.

Total chaos broke out when the prisoners began to converse and strategize about which line to join. After being crammed into hot cars all day, the women's strong body odor overwhelmed the senses. The guards waded into the mob, shoving and clubbing the prisoners until they were all in line.

At the front of the line, each prisoner was asked the same questions: name, age, tribal affiliation, names of relatives who might be here, etc. Based on their answers, the guard decided on the prisoners' housing assignment. Behind each table, squads of soldiers stood by to escort the prisoners to their new quarters. They beat anyone who protested.

A shoulder-high platform raised above the ground stood off to the side in the distance. Wooden steps led up to it. Above the platform, a large beam ran across its length. Kaina had seen this before. It functioned as a gallows. If her ISIS mission became known, they would hang her there as a spy.

Kaina picked a table staffed by a young Kurd about her age, hoping to elicit sympathy. She needed to believe Kaina's story. Otherwise, her mission would fail right there. As the line inched forward, the guard became more impatient, asking fewer questions. Kaina would have to state her case quickly to avoid being sent off with all the others. Eventually, she stood face-to-face with the young girl.

"Name?" asked the bored Kurd.

Stay calm. "I am called Kaina al-Badawi, although that's not my true name."

"You are Bedouin?" she said, referring to her last name.

"No. The Daesh kidnapped me six years ago and sent me here. My real name is Natalie Martinez, and I'm an American."

The Kurd looked at her sharply, no longer bored. "American? So you say. Everyone wants to go to America. What proof do you have?"

"I have no papers. The Daesh took everything from me. But I can provide the address where I lived, and the Americans here can verify it," she said.

"You are a liar. Why would the Daesh want you?"

Kaina looked at the ground, embarrassed. "A sheik in Bahrain bought me as a slave when I was thirteen. He liked young girls for sex. After a year, he grew tired of me and sold me to Abu Osama al-Tunisi."

The mention of the name had the desired effect.

"Do you know al-Tunisi?"

"Yes, I've been his property for five years, living in his household."

After some thought, the young Kurd reached a decision. "We will find out if you are American and know al-Tunisi." She signaled to a soldier standing nearby. "Take this one to thirty-two for further interrogation."

Kaina felt the pressure she was under ease and gave an inward sigh of relief. She had passed the initial test, saying just enough to be referred to someone higher in the chain of command. Al-Tunisi told her to mention his name to the Kurds. They despised him because he had taken part in the massacre of the inhabitants of several Kurdish villages the previous year.

Because of this, anyone providing details on his movements would be of interest. How much detail she would provide, Kaina hadn't yet decided. Her relationship with al-Tunisi was complicated. Although treated well from the time she arrived at his camp, he trained her to be a jihadist, a tool of ISIS, to strike at the heart of America. He had tried to instill in her mind that America was an evil place, the home of Satan. The Americans had sold her to the sheik. And how was her life before that?

The soldier searched her, making sure she had no weapons, before marching her to a more remote area of the camp. Eventually, they arrived at the entrance to a large Quonset hut with thirty-two stenciled on the door. The hut looked new. Inside it, another soldier sat behind a table and inspected the papers handed to her by Kaina's guard.

As soon as she stepped inside the hut, the heat washed over her. It felt like she had stepped into an oven. Lacking air conditioning, the guard relied on a fan to cool herself, but there was no relief for the prisoners. The smell reminded her of the basement of the National Hospital.

A well-lit passage extended behind the soldier to the rear of the hut. Rows of sturdy steel doors lined the passage. Small windows on each door allowed Kaina to glimpse women looking out. She realized this must be the camp jail.

The guard behind the desk sniffed. "Another claiming to be American. If you lack proof, you'll be with the rest of the Daesh scum in here until we have killed every one of them," she stated, motioning towards the cells.

Kaina remained silent, not wanting to say anything to irritate the woman. She was only a clerk, not the next official in line to interrogate her.

Realizing she could not goad Kaina into saying something stupid, the guard pushed her chair back with a loud scrape and stood up. She wore the tan uniform of the YPJ and had a pistol strapped to her hip. Grabbing a ring of keys from the desk, she took Kaina by the arm and led her to a vacant cell.

Jammed into the back corner, a sagging cot, covered with a thin blanket, served as her bed. She guessed the bucket on the floor across from the cot was for relieving herself. A single, empty shelf hung from the front wall next to the door. Under it stood a small metal table bolted to the floor. A battered three-legged wooden stool hid under the table.

The cell's walls were smooth and twelve feet high. A chain-link fence stretched horizontally from wall to wall, taking the place of a ceiling. Above the fence, a guard armed with an AK-47 patrolled a catwalk. Industrial lights hung from the hut's ceiling, illuminating the cells.

"This is your new home," the guard said. "Probably a lot nicer than your old one." She shoved her inside and laughed as the door slammed shut. The key turned in the lock, and the guard's footsteps faded away.

Kaina sat on the cot's edge, caressed the rough blanket, and released a deep sigh. Hopefully, the prisoners were allowed outside during the day to enjoy fresh air away from the stifling cells. If not, sitting here with nothing to do would drive her mad. Yet, the guard's remark was accurate. This was a lot nicer than her old home. Nobody was trying to kill her.

CHAPTER 6

The whistle blew, and the guards shouted to the prisoners to prepare for inspection. Cell doors were unlocked, and the prisoners were ordered to stand at attention outside their door. A guard stalked down the row of cells, counting bodies. When she confirmed no one had escaped during the night, the guards herded everyone toward the prisoner's washroom at the back area of the hut.

Upon entering the washroom, an older woman handed each prisoner a plain, white towel, rough to the touch, and a sliver of soap with a faint clinical scent. The sound of running water filled the room as the prisoners rushed toward the sinks and showers. Kaina stopped inside the entrance, uncertain if a protocol needed to be followed. She felt a jolt as the woman behind bumped into her.

"Why are you stopping?" the woman asked.

"Forgive me, it's my first day here. I don't know the procedure," Kaina replied.

"You better learn quick, or you'll miss your opportunity and smell like a camel for the remainder of the day," she said. "There's no procedure. Either wash at the sink or take a shower. When you're done, return to your cell and wait for breakfast. The guards give us only an hour. If you're late getting back, they will beat you."

"Thank you, sister. You're very kind. What's your name?"

"Aisha."

"I'm Kaina."

Kaina took a quick shower, despite not bringing her spare clothing with her. Tomorrow, she would know better. Forty minutes later, she was back in her cell, awaiting developments.

The best outcome imaginable, although unlikely, was being granted another interview that day, conducted by an American who would help corroborate her story. Al-Tunisi warned her it might be a lengthy process. A bureaucrat in America would send out inquiries to local officials able to confirm her story. The replies would travel up and down the chain of command, eventually reaching the Americans here. She couldn't do anything to hasten the process. Meanwhile, she would use her time to learn more about the camp and the guards.

The next whistle blew, indicating the time to line up for breakfast. The prisoners filed through an open door at the back of the building to an outdoor quad with a dirt floor. Multiple picnic tables stood next to each other in the dirt. The ground was dry and cracked, devoid of vegetation, radiating the heat from the sun. Barbed wire surrounding the quad was foreboding. Each corner contained a watchtower from which armed guards watched everything. She hugged herself, feeling trapped and isolated. A tin shed served as the kitchen in one corner, where each prisoner got a plate of food and hot tea.

Outside the fence, women's chatter filled the air around the tents she had seen the day before. Inside that camp, movement appeared unrestricted. She was envious. In Raqqa, she took the freedom to move about for granted. Here, she could go only where the Kurds took her.

Kaina took her plate of food, which was better than anything she had eaten in Raqqa in the last month, and spotted Aisha sitting alone at a table. She would be an excellent source of information about the camp and the guards. As she walked over, Aisha greeted her with a smile.

"May I sit with you, sister?"

"Of course," Aisha said.

"Thank you for helping me this morning. The guards told me nothing. They threw me in the cell and treated me like trash."

Aisha made a face. "They're all hardcore YPJ, who would just as soon see us dead. Only the Americans keep them from slaughtering us all. Did you arrive with the convoy yesterday?"

"Yes, there were many of us."

"They've been enlarging the camp for a week to accommodate everyone. How are things in Raqqa?"

"Not well. The SDF takes more territory every day. The Americans bomb everything while the mujahideen fight until they've nothing left to give. We left to ensure enough food and medicine for the soldiers. How long have you been here?"

"Twenty-nine days. I was living in the al-Mashlab neighborhood when the Americans bombed it overnight. The next day, the SDF launched a sudden and powerful attack, seizing our positions. The Kurds captured me before I could flee. I expected to be shot and buried in an unmarked grave, but they brought me here instead. Why are you here instead of with everyone else?"

"I'm not sure," Kaina said carefully. "I told them I was al-Tunisi's slave, so they must think I know useful information about him as if he would confide anything to a mere slave. Why are you here?"

"A case of mistaken identity. A soldier claimed to recognize me and said I was a spy for ISIS. There's no way to prove otherwise, so here I sit. If I slept with him, he promised to change his story, but I would never have sex with a Kurdish infidel." She sighed. "The YPJ might release me once the battle concludes."

"God willing. What happens to the others?" Kaina asked, waving at those beyond the fence.

"The Kurds determine which village they are from and send them back if possible. Otherwise, they get sent to a refugee camp up north, near the border with Turkey. This camp is a temporary solution. The Americans will dismantle it after the battle concludes. How did you end up as a captive of al-Tunisi? Is he truly as intelligent as people claim?"

Kaina concealed the true story. No one could know she was an American. She had rehearsed an alternate version with al-Tunisi many times.

She explained that her parents were Bedouins, very poor and starving, with two other children to feed. To buy food, they sold her for money. "Then I became Al-Tunisi's maid. I cleaned his house, washed his clothes, and cared for his children. We rarely spoke."

Aisha eyed her new friend. "You're beautiful. Didn't he want you in his bed?"

"No, it was beneath him to have sex with a slave. As a famous commander, he had his pick of anyone he desired. Women threw themselves on him every day, hoping for a favor. I was nothing."

"The soldiers would tell stories of his bravery in battle. Once, I saw his picture and thought he was tall and handsome. I imagined meeting him someday and becoming his wife," Aisha said.

The two sat at the picnic table the entire morning, chatting about camp gossip. The guards were in a good mood, and let everyone stay outside until the hot afternoon sun, and the lack of shade, drove them indoors.

Kaina lay on her cot and thought about her new friend. She wasn't sure she believed the story about being mistaken for a spy. The camp only held women prisoners, and men were prohibited from entering it. When would she have met this soldier who accused her?

Also, her description of al-Tunisi as tall and handsome wasn't right. He was of average height, and she didn't consider him especially attractive. But Aisha saw him in a photograph; perhaps someone touched it up to make him appear that way.

This proved nothing, but an uneasy feeling in her gut told her Aisha was not to be trusted.

Chapter 7

Kaina waited to be interrogated, the uncertainty of her situation becoming more stressful by the day. Did the Kurd soldier refer her case to someone of higher rank? Or did someone forget her claim, dooming her to a lengthy prison stay and the end of her mission?

Three days had passed, and she had yet to see an American. Time was slipping through her fingers. Outside the fence, the women who hadn't been detained for questioning walked around, chatting amongst themselves. Most appeared pleased to have escaped Raqqa. Every day, a convoy of trucks arrived and took some of them away, back to their clans. She sighed, envying them for the limited amount of freedom they had.

On her fourth day of captivity, she was pacing in the quad, feeling like a caged animal. The sun was straight overhead, burning down on her without mercy. A slight breeze brought the spicy smell of kibbeh being cooked to her nose. She had no appetite for food and was losing weight.

As a guard drew near, Kaina felt a rush of anticipation, her heart racing. Perhaps she was being summoned to the next interview.

"Come with me," the guard sneered as she grabbed her arm and led her outside the fence to a small weather-beaten Quonset hut nearby. Though it matched the other huts from the outside, inside, a frigid gust of cold air sent a shiver down her spine. The hut contained four rooms, two on each side of a central passage. Looking very comfortable, two guards were busy shuffling papers on a table inside the front door.

"This is Kaina al-Badawi," said the guard accompanying her to the hut.

A guard seated at the table nodded. "Take her to room two."

Her guard marched Kaina to the second door on the right. After a quick knock brought no response, the guard ushered her inside. The room was empty. A metal table occupied most of the space. Behind it sat two empty straight-backed chairs. Another chair faced the table from the opposite side. A camera mounted on the wall recorded everything.

The guard pointed to the third chair. "Sit."

Kaina did as she was told, trying to slow her racing heart. The guard turned and left her alone as the door clicked shut. The camera watched her silently.

Half an hour crawled by. The lone sound was the quiet hum of the air conditioning. Memories of walking into an air-conditioned room flooded back from Kaina's childhood in America. It ceased to exist in her life after her kidnapping. Having become accustomed to the heat of the desert, the room was freezing. A cup of hot tea to warm up would have been nice.

The scrape of the doorknob turning caused her heart to skip a beat. Two people, a man, and a woman, entered and sat across from her. The woman was middle-aged and dressed in the YPJ's uniform. Bronze eagles attached to her shirt collars indicated to Kaina that she was a major. Her black hair, tied tightly in a ponytail, framed a square face and tired eyes. In her right hand, she carried a brown briefcase.

The man wore civilian clothing, giving no hint of his importance. He wore a white cotton shirt tucked into khaki pants that looked worn and comfortable. He was about six feet tall, with a mop of unruly black hair cascading past his ears, touching a full beard covering his cheeks and upper lip. *Maybe an American,* thought Kaina, *with some Arab ancestors.*

The major spoke first. "You're Kaina al-Badawi?"

"Yes, but that's not my real name."

"We'll get to that," said the major, pulling a file from her briefcase. After studying it for a moment, her gaze returned to the prisoner. "You state that you're a slave of al-Tunisi?"

"That's correct."

"When did you become his slave?"

"Five years ago."

"When did you last see him?"

Kaina considered lying but realized many people might have seen her at the National Hospital before the evacuation. Al-Tunisi had said to be truthful whenever feasible. Every statement proven to be a lie lessens the likelihood of your story being believed.

"The day before the convoy arrived here," she replied.

"What was the purpose of your meeting?"

"He told me I was to be part of the convoy leaving Raqqa in the morning."

The major continued her questioning for another hour, asking only questions regarding al-Tunisi, and the strength of his army. When questioned about troop positions, Kaina evaded answering, arguing that she never had access to that information. The man stayed silent and seemed bored. Finally, the major grew frustrated with the lack of useful information and nodded to him.

He sat up straight, placing his arms on the table. "My name is Ali Nasser. I represent the United States government here in Raqqa, and my job is to evaluate your claim to be an American. Please share as many details about your life there as you can recall. Do you understand?"

He left a powerful impression on her. His Arabic was flawless, allowing him to blend in anywhere. In the right attire, he would pass for a mujahideen. Al-Tunisi said that America recruited these kinds of men to become spies. They worked for a department called the Central Intelligence Agency and should never be trusted.

"Yes, I understand."

"Very well. At what age were you taken?"

"Thirteen."

"Share your memories of that day with me."

"I grew up a homeless thirteen-year-old kid in Santa Barbara, California. My mother died when I was very young, and I never knew my father. I had no relatives to take care of me. The police found me and turned me over to Child Services. A woman came and picked me up. She said she would take me to her house until a foster home was available. When we arrived, she locked me in a bedroom. There were bars on the window, so I couldn't escape. The following day, a man named Frank showed up at the house. I didn't want to go with him, so they tied me up with duct tape and carried me out to his van. We drove around for a while, then he stopped. Another man took me in his car. He gave me a shot, and I fell asleep, so I don't know what happened after that."

Kaina noticed Ali leaning forward, fascinated by her story. The plan was unfolding smoothly.

"The next thing I remember was waking up on a small plane. Only two men, excluding me and the pilot, were aboard. No one would tell me our destination. I got angry and started throwing things, so they sedated me again. When I woke up, the plane was landing somewhere in the desert. A man forcibly removed me from the plane, and then some money changed hands. He handed me over to the people waiting for us. They covered my head with a hood, leaving me clueless about our destination. We drove to this big house that had walls all around it and guards with guns. The guards took me inside and said I belonged to Sheik Abdul-Wadid Diya al-Din. I had to do anything he wanted me to do, or they would kill me."

She paused. This was the part she dreaded telling, especially to a man. The pain she endured over and over for a year would always be fresh in her mind. Despite the chill in the air, sweat broke out on her brow, and she found it difficult to look at Ali. She clasped her hands tightly together and began.

"All he wanted from me was sex. He liked doing it with kids. The more I fought, the better he liked it, so I learned to let him do whatever he wanted without reacting. He used to beat me for that. After a year passed, he sold me to Abu Osama al-Tunisi. I became his maid and took care of his house and kids. I followed him whenever he moved, and we ended up in Raqqa. So here I am."

Ali thought for a moment. "Are you aware of the identity of the person from Child Services who brought you to her house?"

"I'll never forget that. Her name was Angela. The man who picked me up the following day was Frank. I never heard the other guy's name.

"Okay. This is a very unusual case, but you've given me solid information that should be easy to verify. I'll write up my report and get it off to Washington. It may take a while to contact the people who can verify your information."

He paused, deep in thought. "It's safer for you to stay in unit thirty-two for now. Most women here harbor strong hatred towards Americans. If they discover your true identity, they may try to kill you. Unit thirty-two is a more controlled environment. Once we confirm the truth of your story, we will arrange for your immediate evacuation. If you think of anything else, inform the guard you desire to speak with the major, not me. Don't tell anyone else this story. Meanwhile, enjoy not being shot at. You wouldn't have lasted much longer in Raqqa."

Ali nodded to the major, and they both exited. A heavy silence hung in the air before a guard appeared and led her back to her cell. Kaina's heart was full of hope. At last, she had spoken to an American.

CHAPTER 8

The late afternoon sun was so hot that even the scorpions stayed in the shade, but Kaina didn't want to go inside. She sat at one of the picnic benches in the quad, with the ever-present sand swirling around her ankles from a slight breeze. The brief moments outside the fence earlier that day had stirred a longing for freedom in her soul. She imagined herself free from all the constraints of her life, with the salty smell of the ocean filling her nose as she lay on a beach, seagulls crying in the distance, and no worries of any kind. But that wasn't reality.

The reality was being a POW in a Kurd camp, at the mercy of their every whim, constantly guarding against one slip of the tongue that would destroy her plan. Her goal was to stay alive long enough for the Americans to confirm her identity. Without an American rescue, she might be here for years and all her training would go to waste.

She replayed the interview with Ali in her mind, analyzing every word for mistakes, but found none. Al-Tunisi had pounded the story into her brain to the point it became automatic. It needed to be presented in a way that evoked sympathy. Focus attention on her abduction, which, when proven true, would lead credence to the rest of her story.

Her claim to Ali of being al-Tunisi's maid was valid only in her first year with him. When it became clear he had no sexual interest in her, she relaxed and devoted herself to caring for him and his children. Her acceptance of Islam earned his trust, which led to him presenting his plan to her. Kaina readily agreed, seeing it as her only path to freedom. Thereafter, she spent most of her time in training camps.

Aisha's sudden arrival interrupted her thoughts. "Here you are. I've been looking for you. I saw the guard taking you away earlier. Did you finally get an interview?"

"Yes," Kaina said without elaboration. She was wary of talking to someone she didn't trust.

"How did it go? Did they force you to disclose al-Tunisi's favorite food?" she said with a smile.

"Yes, they tortured me until I gave it up."

"You were gone for hours."

"The interrogator kept digging, trying to get me to say something important. I kept reminding her I was only the maid and didn't know his movements or tactics. Would he have let me leave if I knew anything about him? I must not have convinced them because they brought me back here."

Aisha reached over and touched her hand. "It's a tactic the YPJ uses to crush your spirit, get you to tell them more. They informed me I could leave this place if I confessed to being a spy. More likely, they would have shot me."

"I've nothing more to say. What harm can I do? Why not set me free so I can go home?"

"Where is home, my sister?"

The instant she mentioned home, Kaina knew she made a mistake. She remembered al-Tunisi's admonishment never to tell anyone her nationality. She was talking too much to Aisha.

"I'm not sure anymore," she said. "We were Bedouins, always moving when the grass for the animals ran out. I was only thirteen. Too young to pay attention to geography."

"Don't you remember where they sold you?" she pressed.

"All I remember is a small village. I had never been there before. My parents went there to trade, and I was the one who got traded. The next day, they left."

"You weren't aware of this in advance? It must have been a terrible shock."

"Yes, it was. Aisha, the sun is giving me a headache. I'm going to lie down now. God be with you."

"And with you, my sister."

Kaina hurried away to her cell, upset with herself for her mistake. The woman's intense curiosity about her was unsettling. Did she work as a spy for the Kurds, attempting to gather information on al-Tunisi? Or was she just one of those nosy women who likes to know everything about you?

She resolved to avoid Aisha as much as possible while Nasser checked her story. *Do nothing to draw attention to yourself.*

CHAPTER 9

Weeks later, as Kaina sat on her bed, depressed about the lack of progress, footsteps grew louder outside her cell door. A guard stopped and peered inside. "Come with me," she commanded.

Five days ago, Ali Nasser took her fingerprints, filing away the cards containing them in a binder. He assured her this was routine in situations like this, trying to temper her excitement regarding potential progress. She believed he was lying about that. Someone in America must have requested them, meaning her story was being taken seriously. Since that day, nothing had happened, and it was wearing on her patience.

Kaina's heart raced as she followed the guard out of the room, their footsteps echoing through the hallway toward the front door. The possibility of being rejected by America and becoming homeless in Syria haunted her. If they released her, she had nowhere to go.

She shivered in the cool interrogation room, her body drenched in sweat from the scorching sun outside. Silence weighed heavily in the room as she settled into a chair and waited. Fifteen minutes later, the door opened. Ali walked in alone and sat behind the desk. He wore khaki pants identical to the ones worn at their last meeting, and a black t-shirt. Kaina thought he looked weary, his eyes sunken, with dark circles underneath. *The job must be getting to him.*

He placed his briefcase on the desk, sat down, and withdrew a thick stack of paperwork. Giving her a quick smile, he got right to the point.

"Kaina, we have completed the investigation into your claim of American citizenship. I sent your fingerprints back to headquarters. Our experts compared them to a set belonging to Natalie Martinez, which were on file with Santa Barbara County Child Services." He paused, allowing the tension to grow. "The prints matched. You're indeed Natalie Martinez."

Kaina leaned forward to touch his hand. "Can I go home now?"

"Yes. Tomorrow morning, a helicopter will transport you to our airbase at al-Tanf. From there, a plane will take you back to America. Once you arrive home, we will provide temporary lodging while you decide how to support yourself. The kidnapping deprived you of an education. I suggest returning to school to learn a trade and get a degree. Without a good job, living in America can be challenging."

Kaina's eyes closed. A smile spread across her face as she melted into her chair. A feeling of pure joy overcame her. Nothing could keep her away from America now.

"Now there's your kidnapping case," Ali continued. "The police will launch an investigation to identify the perpetrators. We expect you to cooperate in this matter. Are you willing to sit down and tell them everything you can remember?"

"It's my greatest desire to find the bastards that did this to me. They took six years of my life away from me. Send them all to Hell, where they can no longer prey on young girls."

Her forceful answer left Ali taken aback. "Yes...well, it's settled then. Pack your belongings. The helicopter leaves at eight tomorrow morning." He stood to shake hands. "Welcome back, Natalie."

Back in her cell, Kaina packed her few meager belongings. Lost in happiness, she remained oblivious to the sound of approaching footsteps at her door.

"Are you leaving, my sister?" Aisha asked.

Startled, Kaina straightened and turned to face her friend. "By the grace of Allah, yes. The Kurds have determined that I know nothing about al-Tunisi, so they're releasing me."

"That's wonderful news. Where will you go?"

"I'll try to make it to Jordan," she lied." I can search for my clan in the refugee camps there. There's no future here. Soon, the SDF will defeat ISIS, and I'll have nowhere to go."

"I shall miss you, my sister. When do you leave?"

She hesitated before answering. The constant barrage of prying questions grated on her nerves. But what did it matter? Soon, she would be gone and never see this meddlesome person again.

"Tomorrow morning."

"I shall pray for your safe passage, God willing."

"Thank you, my sister. May Allah watch and protect you."

CHAPTER 10

Kaina lay on her bed, tossing and turning, too excited to sleep, when she heard a faint sound outside her door. *Who would be outside at this hour?* The sound of a key inserted into the lock froze her in place. Something was wrong. No one visited the cells at night. The key turned slowly, being as quiet as possible. She tensed, feeling a prickling sensation on the back of her neck. Frantically, she searched for something nearby that had the potential to serve as a weapon for her defense. Her hand moved without a sound, picking up a heavy book from the floor beside her bed. It was the only thing within reach.

With a soft click, the door unlocked. Silence followed. Kaina waited, certain that the intruder was listening for any sounds inside the cell. The door swung open. A shadowy figure, clad in black, with a face hidden by a scarf, stood in the doorway. A stiletto gleamed in the dim light from the hallway. The person was thin and petite. It flashed through Kaina's mind that this was a woman, likely one of the Kurdish guards, since she had a key to the cell. Shouting for help would, therefore, be a waste of time and reveal to her intruder that she was awake, negating the element of surprise.

Someone didn't want her to leave here alive. Her choices were bleak—either she would kill the intruder, or the intruder would kill her. She liked her odds of surviving. During her months at the camps, a battle-hardened jihadist taught her Krav Maga, the Israeli method of self-defense. Plus, she had the advantage of catching the intruder by surprise.

As the assailant entered her cell, Kaina sprang from her cot, took aim, and threw the heavy book at her. Confused by the sudden turn of events, she froze as the book glanced off her head. Kaina kicked her assailant's hand, making the stiletto fly across the cell, evening the odds. They circled each other warily. Kaina kicked again, aiming for the belly, but her assailant caught the foot and flipped it back, causing Kaina to lose balance and fall to the hard floor. Her assailant stood over her, aiming a head kick, but Kaina whipped her foot around, tripping her. The assailant fell on top of her, wrapping her arm around Kaina's throat in a chokehold and cutting off her air supply. She would be dead in minutes if she didn't escape. Thrashing around and gasping for air, she felt a glimmer of hope as her fingers touched the stiletto handle. With her last strength, she drove the knife into the assailant's side. Her attacker groaned, and her grip loosened. Kaina pushed her away and crawled into a corner, her ragged breathing the only sound in the cell. She watched her foe, her eyes scanning for any sudden movement.

She waited, expecting her assailant to have a backup ready to continue the fight, but the building was quiet. Despite the noise made during the fight, no guard came to investigate. Someone had bribed them to ignore it, or her attacker was one of the guards. Either way, she knew she couldn't rely on anyone to protect her if she called for help.

After a moment's hesitation, she crept toward the body. A pool of blood was expanding on the floor, staining the concrete a dark red. Raspy, shallow breathing indicated the intruder still lived. Determined to find out who tried to kill her, she ripped the scarf off the intruder's face. What she saw left her speechless.

"Aisha! This can't be true."

"My sister," Aisha whispered.

"Why have you done this?"

Aisha hesitated. "My employer ordered me to kill you. If I had refused, they promised to kill my family. Then they would come for me. I had no choice. Now I'll die anyway."

"Your employer? Aren't you a prisoner here?"

Aisha's eyes were closed, her face chalk white. Kaina shook her gently. "Talk to me."

After a moment, her eyes opened. "What I told you wasn't true. They placed me here to watch you. They wanted to make sure you didn't return to America."

"Who do you work for?"

She offered a faint smile. "Can't you guess? The people who kidnapped you. Teddy Bear Fantasies."

Startled, Kaina sat back, shocked that her kidnappers had kept a close eye on her even after selling her to the sheik. *Did they do this to every slave they sold? How many had they killed to keep them from talking?*

"Tell me the identity and location of these people. I'll seek revenge for both of us," said Kaina.

A lengthy silence preceded her response. Her voice was but a whisper. "I...I can't tell you. We handled our business over the phone. There's a phone number...in my pocket. Forgive me, and may Allah guide you always."

"I forgive you, Aisha, and I swear to make them pay for what they have done to you."

Kaina's gaze remained locked on Aisha, eyes betraying no emotion, as her last moments of life slipped away. A thorough search of her body uncovered the phone number on a folded piece of paper. Besides the key to her cell, she found nothing else. After memorizing the phone number, she tore the paper into small pieces and swallowed it. She winced as she touched her neck, the bruises from the chokehold tender.

She felt tempted to leave her cell and seek help. However, one of the guards might have given Aisha the knife and key to her cell. Maybe they planned to have Aisha kill her, then leave and lock the cell door. Morning roll call would reveal Kaisha's body, leaving her time of death uncertain. If she raised an alarm now, the corrupt guards would kill her to save themselves.

CHAPTER 11

At the morning's scheduled time, Kaina heard a guard working her way down the row of cells, unlocking each door. She steeled herself for the upcoming confrontation. In a few moments, she might be dead.

The guard was instantly alert when she arrived at Kaina's door and saw it unlocked. With her AK-47 in firing position, she pushed open the door with her foot. Kaina sat on her bed, her hands raised in the air. A pool of blood surrounded a motionless body on the floor with a stiletto protruding from its side. The guard's eyes widened in astonishment. Backing out of the cell, she fumbled for her whistle and blew it urgently to sound the alarm.

Kaina felt relieved. The guard hadn't attempted to kill her, so she was likely not part of the plot. There was safety in numbers, so the more guards she called, the better. They arrived at the cell in force, but instead of restraining the prisoner, they watched her, weapons at the ready. After a brief wait, Kaina heard running footsteps in the hall. The guards shifted to the side, creating a path for the major who had interrogated Kaina weeks ago. She stopped inside the cell door, breathing heavily, shocked by what she saw. The lights flickered overhead, casting eerie shadows over her as she kneeled beside the body. Her hand trembled as she tried and failed to locate a pulse.

Kaina relaxed, feeling out of danger for now. No one would try to kill her with so many witnesses.

"Kaina!" the major hissed in a rage. Rushing to the bed, she towered over her prisoner. "What's happened here? Why is Aisha dead in your cell?"

"She arrived in the night, intending to kill me while I slept. We fought, and I killed her to save my life."

"How did she enter your cell through a locked door?"

"With this key," Kaina proclaimed, displaying it for all to witness.

The major's face turned white. "Bring her to interrogation," she snapped at the guards as she pushed past them and stomped out of the cell.

The guards swarmed her, grabbing her arms and attaching a pair of handcuffs to her wrists to ensure her compliance. She was duck-walked from the building to an interrogation room in the Quonset hut. For the next hour, they left her alone with her thoughts.

Aisha had given her the name of the organization her kidnappers worked for and a phone number that she could trace with the right connections. Allah had presented this to her, as a sign that he favored her quest. She prayed for Aisha's soul to rest in peace and for the Kurds to set her free.

As she sat silently, wondering what would happen next, footsteps approached the door to her interrogation cell. A guard glanced inside, then made way for the major's arrival. Kaina breathed a sigh of relief as she saw Ali following the major. He looked grim, avoiding her gaze as he sat across the table.

The major appeared to be under enormous stress, taking a moment to compose herself. The air conditioning unit hummed in the background.

"This incident was an unprecedented breach of security. We must identify and punish the traitors who made this possible. You must tell us everything you know. What can you tell me about Aisha? The guards say you two appeared to be friends and talked frequently."

"When I first arrived here, she befriended me," Kaina replied. "She claimed that several weeks earlier, she had been captured and accused of being a spy. When she denied that, you placed her in the unit to which I was assigned. Initially, I appreciated her advice, but she constantly probed for personal details of my life and plans upon release. This made me suspicious of her motives, so I avoided her as much as possible."

"Why would she want to kill you? Did she say anything during the attack? Did you tell her you were an American?"

"I know why she attacked me. During the fight, she called me an American pig. Yesterday, I told her I was being released, but not because I was an American. Only those present here knew that."

The major looked uncomfortable. "So, you believe one of my staff leaked the information on your nationality to her?"

"It's one possibility worth considering. I believe that telling her of my pending release triggered the attack. She didn't want me to leave here alive."

"I handpick my guards for their loyalty to me. The Americans would have no reason to want you dead."

Kaina said nothing. The room grew quieter. The major, looking frustrated, pinched her nose and waved a hand at Ali.

"This is a tough situation," he began. "The major needs to find the source of the leak, and why Aisha tried to kill you. It may be because you are an American or for some other reason. Perhaps a grudge against al-Tunisi, your former commander."

His eyes flicked to the major, who gave a slight nod of approval. "Against that need, we considered your safety. There may be others here who wish to cause you harm. Since you have shared all your knowledge, staying here longer serves no purpose. Therefore, the major has agreed to proceed with our plan for repatriation to America. The helicopter leaves for al-Tanf in fifteen minutes.

Guards will escort you to gather your belongings, and then you'll leave on the flight."

Kaina looked up at the ceiling. "Thank you both for saving my life. May Allah's mercy protect and guide you." Silently, she thanked Allah that her mission was still intact.

CHAPTER 12

Twinkling lights filled Natalie's window as the Boeing 787 made a nighttime final approach to Washington. City lights extended as far as she could see. The plane was enormous, seating nine people across and still having room for two aisles. In the pocket on the back of the seat in front of her, she had found a plastic card that told her the plane could hold two hundred fifty-seven people, plus the crew. It rivaled the size of a small Syrian village. She didn't understand how something this large and heavy could fly.

The plane banked left and crossed a large river. The steward announced they were landing at Ronald Reagan International Airport in Virginia. After the plane touched down and reached the gate, she gathered her carry-on bag and followed the other passengers into the terminal.

She was approached by a middle aged woman in a dark blue pants suit. "Hi, I'm Sara," she said, shaking her hand. "I'm here to escort you to your new home. Let's get you through customs."

Natalie nodded and followed her towards the exit. She felt conspicuous in the Western clothes the Americans had given her, even though every woman around her was similarly dressed. Her niqab was left behind in al-Tanf. It was likely in a trash can by now. She smiled when she realized she would never have to wear it again. The chains that bound her to ISIS were falling away.

The airport resembled a bustling city, with people rushing everywhere. It overwhelmed her senses. Hundreds of people were boarding and disembarking planes. Brightly lit shops sold goods that would have been luxuries in Syria. Restaurants were everywhere, some offering food she had never heard of. *What was Thai food like?* Signs everywhere kept you from getting lost, and constant announcements over the paging system alerted passengers that a flight was about to board.

A sense of unease came over her. ISIS had trained her to avoid crowds like these, as crowds were easy targets. Any suitcase or backpack could contain a bomb. One suicide bomber, willing to give his life for the cause, was all it took. *Weren't the Americans aware of this?* She scrutinized each passing face, looking for the signs of a person who didn't quite fit in.

She was further unsettled by seeing things that sparked buried memories from her childhood. A short distance away was a

McDonalds, which she knew served hamburgers, although she couldn't remember how they tasted. A small child walked by her eating an ice cream cone, her favorite thing to eat when she was that age.

She felt like two different people were pulling at her, demanding attention. Her training told her this was all wrong, while the rational part of her brain reminded her she wasn't in Syria anymore. Her entire thinking process needed to adapt. She reminded herself to be patient and learn all she could. Eventually, she would feel at home.

After clearing customs, Sara guided her out to a waiting car. Natalie put her small bag, containing everything she owned, into the trunk. The humidity was stifling, something she never encountered in the desert. The sound of honking horns as cars maneuvered for position at the curb echoed through the area. People shouted for taxis while others shoved suitcases into trunks. The stench of diesel exhaust belching from passing buses made her feel ill.

Everything was happening so fast. She slowed her breathing in the car's backseat, trying to calm her anxiety. Her heart rate didn't slow until they were far from the airport.

In a safe house near Arlington, Virginia, she met Karen, the "housekeeper" who lived there and was in charge. She was a large woman, with wide hips and a kind smile.

"Welcome to your new home," said Karen. "I'm here all the time, so if you have any questions, just ask. Let me show you to your room."

She took her to a room containing a small bed, drawers, table, chair, and lamp. Printed curtains, matching the bedspread, framed a window that looked out onto a flower garden in the backyard. The bathroom was across the hall, reserved for her private use. Though modest by American standards, she considered it luxurious.

The next morning, her debriefing got underway. Two men wearing dark suits and ties appeared at her bedroom door, introducing themselves only as Carl and Steve. Carl set up recording equipment in the dining room and Karen disappeared. Natalie sat in a chair and tried to remain calm while staring at the camera. She had rehearsed this part with al-Tunisi hundreds of times. Nevertheless, she was nervous as the questions began. Like the major at the Kurdish camp, the agents focused on her involvement with al-Tunisi and ISIS rather than her kidnapping. They bombarded her with questions, trying to poke holes in her story. But she held firm, insisting she was just a maid without insight into his actions or strategies. After several days, the agents ran out of questions, packed their equipment, and left.

After breakfast the next day, Karen sat down with Natalie. "I noticed you brought very little in your bag when you arrived. The government has given you an allowance to purchase things you might need. Would you like to go shopping?"

Natalie thought that was an excellent idea. Karen drove to a nearby mall with stores on two levels, eliminating the need to go anywhere else. Natalie let Karen pick out her clothes since she did not know what styles women wore in America.

As they were leaving, they walked past an electronics store with a display window featuring a selection of laptop computers. Natalie had used one occasionally in Syria during her training and knew how useful it could be.

"Is there enough money left to buy one of those?" she asked, pointing to the laptop. "I have a lot to learn about America, and this could be helpful to me."

Karen looked at the price tag and thought about it. "It's a stretch, but I think I can justify it. Everybody in America has some kind of computer, even if it's just their cell phone. Let's get it."

Natalie smiled. Now, she would have access to the Internet, which she would use to research her plan. Almost anything was discoverable on the Internet, and she would take full advantage of that.

CHAPTER 13

A week later, because Karen pushed her to, Natalie met the owners of a halfway house for women reintegrating into society. They had a room available, and Karen thought it would be the logical next step for her to take towards independence. The safe house was only a temporary residence.

On the drive over, Natalie shivered in her light jacket. The fall days were getting cooler, and the summer humidity had disappeared. Her body had yet to acclimate to cold weather. It was going to be a long winter.

Most of the residents of the house were former drug users, but a few battered women lived there too, all trying to put their lives back together. Natalie felt some empathy towards them. If Teddy Bear hadn't kidnapped her, she might have used drugs to cope with her miserable life and ended up just like them. But her life up until now hadn't been easy either.

Karen encouraged her to move in. "The next step for you is to learn self-sufficiency. Since you're nineteen, you're legally an adult in this country. But you aren't ready to take on the responsibility that entails. The government will cover your room and board, but you need a job to support yourself."

Natalie wondered how long it would be before Mohammad contacted her. A job wouldn't be necessary once she had everything she needed from him.

Karen was still talking. "To get a good job, you need an education. The best thing to do is to enroll in an adult school where you can learn with others your age. It may take a while, but it's necessary to survive in this country. Once you get a high school diploma, you can enroll in college or master a trade."

She agreed to do everything suggested, seeing it as a chance to break free from Karen's supervision. She was constantly asking questions about her life and, most likely, reporting everything she said to the FBI. Without her around, it would be easier for Mohammad to contact her.

In her new home, her room was much like her last, with sparse furnishings: a single bed, a dresser, and an end table with a lamp. A closet, hidden behind a sliding door, was roomy, but the clothes she owned filled only a quarter of it. Down the hall was a large community bathroom shared among all the residents. A window, framed with white curtains containing prints of blue flowers, looked out into a small but well-kept backyard filled with roses and jasmine. With her window open, she could smell them.

The local adult school was located a short bus ride away. The halfway house owners helped her fill out the paperwork to enroll. She marveled at the freedom she enjoyed. In Syria, she could not have traveled alone or attended school. Here, no one seemed to care where she went.

The subjects taught in school held no interest to her. She saw no use for math or social studies. Her mind remained in Syria, where survival was a daily struggle. Few, especially women, ever went to high school there. She felt uncomfortable sitting among the other students, who seemed preoccupied with their cell phones and social lives. They knew nothing about life, how fickle it was. Death could come tomorrow, and they would be unprepared to meet it. She had her faith, and Allah would welcome her to paradise when her time came.

Natalie waited, her phone always within arm's reach, for a message or call from the enigmatic Mohammad Mustafa. Only he could provide the equipment she needed. She didn't know how he would find her, but al-Tunisi had told her it would happen. He wouldn't have sent her to America unless he was sure. Hopefully, Mustafa was watching, waiting for the perfect moment to approach her, knowing that she was still under the constant supervision of the housekeeper. Another possibility, that the police had discovered him, was too frightening to contemplate.

Time slowed with each passing week. Mustafa remained silent. The days became dull and repetitive: wake up, eat breakfast, go to school, come home, take a walk, browse the Internet, and sleep. She was worried that this would become her life. *Had Mustafa changed his mind about helping her?* The thought made her depressed for days. The mission would be impossible to pursue without him.

For the past five years, she had lived in constant stress, always on edge, unsure of her survival. Now, the worst thing that could happen to her was missing the bus to school. *No, that's wrong*, she thought. Teddy Bear attempted to murder her in Syria, and if they were aware of her presence there, they likely knew she was here as well. They might try to kill her again. That brought up another worry. *Was she losing her edge?*

In Syria, she had practiced firing weapons every week. Here, she hadn't even seen a pistol. No one to practice hand-to-hand combat with, no camps to infiltrate unseen. The sole option available was exercising to keep herself strong.

Her spare time was used to browse the Internet, seeking information about Teddy Bear Fantasies. But her searches yielded no results. They seemed nonexistent. *How did they find clients who were interested in buying young girls?* Needing the help of an expert, she found herself without anyone trustworthy within her limited circle of acquaintances. Her only hope was Mustafa, but where was he?

A helpless feeling came over her. Free from ISIS, yet still unable to carry out her mission. Free of the police, yet stuck in a halfway house to reintegrate into society. She was part of a superficial society focused on attaining things, not serving as a shining example for others.

Islam remained the sole constant in her life. After buying a prayer rug at a local store, she kneeled daily on its rough surface in her room to pray and read the Qur'an, finding peace in its passages. She ached to attend a local mosque but worried that would draw attention to herself. Everything was in Allah's hands. Perhaps he was testing her faith to determine if she was worthy of the mission. Or perhaps he had already decided she was not.

***

She could accomplish nothing without funds, weapons, and knowledge of the mission. A backup plan didn't exist. She settled into a dull routine, her hope that Mustafa even existed fading fast. Even al-Tunisi, who had assured her contact would happen, had let her down.

As October transitioned into November, the days were crisp, the nights were wintry, leaves had fallen from the trees, and preparations for Thanksgiving were in progress. She was not in the mood to celebrate it.

One day, as Natalie left her bus and trudged towards school, a small boy on a bike stopped beside her. "I'm supposed to give you this," he said, offering her a cell phone.

She glanced at him, then at the phone, sensing it might be a trick. "Who told you to give me this?"

"Some man. He said he will call you later when you are alone."

Was it Mustafa? She snatched the phone out of his hand. "Thank you," she said.

The boy shrugged, wheeled his bike around, and pedaled off.

Natalie looked around but saw no one paying her any attention. She walked into a nearby park and sat alone on a wooden bench. The wood was rough, and a splinter poked at her. Dead leaves from nearby maple trees covered the grass. A squirrel chattered at her from a nearby tree limb. People strolled by, talking to each other. She rechecked the area, her heart racing, but still saw nothing unusual.

After ten minutes, the cell phone hadn't rung. She wondered if the park wasn't private enough for him to call. *How would he know when she was alone? Was he watching her?* After waiting another five minutes, she got up and went to class. It was important not to interrupt her daily routine. *Do nothing to draw attention to yourself.*

The day dragged on as Natalie attended her classes and ate lunch in the cafeteria. She prayed Mustafa *wouldn't* call now as she was never alone and didn't want to tell him that. The phone remained silent.

She finished her last class late in the afternoon and walked outside to the bus stop. Other than a stray student passing her, she was alone. *Would he call now?* The phone remained silent while she waited for her bus. The bus arrived full of people, disappointing her. She couldn't talk to him now, but the phone did not ring.

She reached her stop, exited the bus, and started walking the few blocks to the halfway house. *Now would be the perfect time for him to call.* As if reading her mind, the phone rang. Her hand shook as she answered it.

"Hello," she said.

"Is this Kaina al-Badawi?" a male voice asked in Arabic.

"Yes," she said, hope soaring.

"This is Mohammad Mustafa. Do you remember that name?"

"Yes. I've been waiting for your call for months."

"I couldn't proceed until the FBI had finished with you," he said, his voice filled with caution. "They watched you all the time. Some didn't believe your story."

She wondered how he knew this. *Did he work for the FBI?* Al-Tunisi told her not to believe anything the police said. But this man, he said to trust. Maybe he was an FBI operative loyal to ISIS, working undercover to gather intel for the cause.

"Praise be to Allah that you could contact me," she said. "I'm ready to strike the infidels, but I need the proper equipment before that can happen. If I make a list, can you help me?"

"Of course. Preparations started long ago."

That was a stupid question. He needed to have faith in her abilities for her plan to succeed. "Forgive me, Mohammad. Al-Tunisi gave me only your name. I didn't know what to expect."

"No matter. I'll try to provide what you need, no matter the obstacles that may present themselves. Allah has commanded it. You may leave your list in a safe place I've found. Once everything is ready, I'll call you with additional information. A meeting is unnecessary. It's safer that way."

She worried about his reluctance to meet, wondering if something was wrong. Five years with ISIS had taught her that when entrusting your life to others, it's essential to meet the person first. Look them in the eye, observe their body language, and gauge their reliability. However, she lacked the leverage to make demands. Nothing was possible without Mustafa.

"Very well. Tell me of this place, and I'll leave my list for you."

He gave her the information, cautioning that it might be several weeks before everything was ready.

"How may I contact you if I need something else?"

"Make sure your list is complete, so it's unnecessary to contact me," he said curtly.

Once again, others did not trust her, leaving her in limbo without a backup plan. But what choice did she have? She sighed and consoled herself, knowing this was the last thing she required from him. Then, she would be the one making the decisions.

Chapter 14

While everyone else was asleep that night, Natalie sat at her desk, composing her latest weapon list. She had thrown away the previous three, deciding they were too narrowly focused. She needed a wide range of weapons suitable for her plan and mission. Not knowing what it was made it more difficult. The mission could be anything, but it most likely involved an important person's assassination or blowing up something to make a political statement. That was what she trained for, so it made sense to her.

Most of what she wanted was high-tech weaponry: a McMillan TAC-50 sniper rifle equipped with a Leupold Ultra M3A 10×42 mm fixed power scope, an AK-47 assault rifle, two Glock 19 pistols with multiple extended magazines, silencers, and laser sights, a Ruger Max 9 for backup, two pounds of C-4 explosive with remote detonation equipment, a box of grenades, and a thousand rounds of ammo. In addition, she wanted night vision goggles, body armor, new identity documents, credit cards, twenty thousand in cash, an unregistered cell phone, a safe house, and a car. The list was extensive, and she didn't expect to get everything, but if you don't ask, you don't get.

The TAC-50 gained a reputation for its accuracy at long range, including a confirmed kill in Afghanistan from 2.2 miles away. If her target was well-guarded, a long shot might be necessary. She picked the AK-47 because she had trained with it and found it superior to the American M-4 in a firefight. The pistols were for close-in work. She could hide them under her clothes for a surprise attack. If ambushes or building destruction were called for, the C-4 and grenades would do the job.

Outside her window, a full moon illuminated the backyard. After sunset, the temperature plummeted, and the window glass felt cold to her touch. Two dogs barked nearby, disturbed by something they saw. She scanned the backyard, looking for movement, but saw nothing. She had been on high alert, wondering if she was being watched, since the kid handed her the cell phone.

Content with her list, she went to bed and stretched out in the cozy warmth of the comforter. She trained with all the requested guns, earning a reputation as an expert marksman with each. Tomorrow, she would leave the list at the dead drop. Then, one last delay while he procured the weapons. She offered a prayer of thanks to Allah for guiding Mustafa in contacting her. Finally, a path forward. Once she possessed weapons, the next move was hers.

Natalie waited patiently as the "several weeks" Mustafa had requested came and went. There had been no further communication from him. She thought about him constantly. Did he celebrate Thanksgiving with his family? Were they aware he worked for ISIS, or would he keep this a secret? Was he born an American, or had he immigrated to the country? How would he get the weapons she desired? There were so many unanswered questions.

After Thanksgiving, the waiting game continued. Winter arrived, chilling her to the point she dreaded going outside. Her body refused to adapt to the climate, forcing her to wear several layers of clothes to keep from shivering constantly.

A week before Christmas, the burner phone rang as she was getting ready for bed.

"Kaina, I'm sorry it's been so long since we last spoke," said Mustafa's soft voice. "The list contained some items that were most difficult to obtain. Despite my best efforts, one item was impossible. The rest is at the safe house. Tomorrow, at the drop point, you'll receive detailed instructions on where it is. Before you go there, destroy your old cell phone so no one can track it. I'll call again after Christmas to confirm the delivery was satisfactory."

The phone clicked dead before she said a word.

Natalie's excitement was so overwhelming that she tossed and turned all night, unable to sleep. Tomorrow was going to be the most important day of her life.

CHAPTER 15

What would she find at the drop site? The next morning, despite her desire to visit it, she forced herself to go to school. The FBI might still be watching her, and her absence might attract attention. After school, she loitered around the drop site, pretending to be waiting for someone while she scanned the area. Far away, she could hear the sounds of children laughing in a nearby park, but no one was near her. She took a deep breath and walked to the drop site, where an envelope awaited. Stuffing it into her pocket, she hurried away, unsure she wasn't being watched. She took a different route home, scrutinizing the bus passengers and searching for any familiar faces. As night fell, she locked her bedroom door and settled onto her bed, anticipation building as she tore open the envelope.

A set of keys fell out, attached to a car fob. Along with it, a scrap of paper showed the safe house address. The location was in Arlington, Virginia, which wasn't within walking distance or on a bus route. This didn't worry her. Additional means of transportation existed. She began to plan her escape.

She visited the school library to use their computers. Typing in the address Mustafa gave her, she found it belonged to a house. Using the satellite view, she familiarized herself with the neighborhood.

She planned to walk out the front door, like she did every day, then disappear. She would take only the small amount of her clothes that would fit in a bag, not a suitcase. Anything more would invite questions if anyone saw her leaving.

The next day was Saturday. Natalie left the halfway house with a large bag containing her essential belongings. Bundled up in her heavy coat and gloves, she walked towards the bus stop. As luck would have it, Tina, one of the other women staying at the house, walked toward her. There was no way to avoid her. She would have to bluff her way through questions.

Tina stopped in front of her and smiled. "Hey, you going shopping?" she asked, pointing to Natalie's bag.

"Yeah, I've got to return a few things that didn't fit," she replied. "I figured now would be a good time to do it."

Tina shrugged. "Well, good luck. It's way too cold for me. I'm going home to get warm." She waved her hand and resumed walking.

Natalie blew out a long breath and headed toward the bus stop. As soon as she was out of sight of the house, she called Uber. Standing on the sidewalk waiting for the driver, she half expected the FBI to appear and arrest her. *What was taking him so long?* Fifteen minutes later, the driver arrived. He looked Arabic, which made her hesitate. *What if Teddy Bear or ISIS sent him? Get a grip, Natalie. How would they know she would call Uber?*

She scanned the area one last time and said a quick prayer to Allah to protect her. This was the point of no return. If the police followed her to the safe house, they would find the weapons. There was no rational explanation for that. The FBI would throw her in jail, and her carefully crafted plan would be over before it started.

Steadying her nerves, she climbed into the backseat, leaned forward to give the driver an address, and settled in for the ride. The day was bitter, and a gray, overcast sky threatened rain or snow. She preferred snow, to experience it for the very first time. Gusts of wind rocked the car, but the heater kept everything warm inside.

The driver headed southwest across the Potomac River, and the traffic thinned out as they entered Arlington. A short time later, he left the freeway and drove into a subdivision containing modest brick tract homes built some time ago. The neighborhood, once middle-class, had fallen on hard times. The homes showed signs of deterioration, with peeling paint, roofs that needed replacement, and lawns full of weeds that nobody mowed. Natalie noted the similarity of the houses. Upgrades made by owners over the years were all that distinguished them.

Natalie noted every car she saw once they entered the subdivision. No car followed them beyond a few blocks, but she still felt unsafe. The FBI might be using multiple vehicles to follow her, or a drone, too high in the sky to notice.

The driver weaved through the subdivision for fifteen minutes before stopping in front of a house indistinguishable from the rest. "This is it," he said.

Natalie paid in cash and stood on the sidewalk looking at the house, her breath condensing in the cold as he drove away. Once he turned the corner, she walked back a few blocks to the address Mustafa supplied.

The house stood atop a sloping hill, excavated by the developer for a garage and basement. The living quarters were built above it. There was nothing about it that would draw anyone's attention. The front was a plain brick exterior with a couple of windows. A weathered asphalt shingle roof needed repair. The paint was peeling off the fascia. Cracks marred one of the window panes. Plain white curtains covered all the windows, giving off an unwelcome vibe while providing privacy. The only cared for part of the property was the freshly mowed lawn. She wondered who mowed it.

She scanned both sides of the street before climbing the worn stone steps to the front door. She felt totally exposed, as though a thousand eyes watched her. Pausing, she pressed the doorbell. Chimes sounded in the distance, yet no one answered the door. From her purse, she retrieved the collection of keys Mustafa gave her. Among them was one with the name "Schlage" stamped on it. It looked like a house key, so she inserted it into the lock. The key turned, and the door swung open.

Stepping inside, she found herself in a hall next to a carpeted living room. The room was furnished with a couch flanked by two end tables, each with a lamp. A battered coffee table stood in front of it. Two leather armchairs faced the couch from across the room.

The hallway led to a half bath and a small kitchen. Another hall angled left, leading to bedrooms. Next to the kitchen, a breakfast nook, containing a bay window framed by lace curtains, provided a picturesque view of the backyard. The nook contained a round, rustic pine table, and a couple of well-loved chairs. An unaddressed manila mailer lay on the table, its contents a mystery waiting to be unveiled.

A lingering, musty smell permeated the house, suggesting a lack of ventilation. A thin layer of dust covered everything. Cobwebs filled the corners of the rooms. Floorboards creaked as she walked through the rest of the house, discovering two bedrooms and another bathroom.

She peeked through the curtains in the living room, studying the street outside. A car drove by, but the driver didn't even look in her direction. Other than that, the street was empty. Either no one followed her, or they hid nearby, waiting to see what she did next.

Her mouth felt dry, and a headache was throbbing in the back of her brain. The uncertainty of her safety grated on her nerves, but she was powerless to change anything. The risk of coming here was unavoidable, so she would have to live with whatever came next.

Turning on the heat, she shrugged off her coat, sat at the table in the breakfast nook, and tore open the mailer. Inside was a passport, a credit card, a cell phone, and a driver's license with her picture on it, all in the name of her new identity, Amy Sanchez. *Where had Mustafa gotten her picture?* It also contained bundles of cash and a typed letter.

If you're reading this, everything has gone according to plan. I have provided all that you asked for except the grenades, which were unobtainable. Everything else is in the basement. The key fob will start the car parked in the garage. The refrigerator has sufficient food for two weeks.

This is where you will live until you carry out your mission. Stay inside as much as possible. Once the police realize you've left the halfway house, they will search for you.

Allah has selected you to deal a decisive blow to the Great Satan, a task reserved only for the chosen few. The faithful will remember your name forever. Get familiar with the weapons and learn how to drive the car. I'll call soon with further instructions. Burn this letter now.

Natalie read the letter twice, her eyes scanning each word before she bowed her head in silent prayer. Her mind was a whirlwind of conflicting emotions. Now, she had everything needed to complete her mission, but did she want to do so? She was also free to undertake an alternative plan, which was full of risk. If anyone in ISIS discovered it, they would brand her a traitor and hunt her down.

She was at a crossroads, torn between two paths, each beckoning with unknown possibilities. The people working for Teddy Bear were the worst of the worst, preying on innocents unable to defend themselves, who had done nothing to deserve their fates. *How many*, she wondered, *had they enslaved? Who else could end it if not me?* On the other path stood the oppressors, who had stolen Arab lands, killed millions of believers, and supported corrupt regimes. *Did she not owe it to Allah to strike back in some manner?*

It was impossible to do both things simultaneously. If she pursued her original mission, she understood that martyrdom awaited her. If she sought revenge instead, al-Tunisi would soon learn of her betrayal and send men to kill her. Allah alone knew the right course, yet he gave her no sign. What should she do?

CHAPTER 16

Although he would deny it, Ron Jackson was a regular at the neighborhood bar in his hometown of Carpinteria, a thirty-minute drive south of Santa Barbara, California. His favorite seat was towards the end of the bar in a dark corner where he could be alone with his thoughts. This was not a good thing. With each passing day, his self-respect diminished. Remnants of his past plagued him. Things that he desired to fix, but lacked the means to do so. Sometimes, he had nightmares about them, along with a massive amount of guilt.

He was in a bad mood today because he was in his car instead of the bar. On a street half a block from a seedy motel, he was gathering evidence for his latest client, Monique Young. A pistol lay within easy reach on the passenger seat beside him, just in case he needed to discourage one of the locals from bothering him.

It was a sketchy neighborhood near a busy freeway. Full of alleyways where someone could go to buy drugs from dealers who set up shop there. It was getting dark, the streetlights had just come on, and business was picking up. Although near the beach, it wasn't a place to stop to admire the scenery, unless you liked getting mugged. Sometimes there was no choice.

Monique's unhappiness in her marriage led her to take action. She suspected another woman, but needed confirmation. That would provide a convenient reason for divorce and a fat settlement to tide her over until the next husband came along. Her girlfriends, most of whom had already been through this process at least once, recommended Ron Jackson as Santa Barbara's most trustworthy and discreet private investigator. Referrals were his primary method of acquiring clients.

Last week, she had paused outside his office, reading the plaque next to his door, which had only his name on it. Ron watched her through a spy camera he had installed discretely above the door. She seemed to be having second thoughts before finally opening the door and stepping into a modest waiting room.

There wasn't much to see. A former client once told Ron that his office looked like someone with no money or no taste decorated it. He qualified on both counts. Straight-backed chairs lined the cream-colored wall to the right of the door. A worn leather coach leaned against the opposite wall. In front of it, a coffee table held a bowl of fake flowers and a few dated magazines. On the walls were prints of unrecognizable landscapes. A worn linoleum floor, unpolished in months, completed the look.

Another door, labeled private, stood at the room's rear. A sign tacked to it advised all visitors to take a seat. Someone would be with them soon. Monique sat on the couch. A faint odor of tacos from Ron's earlier lunch permeated the air.

Ron let her wait for ten minutes before he opened the door from his private office. He didn't want to give her the impression he had nothing else to do, even though business was a little slow. He gave her his best smile.

"Hello, I'm Ron Jackson. How may I be of assistance?"

Monique rose from the couch and shook his hand. "I'm Monique, I called earlier to make an appointment. I suspect my husband is cheating on me and my girlfriends suggested I talk to you."

For an hour and a half, Ron handed out tissues as Monique tearfully recounted the discovery of suspicious text messages on her husband's phone and the fact that he was always gone. Although she adored her husband, Monique would not tolerate infidelity.

She wanted irrefutable proof her husband, a.k.a. the lying dog, was cheating, to boost her chances for a generous settlement in the divorce. Irrefutable proof meant pictures, which was why Ron was sitting in his car, watching a room at the Paradise Beach Motel, a run-down place near the 101 freeway on the outskirts of Santa Barbara.

Monique's husband had driven there earlier, forcing Ron to follow just as he was about to end surveillance for the day and head to the bar. He was parked half a block away and had a telephoto lens on his camera. He didn't understand why a guy worth millions wouldn't spring for a decent hotel room to meet his mistress.

The camera captured every detail, from the lying dog knocking on a room door to his passionate kiss with his girlfriend when she opened it. Routine stuff that he had done many times before for his multitude of clients.

This job was coming to an end. He knew the woman's identity and had plenty more pictures for his client. There was nothing more to be gained from surveillance. Tomorrow, he would type up the report and email it to Monique. Another satisfied customer who would give glowing reviews to her girlfriends. He couldn't have cared less. The work gave him no satisfaction.

Near nine o'clock, Ron decided the lying dog was playing hide the wienie with his girlfriend and not planning on going anywhere that night. The lights had gone out in the motel room an hour ago. The smell of char-broiled hamburgers wafting down the street from a fast-food place on the corner made his stomach growl. There was no point in hanging around longer. He could get a cheeseburger at the bar.

The area was quiet, except for a homeless guy wandering by on the sidewalk, his belongings crammed into bags hanging on a shopping cart. The cart seemed to have lost a wheel, causing it to tilt to the side and scrape loudly as he pushed it down the sidewalk. *Somebody needs to throw a net over that guy and send him to detox. Everyone has problems, but some people just can't deal with them.*

The homeless guy threw up his arms, arguing with an imaginary person next to him. Ron watched, ready to react if the guy approached him. People on fentanyl were unpredictable and became violent in a heartbeat. The man continued onward, unaware he was being watched.

Ron started his car and drove onto the 101, traveling south towards home.

He was the last patron to depart at the bar's closing time of 2 am. The bartender knew him well and refused to give him his car keys, which Ron, by previous agreement, always deposited in a jar when he arrived. He staggered the three blocks to his home and passed out on his bed. There was no guarantee the nightmares would stay away.

Chapter 17

The next day, the sun was straight overhead by the time Ron got his shit together. Hours earlier, he'd awakened with a pounding headache and an urge to vomit—a familiar feeling. He knew what to do.

He stumbled to the kitchen and started his coffeemaker brewing. Then he went to his bathroom and turned on the shower, cold water only. Next came the hard part. Steeling himself, he stepped into the shower, gasping as the cold water had its intended effect of clearing his mind. Sometimes, he would puke in the shower, but he fought the urge today. A few minutes later, with his teeth chattering, he stepped out of the shower and dried himself off to warm up. Returning to his bedroom, he dressed in an old T-shirt and sweatpants.

The smell of brewing coffee drew him to the kitchen. He opened a cabinet and removed a bottle of aspirin, a coffee cup, and a bowl.

Pulling a carton of milk from the frig and cereal from another cabinet, he took it all to the kitchen table. He ate slowly, his stomach still queasy from last night.

An hour later, he felt close enough to normal to consider his next task. His laptop computer sat next to him on the table. He couldn't put it off forever. With a heavy sigh, he booted it up and began typing his report to Monique.

He was close to finishing it when his cell phone rang. A glance at the display created a mix of surprise and curiosity. The name on the caller ID was his ex-partner, Mary Ann McDonald.

Years ago, he and Mary Ann were Santa Barbara Sheriff's detectives. Things changed forever when they caught a case involving two dysfunctional siblings. The siblings targeted children who were wards of the state, with no family and no one to miss them if they disappeared. Then, they kidnapped the children and sold them into slavery.

When authorities found the sister dead, the scheme unraveled. The detectives took on the murder investigation, which led them to uncover the kidnapping business. Ron still found it hard to believe that under his watch, eight local children, four of them babies, went missing. The case devastated him, but despite his best effort, they never found the children.

When the leads ran out, the chief of police and the chair of the Board of Supervisors ordered the case closed. He quit the force, determined to open a detective agency and find the eight missing children. He took it personally; closure was needed to banish the guilt that haunted him.

The lofty goal commanded respect but proved impossible to achieve. Making a living was necessary, and investigating a case without a paying client wasn't helping. He told himself the divorce work was just a temporary job. The children would get his full attention as soon as he saved a little money.

Six years had passed, and he was still doing divorce work. Not one clue had surfaced since the case was closed. The missing children became a part of him, gnawing at his conscience. He considered himself a fraud for not searching for them. They were young children when they disappeared, all but forgotten now. And there was something else, even worse, that haunted him.

It had been a long time since he and Mary Ann had last spoken. There was an undeniable distance between them, a clear sign that their relationship was strained. Mary Ann had claimed that the case had reached a dead end, and she wasn't willing to throw her career away to pursue ghosts. Looking back, he had to admit that she might have been right.

"Mary Ann! Long time no see. Did you make chief yet?"

Silence filled the line. "Still the LT, running the sheriff's station here," she replied eventually. "I've gained valuable insights in the past few years. I'm not sure I'd want to be chief anymore. Too much politics at that level."

"No kidding. It's difficult to look in the mirror each morning when that's your only concern."

"Look, this isn't a social call," she said irritably. "I received a piece of information regarding our last case and thought you might be interested. If you're not too busy chasing down cheating husbands."

Ron froze, his breath catching in his throat. *A lead after six years of nothing?* A motorcycle roared by outside his house, snapping him back to the present.

"Anything about that case interests me. What did you hear?"

"Do you remember Natalie Martinez?"

"Of course. She was the key to tying Art Garcia to the kidnapped kids."

"Someone important in the CIA requested a set of her fingerprints."

Ron absorbed this information. There was only one reason anybody would require that. "Did they find her?"

"Here's where it gets weird. The CIA had a woman in custody in Syria claiming to be her. They needed her fingerprints to prove it. They matched, so she's in a halfway house getting acclimated to being in America again."

"Found in Syria? How the hell did she end up there?"

"She got sold to a sheik in Bahrain. He molested her in his home for a year, then sold her to Abu Osama al-Tunisi, a commander in ISIS. The Kurds captured her during the Battle of Raqqa."

"That's an amazing story," said Ron. "That'll mess you up for life. Don't know how she survived it. She's going to need a lot of help to reintegrate into society. Thank God she provided us with names we can squeeze for information. Uncover the identity of the person who supplied them with the children."

"Easier said than done. Al-Tunisi commands the jihadists in Raqqa. There's no way you can touch him. The best course of action is tracking down the sheik. The CIA told me he's a wealthy member of the ruling family in Bahrain. He's well protected, but maybe we can get to him with some help from our CIA friends."

Ron signed the report to Monique and hit the send key. After six miserable years, he felt a chance for redemption. "We can make it work, Mary Ann. You can count me in. What's the plan?"

"That is the question," Mary Ann said. "How do we lure him here? Then he'll be subject to our laws, and the FBI can charge him with kidnapping, rape, and other stuff that will scare the shit out of him. He'll want to avoid the publicity at all costs. Then we offer him a deal to tell us everything he knows about Teddy Bear, or have the media ruin his life."

"We're going to require a lot of help to make that happen," he pointed out, still sitting at his kitchen table. "Wouldn't the FBI have to set up the phony investment opportunity? Who'll watch the sheik in the meantime? What happens if the Feds freeze us out of the sting?"

"All good questions," she replied. "Since I'm the only one with official access to the CIA and FBI, it will be on me to convince them to cooperate. The federal government is a vast bureaucracy, so it won't be easy and may take a while. In their minds, the local police are amateurs. Please be patient. This will be difficult for you."

"That's the only plan that makes sense. Nobody can go to Bahrain and make him talk there. But getting the Feds to go along with it is a long shot."

"There are people who owe me favors. I'll start making the calls today. Try to keep busy and not think about it. There are plenty of pretty young things that need your help with their divorce."

Patience wasn't one of Ron's strong points, so he called Mary Ann every few days for an update. Weeks passed with no word from the Feds. Concentrating on his divorce work was difficult when all he wanted was to help the FBI arrest the sheik. His greatest fear was the plan would fall apart somewhere, crushing any hope he had to fix something that had been eating him alive for six years. One afternoon, while he was in his office typing a report to a client, he thought of a different approach. The idea would require Mary Ann's help.

"Hey, Mary Ann," Ron said when she answered the phone. "Waiting forever while the Feds get their shit together isn't a good idea. The kidnappers are searching for more kids to victimize. Plus, they could shut everything down and disappear if they get wind of an investigation. Why can't we have a chat with Natalie? Perhaps she'll remember something she forgot to tell the Feds."

A silence hung on the line. "I already thought of that. I made the request to the FBI two days ago. When they called the house to set it up, the housekeeper said she hadn't seen her in days. She doesn't answer her phone, and it doesn't appear to be on. Since Natalie was there voluntarily, she didn't think it was necessary to report it. The FBI is looking for her, but since she has broken no laws, finding her isn't a priority."

"Shit," said Ron. "What if her kidnappers found her? She might be dead."

"The FBI gave her a new identity at the halfway house, so they don't believe anyone found her. They theorize she left because she was tired of the living situation."

"Disappeared without a trace? What about friends or her job?"

"Nobody in the house knew her well. Though polite, she kept to herself. She didn't have a job. A government stipend helped her while she attended school. The school hasn't seen her either."

Panic rose in Ron's chest. "Why would she just disappear? How would she survive with no income? Why wouldn't she have told anyone she wanted her own place?"

"These are good questions to which I have no answers," replied Mary Ann.

It seemed more likely to him that someone wanted her gone and abducted her. If true, there was a leak within the FBI. Given a new identity, she should have been impossible to trace. He theorized that the FBI felt embarrassed that she disappeared on their watch and pretended to be indifferent to save face.

With Natalie missing, everything depended on getting the sheik to America. So far, they had made no progress. Was the FBI reliable? Whoever leaked Natalie's location might also tip off the sheik. The success of their plan hinged on getting him here. If he didn't come, there weren't any other options. Ending the case again would be unbearable. He couldn't go back to an empty life working divorces.

CHAPTER 18

Despite her impatience to take action, Natalie stayed at the safe house, awaiting a sign from Allah. She had spent Christmas alone, which was not a big deal. She was a Muslim, and this was a Christian holiday. But everyone on TV seemed happy while she sat like a hen on a nest waiting for an egg to hatch. Mid-January had arrived, and she felt time dwindling. If Allah didn't send a sign soon, she would have to make the decision herself. An unexpected phone call from Mustafa changed everything.

"Kaina, I have important information to share. Do you remember a sheik named Abdul-Wadid Diya al-Din?"

Natalie froze at the mention of his name. "Y...yes," she stammered.

"I'm aware he caused you great harm. You meant nothing to him, and he treated you like garbage. I have learned that in two days, he's flying into New York to meet with the FBI and provide them with valuable information about you and ISIS. For this reason, al-Tunisi has declared him a traitor to the jihad. The penalty is death. He has selected you to carry out the sentence. Although this is not why we brought you here, it's a chance to serve Allah and exact your revenge."

She was dumbfounded by the opportunity being handed to her. "Praise be to Allah. I never imagined this opportunity would come. How will I accomplish this, Mohammad Mustafa?"

"I will leave his itinerary at the dead drop. There isn't much time. He has a flight scheduled back to Bahrain in a few days. If you don't strike quickly, you will lose the opportunity."

The following day was frigid, forcing her to wear all the warm clothing she had to visit the dead drop. A light dusting of snow covered the ground, and the sidewalks were slippery with ice. At the drop, the itinerary Mustafa left her was sketchy, only mentioning the location and time of his meeting with the FBI, the hotel and room number where he was staying, and flight information. The sheik also traveled with two bodyguards, which might complicate things.

With limited information and time, planning an attack was challenging. Her first action was soundproofing her basement and preparing it for the sheik if she captured him alive. She had to prevent his screams from being heard.

The next step was to drive to New York and scout the locations. The address for the meeting with the FBI, a modern office building across the street from Central Park, posed problems. Launching an attack inside a building full of FBI agents didn't seem wise. Her chances of getting close enough to get off a shot were remote. The only possibility was to hide in the park across the street and shoot him upon his arrival. With people walking everywhere in the park, staying hidden would be difficult. There would be only seconds to shoot before he entered the building. She would only get one shot. The bodyguards would be screening him, possibly preventing a shot at all. Shooting him there would eliminate any opportunity to interrogate him about Teddy Bear. Her escape afterward through Central Park would be harrowing.

Her next stop was the hotel where the sheik would be staying. Pretending to be a guest, she entered the lobby wearing a wide-brimmed floppy hat to hide her face. The lobby was too busy to mount an attack, filled with front desk employees, luggage handlers, and guests moving about. She found the bank of elevators and rode one to the fourteenth floor.

Stepping out of the elevator, she noted the security camera mounted near the ceiling and kept her head bowed away. She scanned the room numbers and determined the sheik's suite was at the end of the hall, next to a convenient fire escape. A maid was cleaning a room nearby, her cart parked in the hall, with the door to the room open for her safety. It gave Natalie an idea for a bold attack that the sheik's bodyguards would least expect. And if everything went according to plan, she would capture the sheik alive.

CHAPTER 19

Flight 348, non-stop from Bahrain, lumbered low over the Atlantic Ocean on final approach to LaGuardia Airport. Sheik Abdul-Wadid, comfortably lounging in first class, was on his way to a meeting that would secure his financial future. He sipped his glass of wine, stretched, and glanced out the window. Whitecaps were atop the waves below, and he knew from experience that the plane would land in ten minutes.

The thought of arriving in New York filled him with excitement. A broker had pitched a new limited partnership to him that promised a huge return within a year. The caveat was a requirement to attend a meeting of the partners in New York, where he would sign the final papers. Although his yearly trip to America to check on his investments was not for another five months, he couldn't ignore the potential profit from this deal. No more having to kiss the king's ass to get his allowance every year.

After clearing customs, he and his two bodyguards, who flew with him in coach, climbed into a stretch limo waiting at the curb. It was mid-morning on a cold winter day in February. A strong wind blew from the Northeast, scattering the cumulous clouds in the sky. Small patches of snow clung to shady areas under trees. He shivered in his thick jacket. He had always scheduled previous trips to New York during the summer.

A black sedan idled at the curb a short distance behind the limo. Two FBI agents were inside. "He just got into his limo," one of them reported to the command post. "Following him now."

A ride into Manhattan at this time of the day took ninety minutes. The Brooklyn Bridge, always congested with bumper-to-bumper traffic, caused a slow commute. The only alternative was the train, which was unacceptable to a man of his status. After crossing the East River into Manhattan, the driver turned north onto FDR Drive and drove along the river, avoiding the more congested inland traffic.

The sheik found their slow pace irritating. In Bahrain, the police stopped traffic when a member of the royal family traveled by car. They treated him like a commoner here. He wondered what arrangements the government made when the king visited.

It was a non-negotiable requirement that every limo he rode in contained a bar. "Abdul," he said. One of his bodyguards looked at him. The sheik tapped his empty glass. "Get me a refill."

The embarrassed bodyguard took his glass, filled it with ice cubes, poured whiskey into it, and handed it back to the sheik. The sheik made a mental note to replace Abdul when he returned to Bahrain. He should have noticed his glass was empty without having to be told. He needed bodyguards that were focused on his needs to make the commute more tolerable.

Meanwhile, CNN's financial news played on a flat-screen TV. The market was up over 200 points. His irritation with the traffic subsided. Life in America was liberating, free from Bahrain's strict morality rules and a greedy king who demanded a cut of everything.

As the limo glided under the portico of his favorite hotel, a team of impeccably dressed hotel staff swarmed the car. Bellhops opened the car doors and retrieved the luggage. The black sedan stopped further down the driveway, and the FBI agents reported the sheik's arrival.

The hotel manager stood at the entrance, fawning over the sheik, known to be a big tipper. He escorted his half-drunk patron into the elevator, which took him to the penthouse on the fourteenth floor, to make sure everything was to his liking. The sheik walked over to the bar and inspected the bottles lined up on a shelf. A smile stretched across his face as he saw his favorite, a very rare, twenty-one-year-old scotch. The sheik waved his hand, and a bodyguard pressed a wad of bills into the manager's hand.

Once the manager departed, the sheik called a woman he knew from a local escort service. She would expect an expensive night out on the town, but that was minor compared to the pleasure she would give him upon returning to his penthouse.

The following day, he was in an excellent mood while dressing for the meeting with his new partners. This would be his crowning achievement, securing the financial needs of generations of his family yet to be born. They would praise his name long after he joined Allah in heaven.

He expected to be in the company of very wealthy men today and worried about fitting in. His partners needed to see him as one of them, not some second-rate royal from a backward country. He picked out his best suit, a gray gaberdine, custom-made for him and imported from Italy. His shirt was black, made from the finest silk. A dark red silk tie with small black diamond designs projected power and wealth. Diamond cuff links flashed near his wrists. Patent leather Gucci shoes gleamed with a bright shine. He was leaving nothing to chance.

A driver drove him and his bodyguards north on Madison, past the hulking St. Patrick's Cathedral. Turning left on West 59th, the limo stopped in front of a large, modern office building. He was impressed. It occupied prime real estate across the street from Central Park.

He and his bodyguards climbed the steps and entered. The marbled lobby screamed luxury and power. A man in a gray suit approached and flashed a smile. "Sheik Abdul-Wadid, welcome to New York. My name is Jim. We are honored by your presence. Please allow me to escort you to the meeting." He waved them into an elevator gleaming with chrome-edged mirrors. They rode up to the tenth floor.

A soft chime sounded as the elevator door opened, revealing double glass doors to a suite of offices in front of them. Behind the glass, a young receptionist, her desk bare of clutter, welcomed the visitors with a cheerful smile. An elaborate sign on the paneled wall behind her said "Walter, Jones, & Carington, LLC". Jim held the door open with a slight bow, gesturing for the sheik to enter.

"The others are waiting in the conference room, down the hall," he said. "Only partners may attend. Your bodyguards are welcome to wait for you here." He pointed to several overstuffed chairs off to the side.

The sheik nodded, and his bodyguards made themselves comfortable. He followed Jim down a hall adorned with pictures of men in suits to an unmarked door, which Jim opened for him. Inside, the sheik observed a long, polished walnut table with leather chairs circling it. The leather smelled new. A pitcher containing ice water sweated beside a silver platter holding crystal glasses on a side table. The wall facing him was glass with a view of Central Park. Four men and two women in business attire occupied that side of the table with their backs to the glass. The other side had only empty chairs.

Everyone rose, and one man reached out his hand. "Welcome Sheik Abdul-Wadid Diya al-Din to New York. Please allow me to introduce myself. My name is Peter Bennington, the general partner. These are your fellow limited partners." While Peter made the introductions, each person shook hands with him. "Please make yourself comfortable."

The sheik picked the chair across from Peter. "It's truly an honor to meet all of you here for this special occasion. New York is a wonderful place to visit, although I must confess, I prefer the summer weather." The partners chuckled. Jim stood by the door. *Didn't he mention the meeting was exclusive to partners?*

Peter placed a thick binder of papers on the desk with a thud, interrupting his thoughts. He removed a small leather wallet from the inside pocket of his jacket. The sheik noticed his piercing eyes and thought, *this man could be dangerous.*

"Sheik Abdul-Wadid, neither I nor anyone else here are investors. We are agents of the FBI." Peter opened the wallet to display his credentials.

The sheik stared at him in disbelief, then at the others gathered around the table displaying their credentials. *What is going on here? Why is the FBI interested in me?* He slouched in his chair, the smooth leather against his back as he tried to remain calm. Outside, a cloud passed across the sun, momentarily darkening the room.

"What's the meaning of this? Why have I been told false statements?"

Peter opened his binder, removed the top piece of paper, and handed it to him. The paper trembled in his hands as he realized it was a warrant for his arrest. "The government is charging you with kidnapping and transporting a minor out of the country, lewd acts with a minor, and false imprisonment. You have the right to an attorney..."

His mind was a whirlwind of thoughts. *How dare they try to arrest me. Don't they realize who I am? Who's accusing me of these acts? The FBI tricked me into coming here. There's no partnership. I won't be rich. How will I explain this to my family and the king?* His mind came back to reality. Peter was asking a question.

"Do you understand these rights?"

His face contorted with displeasure. "As a member of the royal family of Bahrain, you lack authority to arrest me. This meeting is over. Upon returning to Bahrain, I will report your conduct to the king. All of you will be looking for new jobs when he files a formal protest with your ambassador."

Peter looked unworried. "When visiting our country, you're subject to our laws. You have no diplomatic immunity. Everyone is equal here. You are under arrest. After your booking, you have the right to call a lawyer. Do you remember Kaina al-Badawi?"

The sheik was halfway out of his chair. He sat down and cocked his head as if trying to remember her. "Yes," he said after a time. "I employed her in my household as a maid many years ago. I barely knew her. How is she involved in these false charges?"

"She's the reason you are here," said Peter. "Someone kidnapped her in California and sold her to you. Over the next year, you exploited her as your sexual plaything, violating her and keeping her imprisoned until you grew weary of her. Then you sold her to al-Tunisi." He leaned forward for emphasis. "When you bought her, she was only thirteen years old, a mere child. These are severe crimes in this country. Conviction carries a twenty-year prison sentence. The king will show no sympathy for a child molester."

Abdul-Wadid sweated through his shirt. *How were they aware of this? Al-Tunisi was with ISIS in Syria. He would never give this information to the Americans.* Then he figured it out. *Somehow, they found Kaina. Did she escape from al-Tunisi?* "Who told you these lies? Where is the proof?"

"The proof is the sworn statement of Kaina, who we rescued and returned home. During your trial, she'll testify against you. Everyone will learn about the sick, perverted things you did to her. The media will make it a sensation. You'll disgrace your family, and the king will disown you. After you serve your sentence, you'll have nothing. The government will send you back to Bahrain, where you'll be at the mercy of your king. That's not a position I would care to be in. He may wish to make an example of you for the embarrassment you caused him."

Peter's words hit home. He couldn't survive this. The testimony of one girl was hardly enough to convict him, but even if the jury declared him innocent, the constant media attention would be enough to destroy his reputation. He would end up impoverished and a pariah. The contrast between his life of luxury and the harshness of having to start over with nothing frightened him. He was getting old and would never survive it. He shivered when he thought about what might happen. There was only one card remaining to play.

"I wasn't aware someone kidnapped her. The company that sent her told me she came willingly, as she was destitute. I needed a maid to clean my house. That's all that happened. Kaina's lying about everything else. As I remember, she was always a troublemaker, making up stories. Maybe another employee attacked her, and she blamed me to get your attention."

"That could be the case," Peter offered. "Perhaps you're an innocent victim of this crime. Of course, we'd need information about this company you worked with to verify your story."

Abdul-Wadid weighed the risk of disclosing this information. If Teddy Bear discovered his betrayal, he would be signing his death warrant. It wouldn't be safe for him to travel anywhere outside his fortified home. But at least he would be wealthy and free. The alternative was unthinkable. The time had come to strike a bargain.

"This company is very secretive. I signed a contract that I'd never disclose information about them to anyone. If they find out I broke this contract, they'll sue me. Even my life might be in danger. Of course, if they're kidnapping innocent children and selling them into slavery, that needs to be stopped. It would be my duty to help in any manner possible."

He paused, then pointed his index finger in the air. "If I agree to share this information with you, I need a written guarantee that anything said will remain secret and my identity protected from public disclosure. In addition, I demand that you drop these false charges so I can return home to Bahrain. I will inform the king that the partners couldn't agree, leading to the failure of negotiations. This must remain a secret between us."

Peter steepled his hands and nodded. "This is agreeable, depending on what you have to share. Tell us everything, then sightsee in New York while we verify the information. Jim will be your tour guide. If everything checks out, you'll be free to go home."

The sheik told the FBI all he knew, which wasn't much. Mary Ann and Ron watched the whole thing being recorded in the room next door. Teddy Bear Fantasies was the name of the criminal organization involved in the kidnappings. Also shared were the names and phone numbers of the sheik's two contacts with Teddy Bear. The new leads were tenuous at best, but at least they had a place to start.

CHAPTER 20

After talking it over with Mary Ann, Ron agreed to focus on learning everything he could about Teddy Bear Fantasies, as quickly as possible, before they realized they were being investigated and took measures to disappear. Mary Ann, who had access to law enforcement databases that tracked phone numbers, would research the two names and phone numbers of the sheik's contacts at Teddy Bear. Working together, he hoped they would find the criminals running the organization.

They took a red-eye flight back to Dallas. Ron never mastered the art of sleeping in a cramped, uncomfortable airplane seat, so he made plans and ate a tasteless meal while Mary Ann snored in the seat next to him. He would scour the Internet for information about Teddy Bear Fantasies as a starting point, hoping it would yield more information. The plane provided no Internet connection, so his search would have to wait until they landed.

Their flight was uneventful until hitting some turbulence before landing. Ron looked on in disbelief as Mary Ann slept right through it while he gripped the armrests in terror. He wondered what kind of alarm clock she used to wake herself up in the morning.

Their connecting flight landed in Santa Barbara at eleven a.m. the next day. The sun was climbing into a cloudless sky, promising a warm day. Mary Ann headed home, claiming she hadn't slept a wink on the plane. Ron's eagerness to start his research prevented him from doing the same.

Everything else in his life was unimportant at this point. He finally had a chance at redemption for his failure to rescue the eight abducted children six years ago, as well as the other thing that gave him nightmares. So, instead of going home, he drove to his office and plugged into the Internet.

An hour later, the lack of results frustrated him. Teddy Bear didn't seem to exist. But thinking it through logically, the outcome was predictable. If easily found, the company wouldn't have survived. The filth they peddled would've attracted all kinds of unwanted attention from law enforcement.

There was one more place he could look for Teddy Bear, but he was reluctant to go there. Most people were unaware of the dark web, a unique part of the Internet. Servers in unfriendly third-world countries stored all the content outside Western law enforcement's jurisdiction, allowing it to grow and prosper unchecked. Invisible to anyone without special software, it attracted criminals of all types. Everything bad in the world existed there. The depravity of it sickened him. And he hated the disturbing dreams he would have for days after he used it.

Shaking off his hesitation, he removed a laptop computer used only for the dark web from a drawer in his desk and booted it up. He stored nothing else on this laptop in case someone hacked him while browsing. He typed "Teddy Bear Fantasies" into the new search engine. A moment later, a webpage flashed onto his screen.

"Gotcha," he muttered under his breath. The webpage featured pictures of young girls in suggestive poses, wearing very little clothing. None of them looked to be older than fourteen. Page links revealed disturbing information about the site's target audience. From explicit pictures to companionship, everything could be obtained for a price. *That's what Natalie was, a companion.*

He searched the site for a method of contact. All he found was an email address. This he copied down in his notes but didn't send a message. He needed to talk with Mary Ann first—and coordinate their efforts. Powering down his laptop, he leaned back in his chair, closed his eyes, and thought about his next move.

His cell phone rang loudly on his desk, startling him. He was unaware of his location for a moment and almost fell out of the well-padded executive chair he was sitting in. As cobwebs cleared from his mind, he recognized his office. His eyes widened in shock as he looked at the clock on his desk—five thirty in the afternoon. He must have fallen asleep in his chair. The phone kept ringing.

"Hello," he said.

"It's me," said Mary Ann. "Did you just wake up?"

"Yeah, I went to my office, and I dozed off. I found Teddy Bear Fantasies on the dark web."

"Makes sense. Nowhere else they could hide. Find anything that's usable?

"Only an email address. Tracking it down is impossible. You can access email from anywhere. Plus, I don't want to raise any suspicions we're on to them yet."

"Might be too late for that. I got some news from my FBI contact. The sheik is missing. It seems there was an ambush at his hotel. A security camera in the area recorded the whole thing. On his way toward his suite, someone dressed as a hotel maid stepped out the door of a room he just passed. Shot both bodyguards before they knew she was there. The shooter likely used a silencer, because nobody heard anything. She grabbed the sheik and hustled him down the fire escape. Hotel surveillance shows them leaving via a service entrance near the loading dock."

Ron was stunned. "Did they get a description of her?"

"Yeah, about five feet tall, with long black hair. Seemed to know how to handle a weapon."

"Did they see the maid's face?"

"Negative. Unfortunately, the hotel hung the security camera on the wall behind her, and she never looked back. I think she knew it was there."

Ron was silent for a moment. "If it was Teddy Bear, how did they discover he was in town?"

"The CIA, FBI, and local law enforcement were all involved. A leak could've come from anybody," said Mary Ann.

Something seemed wrong. "If you were Teddy Bear and knew why the sheik was in New York, wouldn't you want him dead before he talked to the FBI? They could have killed him as a warning to others not to talk. Why grab him after the fact?"

Mary Ann mulled it over. "Maybe an opportunity to kill him never happened, so they wanted to find out what he told the FBI. Kidnapping implies he had some information the kidnapper wanted, or he's being held for ransom. The surveillance tape lacks sound, so we don't know what the kidnapper said. The police discovered a hotel maid in the room where the shooter was hiding. She said the kidnapper wore a mask and made her strip down to her underwear before tying her up."

Ron grunted. "That explains how she got hold of a maid's uniform. Another possibility is the kidnapping might not involve Teddy Bear. Maybe it's a disgruntled former business partner he screwed over. Or some radical group in Bahrain trying to oust the monarchy. Just a coincidence it happened right after he talked to us."

He paused for a moment, then sighed. "There's nothing we can do except follow the leads we have. The NYPD will handle the rest of it."

"The sheik gave us two names and phone numbers," Mary Ann said. "I'll start tracing the numbers tomorrow and see where that leads. Why don't you search the names, and we'll chat later?"

"Will do. Right now, I'm going home to sleep in an actual bed. Let's catch up tomorrow."

Chapter 21

She attacked on the third day the sheik was in New York. By then, he had already talked to the FBI, but there had not been enough time to act sooner.

His two bodyguards relaxed as they walked with him down the hall toward the door to his hotel suite after an afternoon of sight-seeing. Hidden behind a nearby guest room door, Natalie watched through the peephole as the three passed. Her breathing was quick and shallow, her body tense. She had practiced ambushes many times during her training, but this was real.

She held a Glock, fitted with a silencer, in her hand as she stepped silently into the hall behind them. Before the bodyguards realized she was there, they were already dead, their pistols still in their holsters.

The sheik's hands flew up in a sign of surrender. "Please don't kill me. I've got money. You can have it all if you let me go." Desperation filled his voice as he begged for mercy.

"Shut up, or I'll kill you," said Natalie. She handcuffed and gagged him, hustled him down the fire escape with the Glock in his back, and bundled him into the trunk of her car before driving away. The entire operation took only twenty minutes. She was long gone before anyone at the hotel realized what had occurred.

Traffic was heavy as she fought her way out of Manhattan and across the Potomac River into Virginia. Arriving at her safe house, she drove into her garage, closing the roll-down door behind her. She felt safer here, and some of the tension went away. The sheik looked terrified when she opened the trunk and told him to get out. He searched the area with small darting eyes, looking for an escape.

His eyes settled on Natalie, who stood nearby with her Glock pointed at his head.

"Move," she said, marching the sheik into the basement.

The narrow room reached under the house. Natalie had covered the small windows with soundproof foam. Only a hanging fluorescent light illuminated the room. Under it sat a metal chair, bolted to the floor, with hand and foot restraints.

When he saw the chair, Abdul-Wadid, still clad in his fine gaberdine suit, shrank back in horror.

She pressed the barrel of her pistol to his head. "There are two choices: sit in the chair or die."

Moaning, he sat, shaking like a leaf, while she secured his arms and legs. She removed his gag and squatted down to look him in the eye. "Do you recognize me?" she asked.

He shook his head. "Who are you? What do you want?" he asked.

"My name is Kaina al-Badawi. You bought me from Teddy Bear Fantasies to be your slave when I was thirteen. Remember what you used to do to me? Now, I have the chance to repay the favor. Tell me everything you know about Teddy Bear if you want to live."

"No, it can't be true. How did you know I would be in New York?"

"ISIS has declared you to be a traitor. Did you not share information about them with the FBI? They told me you were coming, and I could do whatever I wanted with you."

A look of confusion crossed his face. "I know nothing about ISIS. Why would I be a part of that? The FBI wanted to know about Teddy Bear Fantasies and how you came to be my slave."

She smiled. "You lie, but you will tell me everything."

She took a savage satisfaction in his interrogation, reminding him about the abuse he had inflicted upon her as he howled in pain. The once fine gaberdine suit was in tatters, while blood pooled on the basement floor.

Hours later, he had given her only two names: Bob Hackman and Franz Meyers, which was disappointing. He denied to the end that he had anything to do with ISIS. But she had her revenge. The sheik was dead, and it felt good. Allah had sent the sign she had been waiting for.

CHAPTER 22

The nightmare would always begin with him scouring the neighborhood for hours, desperately trying to find her. At the end of an unknown street, he turned the corner and caught sight of her standing on the sidewalk far ahead. He shouted and started running towards her, upset that she hadn't stayed at her school. A disapproving frown crossed her face as she cast her eyes upon him. A van screeched to a halt beside her. The door opened, revealing a faceless man who seized her. Ron watched her struggle to get away.

He ran faster, yet got no closer to the van. The faceless man held her close to his chest, forcing her into the interior of the van. She cast one last anguished look over her shoulder at Ron, shouting something he never heard. The van sped away, leaving him sobbing on the sidewalk. At this point, he would wake up.

But tonight, the nightmare was different. He sprinted with all his might, reaching her just in time to prevent the man from tossing her into the van. He pounded the man, screaming at him to let her go. To defend himself, the man released her, escaped into the van, and sped off. His little sister threw her arms around his neck and smiled.

Ron jolted awake, drenched in sweat, his heart thumping in his chest. He could still imagine his sister's arms around his neck and the smile on her face. The bedroom was dark. The clock on his nightstand said four a.m. He swayed to his feet, switched on a light, and headed to the kitchen. He filled a tumbler with ice and Jack Daniels. The glass sweated in his hand while he walked to the living room and sat in his easy chair to calm his nerves. He gazed out the window into the darkness.

His modest home, built as a beach vacation home sixty years ago, contained two bedrooms, one bath, a kitchen, a dining room, and a living room. The back of the property included a detached one-car garage. The house sat just three blocks from the beach.

Outside, a neighborhood cat watching him from his front yard stretched and disappeared. He raised his glass for another sip and discovered it was empty. Lost in his thoughts, he didn't remember drinking the whiskey but decided a refill was in order. He shuffled into the kitchen, refilled his glass, and returned to his living room.

The cold glass numbed his fingers as he sank back into his chair. He raised it to his lips and took a swallow. The whiskey slid down, warming his chest.

His next thought was about the investigation. He had accomplished nothing yesterday besides finding Teddy Bear on the dark web. The names of two people were all he had to research. His earlier euphoria over the sheik's information was wearing off as the reality of how hard it would be to find them became apparent. His mind wandered, and he thought of the dream.

Why did the dream change? He believed dreams had meaning, and this one was telling him something. Instead of the usual despair when he awoke, he felt good because he rescued his sister. Could she have sent him the dream to tell him not to give up his search for Hackman? Was his longshot attempt about to bear fruit if he just kept at it?

Getting back to sleep was impossible. Ron wandered into his kitchen, started the coffee pot, and sat at the kitchen table beside his laptop. He began his research.

The sheik gave them two names during his interrogation by the FBI. The first, Bob Hackman, was his original point of contact with Teddy Bear. He vetted the sheik to make sure of his identity. Hackman spoke fluent American English, which made the sheik think he was American, but Ron knew that was a risky assumption on the sheik's part.

At first, their conversations happened via the phone. Once the sheik passed the background check, they met in person at a secluded sidewalk café in Monte Carlo during one of the sheik's business trips. During the meeting, they discussed what the sheik desired and the payment and delivery details. They met only once more when he flew with Natalie to Bahrain to deliver her.

The sheik described Hackman as short but very muscular, mid-50s, and beginning to bald, with hair cut very short. His appearance and mannerisms suggested ex-military. He had a tattoo on his left forearm, a skull with the words "2d Bn" below it. The sheik said he had a vibe about him like he would have no problem killing you with his bare hands if you looked at him funny.

The second Teddy Bear contact was Franz Meyers. He was the money man, who gave the sheik instructions on transferring the $80,000 payment for Natalie. The sheik approved the transaction based on a picture of Natalie that was emailed to him. Half the money went to a numbered bank account in the Cayman Islands as a down payment. When Natalie arrived at the small private landing strip in Bahrain, he paid the remaining half in cash to Myers, who flew in on the plane, meeting the sheik on the tarmac. He accepted the money, delaying the handoff until he counted it.

The sheik described Meyers as being of average height, in his late 40s, but overweight. Brown hair, turning gray, with a trim mustache. A spiffy dresser in a tailor-made wool suit. He spoke English with an accent that might be German and gave orders to

Hackman. If any issues arose, or he was interested in another girl, he gave the sheik a business card with a phone number to call. A few years later, the sheik called him to start discussions for another girl but was told the demand was high. They put him on a waiting list, but he claimed there had been no further contact since then.

If Meyers was German, it was a common name. Searching would yield an extensive list that would be impossible to narrow down and waste valuable time. Right now, he would concentrate on Hackman while keeping his fingers crossed for Mary Ann's success in uncovering the origins of the phone numbers.

With such sparse information, researching seemed challenging. Bob Hackman was another common name, and an Internet search would generate thousands of hits. He needed to narrow it down somehow.

He stepped out into his backyard, where he kept a set of weights and a treadmill. Working out focused his mind, making it easier to think. Today, a chilly breeze blew in from the ocean, encouraging him to get started. Attired in an old sweatshirt and jogging pants, he ran for twenty minutes on his treadmill to get warm, then did fifty push-ups and sit-ups. After that, he worked with the free weights for another thirty minutes.

By the time he finished, he had made some decisions. Based on his tattoo, he would assume that Hackman was ex-military. "2n Bn" was an abbreviation for second battalion. That alone would get rid of a considerable number of suspects.

If he was in his mid-50s now, assuming he joined the military following his high school graduation, as was most common then, the date of his service would be around the late 80s.

However, there were many second battalions in the armed forces, so Ron made another assumption that Hackman had been in the special forces or Marines. He lacked evidence for this, only a feeling that the job's required skills would have been learned then.

That narrowed the list to something manageable: the Navy Seals, Marines, or Army Rangers. Ron booted up his laptop and went to Google. A search of the Seals revealed they had no second battalion. The Marines had two, one based at Camp LeJeune, North Carolina, and the other at Camp Pendleton, California. The Rangers had one, at Joint Base Lewis-McChord in Washington state.

Half the night slipped away as Ron, sitting at his kitchen table, pored over the records for the Marines. Laughter and music from a party at a house down the street drifted in his open window. It was cold outside, but he loved the faint sound of the waves washing up on the beach and the smell of the salt air. He wondered if any of the people attending the party had children. The monster he was trying to catch might take them next.

Ron completed his search of the Marine database at the late hour of two in the morning, with his heavy eyelids demanding sleep. He had gotten a password a year ago by sheer luck when a client who was an ex-Marine had given it to him. She had hired him to find her husband from whom she was seeking a divorce. He also was an ex-Marine.

His search had uncovered four men named Bob Hackman. Unfortunately, they were all dead. It was a little-known fact that hospitals, doctors, and funeral homes were required to report the death of anyone in their care to Social Security. By implementing this rule, the government prevented the issuance of checks to deceased individuals, avoiding fraud. Investigating dead people would be an enormous waste of his time, so Ron checked the status of all four suspects.

Unless the Ranger's records yielded something, his assumptions about Hackman were wrong. Ron powered down his laptop and retired to bed, discouraged by his lack of progress.

The next morning's chill forced Ron to activate his old wall heater. It creaked and groaned as the metal warmed up. He was sipping his first cup of coffee, willing himself to return to the search, when his phone rang. Mary Ann's name appeared on the caller ID. He answered, hoping for good news.

"Tell me you got something."

"I ran those two numbers," she said. "Meyers has an account with A1 Telekom Austria. The bill gets paid by a shell company in the Cayman Islands, a subsidiary of a Panamanian company called Uberlegen, of which very little information exists."

"Meyers is Austrian, not German," Ron mused. "Doesn't help much. It's too common a name. Searching for him would be a pointless endeavor."

"I talked to the FBI, and they're looking into who's behind Uberlegen. It may take a while. Meanwhile, the news on Hackman was a bit more promising. The number belongs to Verizon, but it was one of a block bought in bulk by a seller of burner phones. The number is active, which is good news. Yesterday, it pinged off a cell tower in Santa Maria. Whoever has it turns it on only for short periods. Then it goes dark for days."

"Santa Maria! That's just up the coast. Hackman might be lurking right in our backyard. This is an opportunity we can't afford to miss. While you were tracking down the numbers, I researched the name. It's a reach, but based on the sheik's description, I'm assuming he's ex-military, special forces, or Marines. If he's in his late fifties and joined up when he was eighteen, that would have been in the late '80s, so I'm looking there. I drew a blank with the Seals and Marines, and was psyching myself up to search the Ranger records when you called."

"Lots of assumptions there." Mary Ann sounded doubtful. "But go for it. We've got no other leads. I set an alert on the number, so I'll receive a notification when someone turns on the phone. If it's close enough, we might track it down before he turns it off."

"Just let me know where it is, and I'll be ready. I will get that S.O.B. if it's the last thing I do. He took those eight kids, and he's going to tell me where they are. It's all I've dreamed about for six years. We're close, Mary Ann; I can feel it."

CHAPTER 23

Someone had forced the lock, leaving the door jamb splintered and ruined. Ron had been humming a song while walking down the corridor to his office on the first floor. The humming stopped, leaving a tense silence in the air, when he noticed his office door was ajar.

After talking with Mary Ann, he remembered some work he needed to complete at his office. He could search the Ranger records from there, so he pulled into the parking lot around ten.

The building was a modest two-story rectangular structure, built for practicality, not style: a stucco facade with large glass windows trimmed by faux wood beams. The lack of visual appeal mattered little to him since the rent was fair, and it was near his clients in Montecito.

Listening with his ear to the door, he heard nothing. He placed his laptop on the floor, braced himself, and pushed the door open with his foot. Light from the hallway spilled into the outer waiting room, which was empty. The door to his inner office hung open, but the light didn't penetrate it.

A more prudent individual might have retreated and alerted the police, but Ron knew from experience the time-consuming nature of a police investigation would take his entire morning and accomplish little. Besides, he doubted that whoever broke in was still around. He stood beside the door to his inner sanctum, stretched his fingers around the doorjamb, and searched for the elusive light switch inside. When he found it, fluorescent light bathed the empty room.

The damage was extensive. Whoever broke in left behind a scene of utter chaos, with papers and belongings scattered everywhere. File cabinets hung open, the contents flung onto the linoleum floor. His desk's locked drawers stood ajar, their splintered wood a testament to the burglar's determination to search everything. A vacant space on the desk marked his computer's former location. He surveyed the office; the missing item was nowhere to be found.

He sat in his undamaged office chair and pondered who to blame for the break-in. The obvious suspect would be the husband of one of his clients. In his line of work, angry husbands always blamed him for their problems. He had two clients divorcing their spouses. One husband was in San Diego at a convention, while the other was vacationing with his mistress in France. Either might have hired someone to do the deed, but it didn't seem likely.

The only other case he was working on was Teddy Bear. If they broke in, they knew who he was, which would compromise his ability to operate incognito.

How did they locate him so quickly? He thought about the missing sheik. If someone on Teddy Bear's payroll grabbed him, he might have told them about the investigation. But the sheik never saw Ron, so he couldn't have told Teddy Bear anything about him.

This left only law enforcement people as suspects. The leak must have originated from there. First, Natalie disappeared, then the sheik got kidnapped, and now the burglar. It's time to call for reinforcements.

"What?" said Mary Ann.

"We've got a problem," Ron replied.

"How so?"

"Somebody trashed my office last night. They left the place a mess, destroyed my desk, and stole my computer."

She thought for a moment. "A disgruntled husband of one of your clients?"

"Don't think so. I've only got two divorces going on, and neither husband looks likely. Another possibility is Teddy Bear."

"Don't see how they would know about you."

"Exactly my thinking. Natalie disappears, the sheik gets snatched, and now this. There must be a leak somewhere. I don't believe these are random coincidences."

He paused. "I'm not filing a formal complaint. We both know that investigating burglaries is a low priority for the police. However, the building has security cameras monitoring both entrances. Perhaps we can identify the intruder by reviewing the tapes. If you can make an appearance here, I'll call the property manager and arrange a meeting. I'll tell him you're investigating and want to see the tapes."

"Do you think you'll recognize the perp?"

"I don't know," Ron replied. "But if there's a shot of his face, we can run it through the facial recognition software."

"It's worth a try," she said. "But leaving the office right now isn't possible. I'm running this place, you know."

Ron choked back a sarcastic reply. His mind flashed back to the end of their last case when she gave up the search for a promotion. But he needed her help. It would do him no good to sour their relationship. Instead, he blew out a long breath. "Okay, so how about this afternoon? That'll give me time to clean up the mess and do more research."

"Let me look at my calendar." Ron heard the clicking of her keyboard. Then she was back. "Yeah, I can do that. Can you arrange a two o'clock meeting with the property manager?"

"No problem. I'll call him now. I'll let you know if he gives me any flack over the tapes. See you then."

His next call was to the property manager. After informing him of the burglary, he said the police would be there at two and wanted him to bring the surveillance tapes. He agreed.

Ron sat back in his chair, taking a moment to survey the wreckage of his office. He estimated the cost of replacing everything broken or missing at several thousand dollars, not including his door. It would wipe out his meager savings.

The invasion of his private domain left him feeling violated. Someone was targeting him. It bothered him he didn't know why or who it was. *Could the surveillance tapes hold the key?*

CHAPTER 24

R on's mood worsened as the morning wore on. His hands were grimy from the dirt and dust covering the floor as he retrieved his files. Inhaling the dust off of them made his mouth taste like cardboard. By noon, he had stacked, sorted, and filed until the floor of his office was nothing but linoleum.

He slammed the file cabinet shut on the last file and slumped into his chair. He drummed his fingers on the desk, wondering what Bob Hackman was doing while he wasted the entire morning cleaning up his office. Perhaps kidnapping another child? Flying to some god-forsaken country to make a delivery? Enjoying a vacation on a beach in Cancun? Covering his tracks so he would never be found? The possibilities were endless.

His growling stomach demanded lunch. Teriyaki chicken from the Chinese takeout would do the trick. He was dialing the number when a locksmith he had called earlier showed up to repair the office door. After a quick look, he announced it would have to be replaced. A steel plate over the break would work as a temporary fix. *One more thing to mention to the property manager when he showed up.*

Shortly before two, Jerome Butler, a young, newly appointed property manager eager to prove his worth, knocked and entered Ron's outer office. Attired in a blue turtleneck sweater and beige polyester pants, he looked like a college professor. Ron thought he had an arrogant look about him as he stared at the ruined door and pursed his lips.

"Shit, Ron, who ruined this door?"

Ron, still hungry, was not in the mood for sanctimonious nonsense. "Did you bring the tapes?"

"Yeah, I've got them copied on a thumb drive. Who's going to pay for the door?"

"Not me. I'm just a tenant here. You should spend some of my rent to hire a security guard."

"Break-ins were non-existent until now. You're attracting the wrong sort of people to my property. The owner may want to reevaluate having you as a tenant."

This was the last straw. On top of everything else that had gone wrong that day, now he was being threatened with eviction? He should evict this punk right out of his office. Ron rose from his chair as Mary Ann appeared at the door. As she caught sight of the furious expression on her old partner's face, she dashed in front of Jerome, determined to keep him safe. Ron stopped a foot away, breathing heavily.

"Let's turn it down a notch here, gentlemen. Our task is to identify the person responsible for this, not fight over who will pay for a door," she said.

Ron glowered at Mary Ann, his anger ebbing as he realized she was right. He turned on his heels and returned to his desk without saying a word.

She turned to the property manager and flashed her credentials. "I'm Lieutenant McDonald, in charge of investigating the burglary here. Let's see the tapes."

Breathing a sigh of relief, Jerome nodded, removed a laptop from his bag, and placed it on Ron's desk. With the computer powered on, he plugged a thumb drive into a USB port and clicked on a filename. A grainy black-and-white picture of the office building's back door appeared.

"We have surveillance cameras at both the front and back doors," he said. "I screened both the tapes before coming here. Nothing happened at our front door all night, but our back door was different. Let's fast forward to the scene where the intruder comes into view."

The timestamp in the upper corner of the screen moved forward. Jerome stopped the tape at three a.m. "Okay, here's where it gets interesting." He clicked the play button, and a figure appeared in the frame, clad from head to toe in a black ninja-like outfit. A black ski mask covered all but the eyes. Removing a set of keys from a pocket, the figure fit one key after another into the lock.

"Skeleton keys," said Ron.

In the end, a key opened the door. Stepping over the threshold, the figure moved down the hall carrying a crowbar, disappearing from camera range.

"That's it until an hour later," said Jerome. "Let me fast forward to when he left."

The time stamp moved forward and stopped at four o'clock in the morning. When the tape restarted, the figure was walking back toward the door, back to the camera, carrying Ron's computer under one arm and the crowbar in the other. The figure exited the building and disappeared.

Ron looked at Mary Ann and nodded toward the door.

"Thank you very much for your help, Mr. Butler," she said. "I'll keep the thumb drive as evidence. Should you discover anything else of importance, please get in touch with me immediately." She handed the property manager her business card, took him by the elbow, and guided him out of the office. Upon returning, she sat in a chair opposite the ruined desk.

"There's no doubt in my mind, that's the same person who snatched the sheik in New York," announced Ron. "There's a connection between the break-in and Teddy Bear."

Mary Ann looked skeptical. "Really? How could you tell? By looking at the eyes?"

"Same height and long black hair hanging out the backside of the ski mask. If you recall, the sheik's kidnapper had the same long hair."

"Not exactly irrefutable proof. Lots of women have long hair. I know how important Teddy Bear is to you, but we haven't determined that whoever took the sheik was working with them. Was there anything on your computer regarding your current clients?"

"No. When I save my work, it automatically gets stored in encrypted files on the cloud. I conducted all my Teddy Bear searches on my laptop, and it's currently sitting right beside me."

"Anything missing from your paper files?"

"Nothing about my active clients. Most of those files were old. I don't recall everything that could have been in them, but I can't comprehend anyone's interest in an old divorce case."

Mary Ann rubbed her brow. "Then it's safe to believe the break-in didn't yield her any useful information."

"Yes, but that's small comfort. I think she's connected to Teddy Bear, and somebody is feeding her information about me, but I can't figure out who. Finding the mole is crucial before sharing any new information with the feds."

"How're we going to do that?"

Ron shook his head. "Hell if I know. Let's concentrate on finding Bob Hackman and hope he leads us to something."

Mary Ann took the thumb drive and headed back to her office. Ron sat in front of his laptop and resumed his search of the army records. He was experiencing a growing sense of desperation. The right Bob Hackman had to be found, otherwise the investigation would grind to a halt unless Mary Ann traced the burner phone. The clock was ticking on that. Criminals often changed phones frequently to avoid the possibility of being traced. If he did that, they would lose their only link to him.

He attacked the Ranger databases, working into the night, swilling hot coffee to stay awake. When he got tired, he thought of the dream and kept going.

Chapter 25

Ron found five Bob Hackman's in the Ranger's database. One might be his target, but he needed proof that might or might not be obtainable from the information he was gathering. The work was tedious, but that was the nature of it. If things were easy to find, no one would need his services.

He dove into the arduous task of conducting background checks. First, he accessed their service records, which were supposed to be confidential. However, the government's outdated database software contained known security holes. Congressional underfunding left the outdated software vulnerable, exposing the men's complete service records. Although illegal, it was the only way he had to find Hackman. He downloaded all the documents to his laptop and printed them out.

Now that he had their social security numbers, he moved to the Social Security Administration database to determine whether each Hackman was deceased or living.

Social Security informed him that three of the five men were dead. With just two possibilities remaining, his research would take less time than expected. The next step was to access a private database that allowed him to gather updated information about both individuals.

Suspect number one joined the army in 1989, right after graduating from high school in Waynesville, Texas. Once he finished basic training, he signed up to join the Rangers. After multiple tours of duty overseas, he left the army in 1992. He returned to his home state of Texas, securing employment with the city of Dallas in the Parks and Recreation Department. Over the next five years, he got a college degree on the GI Bill and married a local girl. Their family expanded to include two grown children and three grandchildren. Currently, he held the title of Director of Parks and Recreation, responsible for managing and enhancing public parks and recreational facilities. He didn't fit the profile of someone who would be running around kidnapping children in California.

Following his 1988 high school graduation in Louisville, Pennsylvania, suspect number two enlisted in the army. He fought with the Rangers during the Persian Gulf War, and later in Afghanistan. His service record included a reprimand given for not following orders during a botched raid to capture one of Saddam Hussein's sons. However, after serving out his enlistment in Afghanistan, he received an honorable discharge. His record showed he received a Bronze Star for wounds sustained in Afghanistan. As a civilian, he bounced around at various jobs, never settling in one location for over two years. Worldwide Ventures hired him about ten years ago. What his job entailed was a mystery. His current address was unknown. No marriage or children appeared in the records.

Ron's interest heightened. Suspect number two looked like a loner with nothing to tie him down. That he bounced around so much after getting out of the army raised concerns. Maybe he had issues following orders because of PTSD suffered in Iraq or Afghanistan. A job with Teddy Bear, which used his combat skills while granting him much autonomy, would've been a perfect fit.

Suspect number two might be the Bob Hackman he sought, but Worldwide Ventures was the key. Linking it to Teddy Bear would prove he had his man.

He returned to the database and typed in "Worldwide Ventures." The results fell short of expectations. Someone incorporated it as a limited liability corporation in the Cayman Islands in 2011. That was it. There was nothing about who owned it or its line of business.

A memory of the Cayman Islands bubbled to the surface. Then he remembered: Half of Natalie's payment went to a Cayman Islands account. Mary Ann had told him someone there was paying Meyers' phone bill, but she hadn't shared the actual business name.

He speed-dialed her number. "Hey, I have a question for you," he said. "What's the name of the company that paid Franz Meyers' phone bill?"

"His phone bill? Why do you want to know that?"

"I think I found the Bob Hackman who works for Teddy Bear. He gets paid by a company called Worldwide Ventures. If the same company paid Meyer's bill, I think I've got the right guy."

Mary Ann whistled. "Hold on, I've got to look it up." Ron waited as the phone fell silent. Then she was back. "Sweet Jesus. It's Worldwide Ventures. What can you tell me about this guy?"

Ron filled her in. "A post office box is his only address. If he's using credit cards, they're not in his name. He doesn't appear to own a car. He's operating stealthily, avoiding any attention. Finding him will be a challenge."

"We've still got the lead on the burner phone," said Mary Ann. "Where's the post office box?"

"In a strip mall in Goleta. One of those private companies that compete with the post office." Goleta was a city next door to Santa Barbara.

"Text me the address," she said, "and I'll pay a visit to the owner. See what he knows about Hackman."

"Will do." Ron paused. "It's possible that this area is his central hub for operations. He was based on the West Coast when he was in the Rangers. He used the cell phone up in Santa Maria, and we know he was involved in the kidnapping of those eight girls six years ago in Santa Barbara. Given your resources, we should be able to track him down."

"What about your leak? The more people we involve, the greater the chance Hackman finds out about our investigation. I'll do what I can, but outside of my jurisdiction here in Santa Barbara, I will need help to track him. Are you okay with doing unpaid surveillance? It may require your absence from the office temporarily."

"I want this scumbag bad, Mary Ann. It's personal with me. Whatever you need, I'm there."

Chapter 26

The persistent ringing of his cell phone jolted Ron awake. Bright sunlight streamed through the shutters over his bedroom window, blinding him. With a groan, he turned his back to the harsh brightness. Whatever he did last night left his head pounding. Squinting through half-closed eyelids, his nightstand swam into view. A near-empty bottle of Jack Daniels sat there next to his phone. That wasn't a good sign. The phone stopped ringing, and he said a prayer of thanks to Jesus.

Crawling out of bed, he staggered into the bathroom, his head spinning. Nausea washed over him as his stomach churned. He heaved its contents into the toilet, relieved to have reached it in time. After that experience, he felt better until a wave of dizziness attacked him. He struggled to keep his balance as he splashed cold water onto the rough stubble on his face. Glancing up, a stranger's reflection stared back at him in the mirror. Some guy with wild hair sticking out in all directions, bloodshot eyes, and a t-shirt smelling like puke. He looked just like a guy who had failed those kids again.

He remembered coming home from the liquor store with a bottle of Jack and deciding to have four fingers on the rocks to calm him down enough to go to sleep. Then he decided he needed some music to keep him company, so he put on Creedence Clearwater's "Bad Moon Rising," which summarized his situation exactly. He sang with the band, which made him thirsty, so he made another drink. "Who'll Stop the Rain" played next, making him sad, prompting another drink.

Feelings of self-doubt had crept into his mind. *Who was he kidding? The Teddy Bear case was a black hole, and he fell into it. He risked everything he had to solve it, but was almost destitute. No income, no office, and, soon, no home to live in. Play it safe and stick to the easy divorce work.*

That's why he went to the liquor store.

He thought back further and remembered that he had gone to his office to check the door and had discovered it untouched. Instead, he found an envelope taped to the door with his name on it. Puzzled, he removed it, trudged into his office, and settled into his chair. Inside the envelope was a single sheet of paper, a thirty-day notice to vacate the premises, signed by Jerome Butler.

Wadding the notice into a ball, Ron hurled it across the room. There must have been a clause in the lease he had never read that allowed him to be evicted. If Butler had been there, he would have strangled him with his bare hands. The little prick's ego had taken over his common sense. He was getting evicted over a lousy three-hundred-dollar door.

Relieved that he could remember the reason for his condition, he was about to step into a cold shower, hoping to revive himself, when his phone rang once more. Cursing it with every foul name in the book, he turned off the water and padded naked into his bedroom.

Mary Ann's name appeared on the display. This was more than unjust. He was nursing one of the worst hangovers of his life, and she picked this time to call. As the phone continued ringing, he hesitated, torn between ignoring the call or answering it and facing the verbal abuse he knew would be coming if she detected his hangover. But perhaps she had discovered something about Hackman. He decided to tough it out.

"What?" he mumbled into the phone.

"Where the hell have you been? I've left you two messages this morning. Don't you ever check voicemail?"

"Ah...sorry. The battery ran down. Forgot to charge the phone last night."

"Are you sick? You sound like Kermit the Frog."

His muddled brain was having trouble keeping up with the conversation. "Kermit? Who's that?"

"What the fuck is wrong with you?" She sounded exasperated.

Poor decision answering her call. There was zero chance of bluff-ing his way out of it. "I might have had a drink when I arrived home last night. Or it might just be the flu," he added as a Hail Mary.

Mary Ann snorted. "Flu, my ass. Last night, you got stinking drunk, and now you're paying the price, aren't you?"

"Look, I had a bad day. Remember that punk property manager who wanted me to pay for the door? He gave me a thirty-day notice to move."

"That's it? Well, boo hoo Kermit. There's plenty of empty office space around. Pick one. Get a long-term lease so you can't get thrown out next time somebody ruins your door. Why'd you allow something this simple to bother you?"

He wasn't about to discuss his financial situation with her. It might create doubt in her mind as to his reliability. Besides, it was none of her business.

"I don't know. I didn't expect it, that's all. What's up?" He was getting cold, standing naked in his bedroom. Activating the speaker, he laid his phone on the table and rummaged in his closet for a robe.

"While you were pickling your brain, I had a conversation with Nicodemus Hernandez, the guy who owns the store with the post office boxes. Hackman's had a box there for seven years. Pays the rent a year at a time, in cash. He doesn't get much mail, so his pickups are erratic. The customers have keys to the front door to access their mail anytime. He comes at night after closing, so nobody ever sees him. That's going to make surveillance tougher."

Ron found his robe, wrapped it around his body, and took the phone into the kitchen with him. He poured water into his coffeemaker and turned it on. In his current condition, he could drink the whole pot. Dizziness struck again, so he eased into a chair at the kitchen table, praying the pounding in his head would fade.

Mary Ann was still talking. "I got a copy of his application for the mailbox. The contact number matches the one we have. The home address he gave doesn't exist. He used a real Nevada driver's license with another fake address for ID. At least we got a picture of his face. It jives with the description the sheik gave us. I'll text you a copy. It's looking like he's the Hackman we're looking for."

"That's good. Knowing what a guy looks like makes it much easier to find him," he said. "Have you gotten any more pings off his cell phone?"

"Nothing so far. I think he has another phone he uses for personal calls, while this one is strictly for business. He only turns it on when he has to."

Ron downed two aspirins he found in a kitchen cabinet while he tried to focus on his thoughts. "Perhaps we're looking at this from the wrong angle. If this *is* his business line, he must give this number out to potential clients when they're being vetted. Since the phone is rarely on, those clients must be leaving voicemails. All the phone companies allow you to call in remotely to access your messages. Just enter your password."

He glanced at the coffee pot, which was almost ready. "Subpoena the incoming call records to the business line. We should be able to pinpoint the number he's using to call in for his messages. He should keep that phone on, so we can trace it. That's much easier than conducting twenty-four-hour surveillance of EZ Postal for who knows how long."

"From a guy who killed half his brain cells last night, that actually makes sense," said Mary Ann. "I'll get the DA to request a subpoena from Judge Hidy. Meanwhile, you can go back to wallowing in self-pity."

He was about to make a sarcastic comment about why he always had to do her job for her when he realized she was already gone.

CHAPTER 27

*O*nce *they found Hackman, he'd slap a pair of handcuffs on him, then take him somewhere and have a private chat where nobody would hear the screams.* Ron ducked back into the cold shower. Anybody who kidnapped and abused innocent children deserved no better. He'd find out where the children were.

The hope of finding him, combined with the cold water, shook Ron out of his depression. If Hackman used two phones, his idea to find him could work. Right now, it was a waiting game. No one could act until Mary Ann received the subpoena. He hated delay. *What else could he do?* He realized he needed a backup plan if Mary Ann couldn't identify the second phone.

His only other option was to stake out EZ Postal until Hackman came to get his mail. He had a copy of Hackman's driver's license to identify him by sight. While he was getting his mail, he would attach a tracking device to Hackman's car if the opportunity arose. Otherwise, he would follow him, but the risk was more significant.

The problem with that plan was time. It could be weeks before Hackman came to get his mail. He could come when Ron was not there. He couldn't watch the place twenty-four hours a day, every day. Hackman might even send someone else to get his mail, who Ron would not recognize. While he was watching, his funds would dwindle to nothing, with no guarantee of success.

He mailed the final reports to his two divorce clients days ago, anticipating the Teddy Bear investigation would eat up more of his time. Instead, he found himself with nothing to do. He decided to buy some boxes to pack up his office files. EZ Postal would have boxes for sale, and while he was there, he could scout the area for a place to watch the building.

While he drove, he relived the memory of his meltdown yesterday. He believed that the pressure of the Teddy Bear case caused it. The eviction notice was just the trigger that released the guilt and self-loathing he kept locked up in his head. He couldn't afford to lose control of his emotions like that again. Swearing off alcohol, he promised himself he would stay sober for the duration of the case.

Traffic on the 101 was light in the late afternoon under clear skies. His tires hummed on the concrete as he traveled through Santa Barbara to Fairview Avenue, the turnoff for Goleta. Exiting the freeway, he found the address for EZ Postal. It was a small storefront in a strip mall anchored by a Dollar Mania store. The property looked worn and neglected; its best days were long gone. Many of the stores were empty, a reminder of the economic downturn caused by the epidemic. Paint peeled off the facade. Faded store signs, some missing letters, needed to be replaced. Trash and empty beer cans littered the area.

Amidst the commotion of the busy parking lot around Dollar Mania, he could blend in while establishing surveillance. But EZ Postal was open twenty-four hours a day. At four a.m., his would be the only car in the lot, so he needed a less obvious observation post.

After locking his car, he walked down a cracked sidewalk to the storefront. A buzzer sounded as he opened the door. Inside was a wall of numbered post office boxes, small ones on top and larger ones near the floor. To the left, a counter contained displays of greeting cards, key chains, and other knickknacks. A security gate divided it from the post office boxes. After hours, the owner would lock the gate, allowing customers access only to the boxes. A short, bald Latino man with a black mustache stretching down the sides of his mouth stood behind the counter. Ron surmised this was the owner, Nicodemus Hernandez. He walked over to chat.

Crammed into a small space behind the man, a pile of boxes surrounded a hopper filled with Styrofoam peanuts used to cushion items being shipped. Beyond that was a closed door, which he guessed led to a bathroom. A fine layer of dust covered everything, either a byproduct of the Styrofoam or a sign there wasn't much demand for shipping.

"Can I help you?" asked the counterman.

"I'm starting a business out of my house, and I need a post office box. Can you tell me the cost?" Ron asked.

The counterman smiled. "This is the right spot, friend. My name is Nick, and you are...?"

"Steve Truman," said Ron, shaking his hand.

"Glad to meet you, Steve. You won't find a better price on a mailbox anywhere else in town. Let me go over our plans with you."

Ron listened patiently to the sales pitch and then asked a few questions. "Can I get my mail anytime?"

"Sure. I'll give you a key to the front door, which gives you access to your mailbox."

"That's great, but what about security? Somebody could get in, pry open the boxes, steal everything in here."

"I monitor the place twenty-four hours a day," he said, pointing to a camera mounted high on the wall. "If the security company sees anything out of place, they call the cops. Been here fifteen years without a problem."

Ron thanked him for his time, bought a few cardboard boxes, said he'd get back to him when his business was ready, and left. He debated calling Mary Ann about the security camera. Depending on how long the company kept the tapes, they might see Hackman picking up his mail. But since he already had his picture from the driver's license, it wasn't worth the time it would take to review a month's worth of tape.

Walking back to his car, he noticed a van parked beside a white sedan a short distance away. Two men sat in the van's front seat, talking to each other. Neither paid Ron any attention. He dismissed them as part of the busy commotion around Dollar Mania.

He still needed to find a suitable place to observe EZ Postal. Exiting the parking lot, he drove around the neighborhood. A large apartment complex stood across the street. A row of carports for the tenants lined the property along Fairview. No one would notice him if he parked there. All he needed was a good pair of binoculars.

When he returned to his office, the broken door greeted him. He threw the boxes purchased at EZ Postal in the corner, planning to do his packing later in the month. He gazed sadly at the ruined desk. His first business purchase, it had served him well over the years. He felt guilty leaving it behind but was happy the property manager would have the hassle of disposing of it. *What goes around, comes around.*

One good thing about being evicted was he would save the three thousand dollars per month he paid in rent until he found a new office. He could work out of his house, although letting clients know where he lived was not a good idea. They could show up on his doorstep at any time. But he had thirty days to make that decision.

Since there was nothing else to do, he locked up and exited the building toward his car, shoes crunching on the loose asphalt. A white sedan with dark tinted windows cruised by, then sped away. He watched it go, then slid behind the wheel before pausing. The sedan looked familiar, but he couldn't place where he had seen it. Then he remembered—the parking lot at EZ Postal.

Ron retrieved a small, metallic black box from his glove compartment. On its face was a digital display with a few buttons underneath it. Before activating the device, he extended a telescoping antenna from the top of it. He walked around his car, pointing the antenna around the undercarriage and observing the digital readout. The device was a scanner for finding bugs, such as tracking devices. He found nothing.

While sitting in the rush hour traffic on the 101, he couldn't stop thinking about the white sedan. Somebody was following him, maybe the woman who ransacked his office. She must have tailed him when he drove from his house to EZ Postal, and then to his office. He felt vulnerable. Whoever was driving the sedan knew where he lived and worked, what kind of car he drove, and maybe had background information on his whole life.

In his usual role, he was the one in pursuit, methodically gathering information and maintaining control of the situation. Now, *he* was being stalked, the reason unknown. What information did he possess that anyone would want? Was Hackman warned Ron was looking for him? Was he in the white sedan? If so, he would take steps to disappear, and they would lose their best hope of cracking the case.

Chapter 28

When he arrived back in Carpinteria, Ron was relieved to find his home undisturbed. He sorted through his bedroom closet until he found his gun safe. After entering the code on the digital panel, the safe unlocked, and he removed his Glock.

Like most retired cops, he had a license to carry a concealed weapon. From that moment forward, he resolved to keep the pistol by his side whenever he ventured outside. He wouldn't go down without a fight if someone came for him.

The next day, his disassembled Glock sat in pieces on his kitchen table. His father had always told him a clean weapon was a reliable weapon, and the advice had stuck. He was oiling the slide when his phone rang. He activated the speaker so he could continue to work while talking.

"Hey, are you still on suicide watch? I've got some news that might cheer you up," Mary Ann said.

"Just hearing your voice is enough to make my heart sing," he said sarcastically. "Does the good news result from my brilliant idea to check Hackman's incoming call records?"

"Yeah, well, I wouldn't characterize it as brilliant. More like standard practice."

"Huh. Funny you didn't think of it," he said as he placed the slide on the rail of his gun.

"Got a station to run here, pal," she said defensively. "Lots of multi-tasking involved. Since no one ever entrusted you with that responsibility, you wouldn't understand. I would have thought about it before you if I wasn't so busy."

"Somebody should recommend you for the Medal of Honor. I'm blessed just to be talking to you." He was enjoying getting under her skin.

"Bite me, dickhead. I'm not telling you anything."

Ron chuckled. "Okay, I'll be nice. Lay it on me. Then I'll instruct you on what to do next." He completed assembling his Glock and snapped an empty magazine into the butt.

A sigh of exasperation came from the phone. "I got the file from Verizon late yesterday. I loaded it on my laptop and took it home with me. Tomas played basketball last night, but I skipped it to review the records. There were quite a few calls. The man keeps busy."

Crap. That made him feel guilty. Tomas was Mary Ann's seven-year-old son, and she had always struggled to spend quality time with him. "Ah, man, you should have waited until today or sent it to me. Time with your kid is more important."

"That information is private. You're not a cop anymore, remember? I had to subpoena it, which means I can't share it without permission from the court."

"Who would know?" Ron said.

"I'm doing this by the book. The subpoena is public information; a defense lawyer would try to quash it. This scumbag won't escape because of a technicality. Last night, I started the analysis and wrapped it up this morning. Three numbers appeared frequently. Per Verizon, two of them belonged to a mail-order company back East. But the third one belonged to another burner phone. I'd be willing to bet that one belongs to Hackman."

He was ecstatic. "Yes! We finally got a lead that panned out. Tell me his location, and I'll go choke the life out of him."

"Easy, boy. Before you choke anybody, we've got to make sure it's Hackman. The number pinged off a cell tower near San Luis Obispo this morning, and then it disappeared. He might have turned off his phone."

This was worrisome. "Do you think he got tipped off?"

"Who knows? I think you should pack a bag for a quick trip. I'll let you know the minute he turns the phone on again. If it stays off a few days, we can assume someone told him about us, and it's game over."

"Well, somebody's following me." He told her about the white sedan. "I thought it might be Hackman, but if he was up north this morning, that rules him out. My money's on somebody in the FBI leaking information. Wiring those chumps to a lie detector would reveal the truth."

"The other possibility is it may have no connection to Teddy Bear," Mary Ann said.

Ron grunted. "Yeah, you're right. It's got me worried, that's all. Some creep might want me dead."

She said nothing for a moment. "Do you still have your Glock? If I were you, I wouldn't leave home without it."

"It's my newest best friend. Hope Hackman gets to see it soon."

CHAPTER 29

The following day, the weather turned funky, with a strong wind blowing in from the northwest. A few daredevil surfers swarmed the beach, relishing the tall waves propelled by a storm far out in the ocean. When the weather was better, Ron would sometimes buy a six-pack of beer, a burrito, and some nachos from Ernie's Tacos, then spend the day on the sand getting a beer buzz and watching the surfers. Today, he spent his morning at the local market, replenishing his nonexistent food supply with canned and frozen items. He was carrying bags of groceries into his house when Mary Ann called.

"Tell me Hackman's back," he said.

"That's what I was going to say," she replied. "Are you ready to travel?"

"I'm packed and ready to go. Where is he?"

"His phone started pinging off a tower in San Luis Obispo, but now it's moving south toward Santa Maria. Maybe he'll drive to us if he's on his way home. But if he stops before getting here, you must confirm he's the right Bob Hackman before we make a move. Once we know for sure, we'll take him down."

"Got it. I'll drive north on the 101, then cut over to meet him. Text me status every fifteen minutes, or if he stops somewhere."

An adrenaline rush hit him as he unloaded the groceries, grabbed his overnight bag, and peeled out of his driveway. Locating Hackman would require skill, patience, and a bit of luck. The phone company could pinpoint the search area, but a dense population would obstruct the search.

Fifteen minutes later, right on schedule, the first text arrived from Mary Ann. *Proceeding south on PCH toward Pismo Beach.* PCH, as everyone called it, was an abbreviation for Pacific Coast Highway, the scenic route south to Santa Barbara. In the 50s, it was the only coastal route between Los Angeles and San Francisco. But then the state built the 101, which bypassed PCH. The road now carried local traffic and ran through small towns with stoplights and quaint shops.

This pleased Ron. Local traffic would slow Hackman down and give him time to get closer. He was hours away from Pismo Beach.

Past Goleta, he reached the turnoff for PCH near Gaviota State Park. The latest text from Mary Ann indicated Hackman was still moving south toward Guadalupe. It was early afternoon, and his stomach growled, reminding him it was time for lunch. But stopping for food was impossible if he was to intercept Hackman before he arrived in Lompoc, where it would be difficult to find him. His best chance would be in a rural part of PCH, north of Lompoc, devoid of nearby towns, and sparsely populated. He needed to get there before Hackman.

Two hours later, he blew through Lompoc and spotted a suitable place to wait on the south side of PCH. He slowed down, made a U-turn, and eased onto a dirt turnout wide enough to accommodate a large truck. It was time to update Mary Ann. "Just parked in a turnout southbound off PCH ten miles north of Lompoc. Here are my GPS coordinates." He read the latitude and longitude off of his phone. "Let me know when he passes, and I'll pull in behind and follow him."

Mary Ann typed in his position on her computer. "Okay, I see you now. He's about fifteen minutes away. Stand by."

Ron adjusted his side mirror for a clearer view of approaching vehicles. Sweat broke out on his brow, and his heart pounded. Everything hinged on spotting the right car among the sea of vehicles. If he followed the wrong one, Hackman might make it to Santa Barbara before he caught up. It would be even harder to find him there. Fortunately, the traffic was minimal at this hour. Only an occasional car or truck drove by.

"He's coming up on you now," said Mary Ann.

He directed his full attention to the side mirror, blocking out any distractions. A small dot appeared on the road behind him and grew larger. Within a few seconds, he recognized the distinct shape of a silver Camaro. Sunlight glinted off the car's chrome accents. It approached at a leisurely pace, well under the speed limit.

Ron slouched down in his seat, making it appear his car was empty, while still being able to watch the approaching Camaro in his rearview mirror. As it passed, he glimpsed the lone occupant, a man wearing a baseball cap that cast a shadow over his face. He memorized the license plate as the car disappeared down the road.

"Okay, I've got him," he said, the excitement clear in his voice. "Silver Camaro, one male." He gave Mary Ann the plate number. I couldn't see his face. I'm following now."

His tires spun on the dirt, raising a cloud of dust as he acceler-ated onto PCH. The Camaro came into sight, prompting him to reduce his speed to match it. Almost at the outskirts of Lompoc, the driver tapped the brake pedal and made a careful right turn onto a secondary road. *Maybe he's not going home. With any luck, he's meeting his boss, and I can bag them both.*

A half mile ahead, the Camaro turned right onto a narrow, rutted road, kicking up a cloud of dust. Further off in the distance, Ron saw the hulking remains of a large factory, likely abandoned years ago. Before making the turn, he hesitated, his hand gripping the steering wheel. The road was devoid of any activity or purpose.

If Hackman noticed another car on it, he would know someone was following him and might set up an ambush.

Caution prevailed. He pulled off to the shoulder of the road near the turnoff and called Mary Ann.

"What's happening?" she said, stress clear in her voice.

"I've tailed him to this isolated access road near Lompoc. I don't know where it goes. He'd spot me in a minute if I tried to follow him. Can you tell me what's out there?" He gave her his GPS coordinates.

"Hold on, let me do some research."

Ron heard the furious clacking of her keyboard. "Okay, I've got an aerial view. It's an abandoned factory. There's a sign that says something about sugar beets. The road dead ends at the factory, so that has to be his destination. There's nothing else around there except farmland."

"Any alternate route to avoid the road?"

"Yes, if you want to hoof it through the surrounding farmland. Looks like about two miles, though. If he leaves while you're out there, he'll be gone before you can return to your car."

He thought it over and reached a compromise. "I've got to know if it's Hackman and what he's doing out there. We may never get another chance like this. Maybe it's a major gathering of Teddy Bear hoodlums. Who knows?"

"Or he knows you followed him, and he's setting you up for an ambush," she replied.

Ron felt offended. "It's not the first time I've done this. I was careful tailing him. There was no way he could have spotted me. I'll drive about halfway in, then park to avoid being seen. If I walk the remaining distance, I can use the buildings for cover."

"Want me to call Lompoc Police for backup? I don't like you all alone out there."

"That might spook him, and I still don't have a positive ID," said Ron. "What if it's the wrong guy? Then we'll both look stupid. Let me investigate, get a look at him, and if it's Hackman, I'll retreat and request backup."

"I don't like it," she repeated, sounding worried. "You have one hour. If you don't contact me by then, I'm calling in the cavalry."

CHAPTER 30

Ron drove down the access road, trying to avoid the potholes without raising a cloud of dust. The tire tracks of Hackman's car were visible, goading him on. Cornfields stretched as far as he could see on each side of the road. A mile in, a small tin building used as an old pumping station sat beside the road. It seemed like a good place to hide his car. He parked behind it, grabbed his Glock and binoculars, and started walking. It was late afternoon; the air was cooling, and he regretted not grabbing his jacket in the trunk. He thought about returning to get it, but he had no time. Mary Ann had given him only an hour to find his target.

A sagging chain-link fence surrounded the factory. A rusty gate that once spanned the road lay flat in the weeds. Next to it, a small roofless guardhouse leaned sideways, ready to collapse if someone gave it a shove. The road continued straight ahead to a cluster of rusted sheet metal buildings. Along both sides of the road, abandoned machinery, shells of cars, and piles of boxes provided excellent concealment. He dashed from cover to cover, getting closer to the buildings. Hackman's location was a mystery. His Camaro was not visible. The only sound was the wind rattling some loose sheet metal on the roof of one building.

The walk from the pump house to the factory had been longer than Ron expected. Hackman needed to be found before time ran out. He hid behind a pile of boxes, his pulse quickening while scanning the buildings through his binoculars, eyes darting from one window to another. He sensed being watched, causing the hair on his neck to stand up. But was it real or his imagination?

The most prominent building loomed ahead, a two-story structure, most likely the main factory. Gaping holes stood where windows had once been. Beyond that was darkness. A feeling of unease crept over him. *That's the ideal spot for surveillance. The view from those second-floor windows extends for miles. If he's up there, he knows I'm here.*

He moved closer, crouching behind a massive motor covered in dirt, and scanned the windows again. There was a flicker of movement on the second floor when the darkness inside momentarily became deeper.

That was enough. It had to be Hackman. He dodged behind a nearby building and ran its length. No one in the main factory could see him. When he reached the corner, he stopped and peered around it. A side entrance to the main factory was a short distance away, and its metal door was slightly open. He paused, listening hard for anything out of the ordinary. All he heard was the wind blowing through holes in the rusting sheet metal.

A quick look at his watch made him realize that the hour Mary Ann gave him was over. He ducked back from the corner and dialed her number. "Listen," he said in a whisper. "I'm at the factory. There's a two-story building next to me. There was some movement in a window, so someone is in there. I'm going to check it out, but I need more time. Give me another hour."

He ended the call and turned off the ringer before she could protest. The factory door beckoned him. His gut told him that Hackman was inside. It was the chance he'd been praying for. *I'll take him by surprise and interrogate him right here, where nobody can interfere. He knows what happened to the kids.*

Taking a deep breath, he cocked his pistol and approached the door. He pushed it open with his foot, relieved that it made no noise. He waited, listening hard, but heard nothing. As he entered the factory, the stark contrast between the bright light outside and the gloomy interior momentarily blinded him. A peculiar odor of decaying beets filled his nose. It was his last thought before a blow struck him from behind, dropping him unconscious to the floor.

CHAPTER 31

Convinced he was drowning, Ron's first reaction was to tread water, only to find someone had tied his hands behind his back. Panicking, he gasped for air and realized he could breathe. He struggled to remember what happened as the cobwebs cleared from his mind.

His eyes fluttered open. He sat on the floor of a large metal building. Water dripped from his face down to his shirt and pants. Weak light filtered in through the ruined windows. Machinery, covered in dust and cobwebs, was scattered around. Beyond that was darkness. *What happened?*

His head pounded. Groaning, he tried to move, but his hands were bound to a steel beam supporting the ceiling. Memories flooded back, one after another. He was stalking Hackman in an abandoned factory. Someone approached him from behind and knocked him out. Whoever did that must have tied his hands to the beam.

His obsession with finding Hackman had clouded his judgment. Any rookie cop would have known to wait for backup instead of charging ahead into an unfamiliar building. Yet that was what he had done. Now, he was a prisoner, trapped in a room with a deranged kidnapper. He remembered telling Mary Ann to give him another hour. *How long was he unconscious?* Perhaps the hour had passed, and the police were on their way.

The sound of something metal thrown across the floor in the darkness drew his attention. A metal pail rolled into view. Behind it, a shadow stopped just shy of the light.

"Nothing works like cold water to wake somebody," said a male voice. "You're probably not feeling too great, so I'll make this quick. I dislike being followed. Particularly by someone as stupid as you. I spotted you at the turnout back on PCH. I'm going to ask a series of questions. My time here's limited, so if you try to bullshit me, I'll shoot you quick and leave your body here for the rats. I've got nothing to lose by ending your miserable life. If you answer truthfully, I'll let you go. Do you understand?"

Ron nodded. Every time he moved his head, a stabbing pain shot into his brain. He didn't believe for a minute that his assailant had any intention of letting him go. Offering hope in exchange for information was a common interrogation technique he had learned as a rookie in the police department. He needed to buy time, praying for the police to arrive before his captor lost interest in him.

"Good. First question: who are you, and why are you following me?"

"Ron Jackson," he said, keeping his head still. "I'm a private detective working on a case you may be involved in."

A hand tossed his wallet from the darkness to the floor before him. "So far, so good. That is what your ID says. Congratulations, you get to live a little longer. Now, tell me about the case you're working on."

"Does the name Natalie Martinez ring a bell?"

There was a momentary pause. "Never heard of her."

"Ah. In that case, you have my apology. I've been following the wrong man."

A snort came from the darkness. "Okay. I'll just kill you now since it's a matter of mistaken identity."

Ron heard a pistol being racked to chamber a round. He kept talking. "That would be a big mistake, Mr. Hackman."

"Huh. It's not a case of mistaken identity, after all. How did you track me down?'

"I'm a PI. It's what I do for a living. Years ago, the Garcia siblings kidnapped Natalie. Doesn't that name ring a bell? They made a living out of abducting young kids who were unlikely to be missed and selling them to you. Eight children that we know about, four of them just babies. Natalie was one of them. She was only thirteen when you took her."

"That's a very sad story, Jackson. Sounds like a fairy tale. Where did you get this information?"

Keep talking. I only need an hour. "You sold Natalie to some sheik in Bahrain, thinking she would disappear forever. But you were wrong. The sheik sold her a year later to an ISIS commander in Syria. When she escaped, friendly forces captured her. The CIA flew her back to America, and she recounted every detail to us. The sheik was very helpful in providing us with a sketch of your face."

Hackman stepped forward into the light. He wore black khaki pants, a long-sleeved black turtleneck sweater, and a black ski mask over his head. A chrome pistol gleamed in his right hand. Reaching up with his left hand, he peeled off the ski mask. "Well, how did he do? Do I look anything like the sketch?"

"Remarkable resemblance, but you've put on some weight since then."

He grunted. "That may be true, but let's return to your story. You keep saying *we.* You're a PI, so who're you working for?"

"That's the interesting part. When the Garcia's were kidnapping the kids, I was a detective with the Santa Barbara County Sheriff's Department. My partner and I caught the murder case when Angela Garcia died. While we investigated that, we discovered the missing kids. Art Garcia died in a mysterious explosion that blew up his house. The explosion almost killed me, too. You wouldn't know anything about *that,* would you?"

Hackman said nothing.

"Anyway, since his sister was already dead, he was the only one who could finger you. When he died, so did all our leads. Did you think it was over? Nobody left to rat you out, right? Despite everything, I never lost hope of getting a break in the case. And six years later, Natalie came back and told us about you. When I began tracing your whereabouts, I came across Teddy Bear Fantasies."

Hackman stiffened. Surprise flickered over his face. "What information do you have about that?"

Ron smiled. "I know you work for them. We've identified several other employees we will soon arrest. It's just a question of time before we bust the whole rotten bunch of you. You can still save yourself, Hackman. Switch sides, confess all, and get freedom in witness protection. Otherwise, you're going to spend the rest of your miserable life in a prison cell."

He laughed. "You got balls, I'll give you that. But I think you're blowing smoke up my ass. I enjoyed the chat, but I must leave before your friends arrive." He stepped forward, leveling his pistol at Ron's chest. "See you in hell."

Ron closed his eyes and braced himself for the end. Shots erupted, echoing through the air one after another, but none struck him. Hackman grunted once, and then there was silence. Opening his eyes, he saw Hackman lying on the floor before him. He was bleeding from his right shoulder and chest, just below his heart. He didn't appear to be breathing.

Ron was stunned he was still alive. The police arrived just in time to save him.

As the echo of the last shot faded away and the smell of gunpowder hung in the air, Ron heard footsteps approaching. "Thank God," he called out to the darkness. "You got here just in time. A minute later, I would have been dead."

CHAPTER 32

The footsteps grew closer, and a figure materialized out of the darkness. Ron gasped in surprise. It wasn't Mary Ann or a member of the Lompoc police. Instead, a figure in black materialized. Only the eyes were visible—the ninja who broke into his office.

She stood studying him, saying nothing. An AK-47 was slung over her shoulder. A web belt held a holster containing a pistol, spare ammo pouches, and other items he couldn't identify. Body armor covered her chest.

As he breathed deeply, his muscles unwound, and his mind settled. Tied to the post, he was at her mercy, but it didn't appear she planned to harm him, or he would already be dead. "Thank you for saving my life. Who are you?"

She ignored him, walked over to Hackman's body, and kicked him in the face. Satisfied he was dead, she spat on his body, then turned her gaze back to Ron. Drawing near, she crouched down beside him, her gaze steady. Her eyes were hard, black as the night, and devoid of emotion.

"You're here today because of me," she said. "We share the same goal."

Her accent was peculiar, suggestive of the Middle East. Then he figured it out and smiled. "You're Natalie Martinez."

"Correct," she said, her eyes never leaving his. "How did you know this?"

"My ex-partner, Mary Ann McDonald, received word of your rescue, and she told me. We thought you might be dead when you disappeared from your halfway house. How did you find me?"

"The Internet told me you and Mary Ann McDonald were the detectives who worked my case six years ago. I saw the website for your detective business, and it gave me your address. No one else would help me find my kidnappers, so I came here to find you. I've been watching to see if you are trustworthy. Then you found Hackman, the man who sold me into slavery, which proved that we are working towards the same thing. I would have preferred to capture him alive, but I couldn't let him kill you."

"I knew someone was following me, but not why. Did you break into my office and follow me in a white sedan when I went to EZ Postal?"

Her eyes narrowed. "Yes, I broke into your office hoping to find information on those involved with Teddy Bear. But I know nothing of a white sedan." A frown crossed her face. "Others may be following you, hoping to find me. You must be careful. They're very dangerous."

He felt a wave of confusion at her admission. "Who are they? How did they find me?"

Before she could answer, the distant wail of sirens filled the room. Natalie rushed to a nearby window and looked out onto the road. "The police are coming. I can see the dust on the road. I must leave now. If I'm discovered here, my mission will fail."

"Wait," he said desperately. "My wallet's here on the floor. Take one of my business cards and call me. There are more people on Teddy Bear's payroll. We can work together to catch them."

She hesitated, then grabbed his wallet and thumbed through it, removing a business card. "Can I trust you, Ron Jackson? You work with the police, and the police cannot be involved."

"I understand. You were never here. Believe me when I tell you I'll do anything to find these cockroaches. It's personal with me, too."

She held his gaze a moment longer, then turned on her heels and disappeared into the darkness. Ten minutes later, Ron heard several cars stop outside the factory, their sirens falling silent. Doors were slammed, orders shouted, and men moved into position. He shouted for help, and soon, officers burst into the room.

"I'm over here," he said, as their flashlights swept the area. "Tied to a post on the floor. There's a dead man near me. Nobody else."

A SWAT team converged on his voice. The sergeant in charge halted before him while the rest of his team swept the room. "Are you Ron Jackson?" he inquired.

"Yes, I am. Who are you?"

"Sergeant Adams, Lompoc Police. The Santa Barbara Sheriff's Department called us. They said you might be in trouble, so we came to check it out. Did you say you're the only one here?"

"That's right."

"A man died over there. Did you kill him, then tie yourself up?"

Ron blew out a deep breath. "It's a long story. How about untying me and I'll fill you in. I can't feel my fingers anymore."

Chapter 33

Ron sat on a large box outside the factory, rubbing his wrists to restore circulation. It was 5 pm and getting dark. The temperature had dropped, causing his body to shiver in the breeze.

The paralyzing fear he felt upon realizing how close he came to death lingered. His reckless actions almost got him killed. The eight missing children drove him to fixate on capturing Hackman to uncover the truth and become a hero. *No, that wasn't it. It went back further than that.* And what was his accomplishment? A dead body unwilling to tell him a thing. He blew his best chance to crack the case because he didn't wait for backup.

The last six years had changed him from someone who worked within the system to someone who didn't respect it. That was fine when all he was doing was divorce work. He operated independently, preparing reports and then moving on to the next client. But that had all changed when Natalie reappeared. He couldn't find the people running Teddy Bear by himself, which, given his mindset, was difficult to admit.

He couldn't help but marvel at how Natalie vanished in ten minutes without a trace. Secretly, he was happy that she got away. If the police had caught her, they would have charged her with Hackman's death. The FBI would have intervened and caused a chaotic mess. He would have had no chance of ever working with her to bring down Teddy Bear. But could she be trusted to work within the system given her distrust of the police?

Mary Ann was the only person he felt he could trust in law enforcement due to their history together. However, after what had happened today, her willingness to continue working with him was in question. He felt himself being squeezed between two opposing forces, both of which he needed to reach his goal.

Sergeant Adams stood nearby with several squad members discussing the rescue, and occasionally glancing his way. The SWAT team had finished sweeping the area, finding no one else. He had told Ron that detectives would be arriving soon to take his statement. Ron was using the time to get his story straight.

A cloud of dust arose far down the access road toward Lompoc. Reinforcements were on the way. A homicide investigation would involve detectives, forensics, and the coroner. The detectives would expect a detailed statement explaining why he was tied up in an abandoned factory with a dead man. That would take hours. Before they arrived, he needed to call Mary Ann.

"Are you all right?" she asked.

"Yeah," he paused, then blurted it out. "Hackman's dead."

"Shit. What happened? Did you get in a shootout?"

He told her the complete story, holding back only his conversation with Natalie. He had made a colossal mistake that could end the investigation. Pretending anything else was pointless. When he finished, Mary Ann was silent.

"Okay, you're right, you screwed this up bad," she finally said. "Do you think the ninja who shot Hackman is Natalie? If so, it's going to ring alarms from here to Washington. The FBI will assume she's a terrorist and hunt her down. And Liz Farmingham could get involved. Remember her? The politician who closed the Garcia case and is now the Attorney General of California? She has the power to pull your license and get me fired. That will stop our investigation, end of story."

Ron felt miserable having to lie to her. "I couldn't say it was Natalie. I've never met her in person. All I could see were the eyes. I won't mention your name either. This is a case I was working on alone."

"That won't fly. Who do you think called the Lompoc police? This is the third time a ninja has appeared in this investigation. The last time at your office, you were positive it was Natalie. What are the chances a different ninja would show up this time?"

Ron started tapping his foot nervously. "Well, remember, we haven't positively identified her as the ninja. I just had a gut feeling it was her on the surveillance tape. This time, seeing her in person, it was different. I didn't get that same feeling," he said, realizing how lame it sounded.

"Are you trying to cover up her involvement in the shooting?" asked Mary Ann.

"No. I'm just saying I couldn't testify in court that it was her."

"Maybe it's time we share our knowledge with the FBI and call it a day. We got the son of a bitch who sold those eight kids, and that's a definite win. The FBI can go after Teddy Bear."

It sounds like she's ready to quit again. "What's the FBI done so far? Sat on their ass hoping the case will go away?" he said. "Natalie disappeared from right under their nose."

A caravan of cars pulled into the area, raising a gigantic cloud of dust.

"The crime team just arrived, so I've got to go. I'm sorry, Mary Ann. This is all on me. If you want to bail on this, I understand. Call me tomorrow and let me know, okay?"

Ron disconnected the call as the caravan halted. Two men in polyester suits emerged from an unmarked car and approached, waving the dust away from their faces. Their sharp, analytical gazes convinced him they were the detectives assigned to the case. One was tall, about six feet four, and thin. He was older, in his early fifties, and looked tired, like someone woke him up to take this case. His partner was much younger, in his mid-thirties, short, with a belly hanging over his belt. He looked eager to begin the interrogation. *Maybe he's being trained by the old guy. They look like Laurel and Hardy.*

The thin man stuck out his hand. "Detective Ramsey. This is my partner, Detective Pickman. You must be Ron Jackson."

"That's right."

Behind the detectives, three people emerged from a van with "Crime Scene Investigation" stenciled on the side, which meant forensics. Slamming the doors behind them, they grabbed their kits, ignored the detectives, and disappeared into the factory. A third van, containing two men, belonged to the coroner. They sat in the van smoking cigarettes, waiting for the authorization to remove the body.

"Tell us what happened here," Ramsey said as he removed a small notebook and pen from the inside pocket of his suit.

"The first thing I should tell you is that I'm a private detective," Ron said as he opened his wallet to display his license.

"Yeah, we know all about your background," said Pickman. "You were previously employed as a sheriff's detective in Santa Barbara. You retired after solving a big case up there involving kidnapping and murder. There was much speculation surrounding your motives. You could have written your ticket. Is there a connection with that?"

Despite being new to the case, the detectives' knowledge of him was remarkable. Somebody must have filled them in. He wondered if Mary Ann was pulling strings and using her influence.

"Alright, you guys have done your homework, so let's cut to the chase. This relates to that old case. Though the media reported otherwise, the case remains unresolved. All the suspects died before they could tell us anything. We never found the kids because we ran out of leads."

Ron let that sink in. Both detectives nodded their understanding.

"Six years passed, and then we discovered that Hackman was the guy the Garcias sold the kids to. I was following his car when he lured me here."

The detectives had stopped taking notes, intrigued by his story.

Ron told them about being ambushed by Hackman. "I kept talking, trying to buy time. He was about to kill me when somebody else hiding in the factory shot him. Then your SWAT team showed up and rescued me."

Ramsey scratched his head and frowned. "Somebody shot him? Did you see this person?"

"Yes, and no. The shots came out of the dark. The shooter entered the light after he shot Hackman. He looked like a ninja, dressed all in black, just like in action movies. Only his eyes were visible."

"Really?" said Pickman. "A ninja? Did he say anything to you?"

"He asked who I was. After I told him, he heard the sirens from the SWAT team coming down the road. That spooked him, and he disappeared."

"How long would you say it was until the SWAT team arrived?"

"Hard to tell when you're tied up, maybe thirty minutes," Ron said, stretching out the time.

Ramsey grunted. "Don't know how he heard sirens if SWAT was thirty minutes away. Did you hear a car leave? Anything like that?"

"No."

"This isn't adding up. As soon as we got the call, we blocked the access road so nobody could leave. SWAT hadn't arrived yet, so your ninja was still here. There's no other way out except through the fields. A chopper is up, looking for runners with an infrared camera. Nobody's seen a thing. How do you suppose the shooter disappeared in less than thirty minutes?"

Ron shrugged his shoulders. "I've got no idea. They train ninjas to avoid detection."

The detectives looked at each other. "Okay, why do you think this ninja saved you?" Pickman asked.

"Good question. I've wondered about that myself. I believe he followed me, hoping I would lead him to Hackman. Maybe he had a grudge against him. Before departing, he kicked Hackman in the face, leading me to suspect he knew him."

This would be evident from the autopsy, so it would boost his credibility if he revealed it now.

Pickman frowned, looking like he didn't believe a word he'd heard. "So, just to recap your story, somehow a ninja followed you here even though there's no evidence he had transportation, shot Hackman, then disappeared by walking miles through open fields, evading a chopper equipped to find him?"

"I know it sounds crazy, fellas, but that's what happened."

"How'd you find Hackman?" Ramsey said. "With all due respect, you're not a cop anymore, so did somebody tell you what that kid Natalie told the cops?"

"Listen, we all have confidential sources. If I disclose that, then I've betrayed a source. Let's just say this person knew that I worked the Garcia case and wanted to catch this guy. Finish what I started."

"Yeah, I think we know who that is since she called us to save your ass."

***

After midnight, a leg cramp wracked Natalie as she weighed the safety of leaving her hiding place. The forensics team had finished gathering evidence an hour ago, and the coroner took Hackman's body away. The chopper had given up its search for her, returning to base to refuel. After conducting a final walkthrough, the detectives were the last to leave.

The ocean breeze had stiffened, rattling the factory's loose sheet metal siding. Except for the wind, a tangible stillness settled over the factory. Only tire tracks in the dirt surrounding the building suggested anything had occurred there.

She waited another half-hour, breathing in the sour odor of decayed beets. From her perch in the rafters, she had an excellent vantage point to observe everything below in the factory. Steel beams crisscrossed in the dark gloom where light didn't penetrate. In her black ninja outfit, she was invisible. She found it amusing that the cops spent so much time trying to find her outside the factory. It didn't occur to them she never left. She had taken a chance that they wouldn't search the rafters with their flashlights, and the gamble had paid off.

It was all part of her training. Doing the unexpected was a key aspect of stealth: understanding the enemy's perspective and then exploiting it.

She felt disappointed when the police discovered nothing of importance on Hackman's body except for his cell phone and a driver's license. She was upset it hadn't occurred to her to take it. One can learn a lot from a cell phone. The detectives were unhappy to find it password-protected. They bagged it and sent it to their lab, eager to see if their state-of-the-art equipment could crack the password.

While waiting for everyone to leave, she thought of Ron's offer to help locate the remaining criminals responsible for her kidnapping. Was it a sincere offer, or a ploy to bring her under the control of the police? If they caught her, they could send her back to Washington, D.C., destroying her plan. But if the offer was sincere, it merited consideration.

She could think of several reasons they should partner and one why they should not. Ron worked with Mary Ann McDonald, who gave him valuable intelligence that Natalie couldn't obtain. How else would he have known to follow Hackman's car? If they partnered, she would insist that he share the information he was getting from Mary Ann with her. That was much better than mindlessly following him everywhere, not knowing what was happening. Her time could be better spent focused on achieving her goals. When he told her he was being followed, she realized ISIS was much closer to finding her than she thought. Or maybe the men in the white car worked for Teddy Bear. Either way, they knew she was in California and followed Ron to find her. She had been naïve to think she was safe from them just because she traveled clear across the country. A partner could watch her back, easing her anxiety.

However, Ron's former partner, a police officer, presented a problem; a bond connected them. Could she count on his loyalty, or would he betray her to Mary Ann if he disagreed with her tactics? He had told her he would not disclose her presence to the Lompoc police, and nothing she had heard from her listening post indicated otherwise. But it could be a trick to earn her trust.

She hesitated to make a decision. He said that finding Teddy Bear was personal. Why was it so important to him? The answer to this question might make it easier to trust him. With no information, her gut told her to delay making that decision and wait to see what he did next.

It was time to leave before someone returned. She hadn't slept in over a day, and her brain was foggy. Unclear thinking could get you killed. Climbing down from the rafters, she followed the access road, settling into a steady jog, while keeping an eye on the sky for any sign of a chopper coming her way. After ten minutes, she veered off into the cornfield near a large rock she used as a marker. She reemerged with a bicycle and rode it to the main road.

Her car was where she left it, in a grocery store parking lot, bringing her a sense of relief. After returning the bike to where she had "borrowed" it the previous day, she drove east to the 101 and then north, back to the extended stay hotel in Santa Barbara where she was hiding. Ron's business card was still in her pocket.

CHAPTER 34

After his close call at the factory, Ron was enduring a second day of isolation at home. The silence intensified his frustration as he waited for his phone to ring. Unable to sit still, he paced back and forth in his living room, his mind imagining the worst. *Did Mary Ann still trust him?* If not, he would receive no more cooperation from her, and his pursuit of Teddy Bear would end.

She begged him to wait for backup, and if he had listened, they would have Hackman in custody, providing names and numbers of those higher up in Teddy Bear. Instead, he placed her in the awkward position of begging the Lompoc police to rescue him. Her anger was justified, but her silence devastated him.

Yesterday, he was lower than a snake's belly, feeling guilty over how royally he screwed up following Hackman. His typical reaction to disaster would be to drown his sorrows with his good friend

Jack Daniels. Only his fear of being drunk if Mary Ann called held him back. Today, he was just disgusted with himself.

Mid-morning arrived. A winter gloom hung over the beach, matching his mood. The air was so damp that his backyard tread-mill felt slick to the touch. The deserted beach parking lot smelled overwhelmingly of the seaweed washed onto the beach at high tide.

Ron stopped pacing, sat at his kitchen table, and buried his head in his hands. There was no other recourse except to swallow his pride and call Mary Ann to beg forgiveness. It was apparent that she had no intention of calling him. Her phone rang for an eternity before she finally answered.

"What?" she said sharply.

Ron gritted his teeth. "I just wanted to say I'm sorry and to thank you for having my back. "What I did was really stupid. I've been carrying all this baggage in my mind for years, and it's eating me up. The chance to redeem myself overrode common sense."

"Can you imagine the anxiety I had sitting here, uncertain if you were alive?" she replied. "You didn't answer my calls. I had to beg Lompoc Police to send out a squad without telling them why you were there. I looked like an amateur, out of my depth. My credibility took a nosedive. Do you understand the importance of credibility for a woman trying to shatter the glass ceiling here?"

Ron felt worse than he did yesterday. He hadn't considered what effect his actions would have on her. Everything he did turned into shit.

Mary Ann continued talking, the anger evident in her voice. "We were supposed to work together. Then you pulled that Lone Ranger shit and almost got killed. Your tendency to lose control makes it hard to trust you anymore. The guilt you carry over your sister, and the belief that you're responsible for these missing kids, badly affects your judgment. Don't you see how messed up you are? You need to get help."

Everything she said rang true. He refused counseling offered during high school when his sister disappeared. After the Garcia shootout, he declined the offer again. He didn't feel comfortable discussing his feelings with a stranger. Things would work out. But now, having reached unimaginable depths of despair, he no longer believed that to be true.

"I see it now," he said. "All these years, I've kept the feelings bottled up inside. Ignored their existence, hoped they would go away. If I could bust this case open, I believed it would fix me."

He halted, desperately trying to think of something to convince Mary Ann of his sincerity. "I'll make you a promise if my word means anything to you. There's a guy I know who runs a group therapy program. He's been trying to get me to attend a meeting, so I'll go until my head gets straight. No more excuses."

"That's the smartest thing you've ever said. It's going to save your life."

"I've just got to ask," he said, after a pause. "Are we done with the case? Did you turn it over to the FBI? Because if you'll give me another chance, I swear I'll be the team player you deserve."

The silence on the phone seemed to go on forever.

"I haven't given the case to the FBI yet," she said. "The Lompoc police lab cracked the password on Hackman's phone. It contained a list of contacts that I'm tracking down. There's still a tap on it, and someone has called him often today. Maybe his boss is wondering where he is. I'm tracing that number. All the calls will stop once these guys realize something's wrong."

"Let me help Mary Ann. If you use anybody else, it will be days before they get organized, which will be too late. Involving more people increases the risk of another leak. I'm already dialed in. Just give me a name."

He could sense Mary Ann was thinking about it.

"What about Natalie?" she said. "Do you still think it wasn't her at the factory?"

"All I can do is give you my opinion. I never saw her face. If she was at the factory, maybe she's watching me to see what I do. She has little reason to trust me."

"You tracked down Hackman. That should count for something in her book."

"True, but she's been screwed over pretty badly by about every adult in her life."

Mary Ann grunted. "My gut tells me this is a mistake, but you're correct; time is of the essence. Therefore, I'm going to give you one last opportunity. I should have the name and approximate location of the person calling Hackman within the hour. Your job will be to find him. When you do, call me immediately. Don't even think about approaching him. You have no authority to arrest anybody. Try to remember we need this guy alive."

CHAPTER 35

Mary Ann kept her word and called back in forty-five minutes with the contact information. Ron made good use of his time while waiting for her call. His car contained everything he thought he might need: clothes, snacks, energy drinks, binoculars, a pistol, and plenty of ammunition. As an extra precaution, he threw some body armor in the trunk. He used his left hand to hold the phone to his ear, and his right to lock the front door.

"The cell phone belongs to a John Anderson," she said. "It's pinging off a tower in Ventura right now. The approximate location is the seven-hundred block of Colvin Avenue. That's an industrial area, mainly warehouses. The phone hasn't moved all day. He may be working or living nearby. I need you to check it out ASAP."

"Any description of the guy available?" he asked.

"Negative. I'll have the DMV search for a car registration under John Anderson in Ventura. It's a common name. The list might be too long, and if he doesn't live in Ventura, we're screwed. I'll call you with an update while you're driving down there."

"Got it. I'm leaving my house now."

"Just to be clear, you are not to approach the subject. We want to keep him alive for a while."

Ventura was a thirty-minute drive straight south on the 101. It was late morning, so the traffic was light. The weather had cleared, allowing the sun to appear. The freeway hugged the beach, providing spectacular views. As Ron drove, seals bobbed on the waves, searching for fish in the Santa Barbara Channel. Farther offshore, oil platforms dotted the surface, and beyond that, the faint outline of Santa Cruz Island.

Mary Ann called with an update. "We got a break on triangulating his location. The phone company rerouted his signal to another tower and gave us an exact address where the two signals crossed: 735 Colvin. Also, there are three vehicle registrations under the name of John Anderson in Ventura. One is a gray Lexus NX, another is a white BMW iX, and the third is a blue Hyundai Ioniq 6. I'll text the license numbers. If you can find one of those cars at the Colvin address, we can get Anderson's home address from the DMV."

735 Colvin proved to be a typical southern California distribution warehouse. It was a white rectangular concrete tilt-up with

loading docks along the right side. Forklift drivers were busy moving pallets of goods in and out of large trucks backed into a few of the bays. The front of the building contained a glassed-in lobby housing several offices where management staff worked. A parking lot covered the remaining area between the warehouse and the street. A large sign attached to the front of the building said "SoCal Logistics."

Ron drove by, searching the lot for one of the three cars Mary Ann described. He knew all three of the ones he was looking for were electric, so he searched for charging stations. He spotted one in the middle of the lot, but the stall was unoccupied. The street ended in a cul-de-sac. He circled, parked on the street near the warehouse, and called Mary Ann.

"One company, SoCal Logistics, occupies the whole address. No sign of the three cars."

"Hang tight," she said. "The suspect appears to have left for lunch. Let me research the company."

Ron tore open one of his snacks and started eating. He reclined his car seat so far back that his head was almost invisible over the dashboard. He wondered if Natalie was following him. She was so stealthy she could be sitting in his backseat getting ready to strangle him. His neck tingled as though a rope was cinched around it. Unnerved by the feeling, he checked to be sure she wasn't there.

Mary Ann called back an hour later. "SoCal Logistics has been in business for a decade, importing stuff from China and selling it on Amazon. It appears to be doing well. The company is owned by Jaden Zhao, a naturalized citizen, who manages its operations. He was born in China, has no known connection to politics there, and lives in a restored mansion built in 1910 near the Ventura Pier."

"Maybe John Anderson works for him," said Ron. "Being in the import business provides contacts worldwide who could be involved with Teddy Bear. He could easily fly a private plane out of Oxnard Airport, just a few miles down the coast. Didn't Natalie say she flew to Bahrain on a private plane?"

"Yes, she did. Let's see what Anderson looks like when he comes back from lunch. He's moving again, coming in your direction."

Twenty minutes later, far up the block, a car turned right onto Colvin and continued towards the warehouse. Ron used his binoculars to confirm it was indeed a gray Lexus NX, with a license plate number that matched the one provided by Mary Ann. As the car drew nearer, he slouched further in his seat, making himself invisible. The vehicle turned left into the SoCal Logistics parking lot and glided into the stall with the electric charger.

Ron sat up straighter and trained his binoculars on the man exiting the car. He was Caucasian, in his late 20s, somewhat short but powerfully built, with black hair combed straight back, a clean-shaven face, and a thick neck. Dark wrap-around sunglasses, a long-sleeved white dress shirt, open at the neck, black khaki slacks, and a pair of gray Sketchers with white sidewalls completed his attire. Sunlight glinted off a piece of gold jewelry on his right wrist as he reached inside the car to retrieve a satchel from the back seat.

Another man emerged from the passenger side, gripping the door handle. He was Asian, mid-50s, taller than the driver but overweight, with thinning gray hair. Square gold-rimmed glasses framed his face. His dress was similar to his companion's, except that a blue patterned tie drooped over his belly, trailing towards his waist. Ron watched his eyes dart around the parking lot before he rushed into the lobby through the glass door. The driver followed behind.

Ron called Mary Ann. "Okay, here's what I've got. The car was the Lexus and the license plate matched, so it belongs to Anderson. Two men were in the car, so I'm unsure which one was him. The driver was Caucasian, and the passenger was Asian. The driver appeared to be a bodyguard, but Anderson isn't an Asian name. If the passenger owns the car, maybe Anderson is Zhao. He could be using Anderson as an alias to hide his real identity. With my binoculars, I got a clear view of his face. Can you get me Anderson's and Zhao's DMV photos?"

"Now that we know the car, that's not a problem," said Mary Ann. "Let me get those photos, and I'll text them to you. Keep watching the warehouse. If he leaves again, follow him."

Ron settled back in his car, lowered the window to relieve the stuffiness, and turned on the radio. Music from his favorite Dire Straits album, "Brothers in Arms," echoed through the car. The weather seemed to be turning again. A cold ocean breeze blew in the window while he hummed to the music.

He pondered the best way to confront Zhao if the photos matched. Only a couple of unsuccessful phone calls connected him to Hackman. He could claim they were just friends. Before questioning him, they needed more evidence linking him to Teddy Bear.

His phone pinged, indicating a text—two headshots sent by Mary Ann.

A moment later, she called. "Did you get them?"

"Yeah. It looks like the same guy, so Anderson is Zhao. He's using an alias to conceal his true identity when working with Teddy Bear. The driver must be his bodyguard."

Ron heard muffled talking from the other end of the line. "Sorry, I forgot to close the door to my office, and somebody had a question," said Mary Ann. "So, we've identified Zhao as someone who at least knows Hackman. There's no connection between him and Teddy Bear yet. Surveillance may reveal something."

"I could sense his nervousness through his body language. Another day without being able to contact Hackman may convince him there's something wrong. He may shut the operation down until he finds out what is happening. Then we'll never get a chance to make him talk. We must give him a reason to call his Teddy Bear contacts."

There was a moment of silence. "I've got an idea," she said. "First, I need to get a court order to tap his phone. There's enough probable cause to get it, seeing as how he's called a proven child kidnapper several times and is using an alias to hide his real identity."

"I like it so far. Then what?"

"Then we call him from Hackman's phone. Tell him we've kidnapped Hackman, and he's told us about Teddy Bear. We'll demand a cut of the profits, or threaten to hand him over to the cops. That should panic Zhao into making a foolish move."

"You're assuming he uses that cell phone for all his calls. If he uses another one, we'll never know what's going on," Ron pointed out.

"True, but think about it. The phone's registered to Anderson, not Zhao, and he's using it to hide his real identity. So, it makes sense that he uses it for all his Teddy Bear business. That way, every time that phone rings, he knows it's Teddy Bear before he answers. He keeps his real name hidden."

Ron remained skeptical about the plan's feasibility, but no alternative idea came to mind. "Okay, you get the court order, and I'll sit on Zhao. Were there any saved numbers on Hackman's phone that look promising?"

"No. He was cautious about that. I checked every one of them, and they are all legitimate businesses. He must have memorized any numbers having to do with Teddy Bear. We only got Zhao's number because he called Hackman."

At six o'clock, when the parking lot was almost empty, Zhao reappeared. His bodyguard was first out the door, scanning the area for threats. Seeing no danger, he motioned for Zhao, and they both jogged over to the Lexus, settling themselves inside. The bodyguard backed up the car, exited the parking lot, and accelerated onto Colvin. Because traffic on the street was light, Ron let them get several blocks ahead before following. He reminded himself that Hackman had spotted him on a freeway that was much busier than this street. And that almost cost him his life.

Zhao stayed on local roads, heading northwest toward the ocean. Ron assumed he was heading home to the mansion near the pier. While driving down a busy street near the beach, the bodyguard turned right into a driveway, stopping in front of a heavy iron gate adorned with a crest of arms from a bygone age. Ron parked a block away to observe what was going to happen next. He had little concern about being spotted. This was the main street to the Ventura Pier tourist attraction, and the traffic was heavy.

After a moment, the gate swung open. The car drove past, and the gate closed. Ron waited a minute, pulled his car into traffic, and glided by the driveway. The gate connected to an eight-foot-high brick fence enclosing the entire property. A security camera sat atop the wall, pointing to the area facing the gate. Next to the driveway, a post held an intercom. Beyond the gate, the driveway split. The left fork stopped at the front door, where visitors could park or turn around. To the right, it curved along the side of the house, disappearing behind it. Ron assumed a garage was back there, since the Lexus wasn't in sight.

A wall of tall trees and overgrown shrubs shielded most of the residence from view. What little he could see revealed a large two-story house of Victorian design. Gables rose at the front corners, soaring past the second floor. Weathervanes stood guard on top of them. Gingerbread cutouts adorned the fascia around the edge of the roof. A screened-in porch obscured the front windows. The pitched slate roof was the finishing touch. The house was in pristine condition.

He drove several blocks, turned around, parked nearby with a clear view of the gate, and called Mary Ann. "I just followed Zhao and his bodyguard home. A tall brick fence surrounds the house, so I couldn't see much. Lots of cover in the yard though, once you scale the fence. Did you file for the wiretap?"

"Good news there. I put a rush on it and got the order an hour ago. The techs are activating the tap now. We'll be able to record any call coming or going from that phone. When we're operational, I'll let you know so you can get some sleep. Tomorrow, we'll make the call."

Ron was uncomfortable, leaving Zhao unwatched. "What if he leaves tonight?"

"That crossed my mind, too," she admitted. "An officer is coming down to relieve you. He's unaware of the reason we're observing Zhao. If anyone leaves, his orders are to call me and be prepared to follow."

He still was reluctant to leave, the need for redemption creeping into his thoughts. *What if he gets away, and it's my fault for not being here?* He shook his head angrily. *Mary Ann gave me a second chance. I'm a team player.* Despite that, he thought of the tracking device in his glove compartment and had an idea. *If I can scale the fence...*

CHAPTER 36

Ron looked at his watch for the third time in the last fifteen minutes. *Where was his relief man?* It was almost ten thirty, and no one had shown up. The guy should have been here an hour ago. The six sodas he downed earlier in the day had settled in his bladder, and he needed to pee in the worst way. He was contemplating a quick trip to a nearby mini-mart when his phone rang.

"Sorry for the delay," Mary Ann said. "I had to inform the local police of the stakeout so they wouldn't mistake our activities for something suspicious. Expect your relief to arrive shortly."

A gray, unmarked sedan glided to a stop nearby. Inside was a uniformed police officer. "He just showed up. I've got to pee, so I'm taking off," said Ron.

"How about we call Zhao tomorrow morning at nine? He should be at work by then."

"Roger that." He started his car and made a quick dash to the mini-mart. After relieving himself, the smell of hot dogs turning on the warmer enticed him. He added some chips and a Coke and had an instant dinner. A slight improvement from the junk food he ate all day. While following suspects, eating well was difficult.

He savored the satisfying crunch of the salty chips between his teeth while he pondered the wall. He needed a box or a ladder to reach the top and hoist himself over it. But how would he return over the wall after he placed the tracking device on the Lexus? His best option would be a rope with a grappling hook, but he didn't have one.

The property occupied the corner of the block. The front wall faced a busy street that was alive with activity. Climbing the wall there unnoticed was impossible. He drove counterclockwise around the block to see if any other opportunities presented themselves. On the right side of the property, the wall ran parallel to the sidewalk on a side street. Across the street, retail storefronts stood dark and silent, closed for the night. He kept driving and discovered that houses blocked access to the back and left walls of the property.

He returned to examine the wall on the side street. Behind it, mature trees rose, their branches stopping short of the wall. He could return tomorrow with climbing gear, but Zhao might be gone by then. Frustration was building when his phone rang.

"What are you doing, Ron Jackson?" a female voice said.

He scanned his surroundings, recognizing the voice, but saw nothing unusual. "Hello, Natalie. Are you here watching me?"

"Yes, I'm nearby. What are you doing?" she repeated.

Ron sighed. "I'm searching for a way over the wall. We've connected the man living here to Hackman. If I attach a tracking device to his car, he'll be easier to follow."

There was a moment of silence. "Do you think he works for Teddy Bear?"

"Yes, I do." Ron was getting impatient with the many questions.

"Are there any police with you?"

"There is one police officer in a gray car out front on the main street watching the entrance. He cannot see this street from there."

"Have you found a way to overcome the wall?" she asked.

"Ah...no. I wasn't aware he had an eight-foot wall around his house until now." *Would this woman ever shut up?*

"Then I'll help you."

A tap on the passenger side window of his car almost caused him to jump out of his skin. Standing outside was Natalie, dressed in her customary black ninja outfit. She opened the car door and slipped into the passenger seat.

"Jesus," Ron said. "Don't ever do that again. Where did you come from?"

She looked at him with her dark, expressionless eyes. "It made sense to follow you here. Your resources to find the Teddy Bear criminals are superior to mine. I knew you'd lead me to them in time. Describe the person living here, and I'll make sure he doesn't see another dawn."

"What? Oh no, that's not the plan," he said hastily. "There're many others employed by Teddy Bear. We need to identify them. Tomorrow, Mary Ann and I will call Zhao, the guy who lives here, pretending to be kidnappers. We'll tell him we have his friend Hackman, who told us about Teddy Bear. If he doesn't pay us off, we'll turn Hackman over to the police. We hope he'll panic and contact other members of Teddy Bear."

"But Hackman is dead."

"Yes. We're gambling that Zhao doesn't know that."

She thought about it. "Yes, this is a good plan. Once we have their names, I can kill them all. It's Allah's will."

Ron believed she could accomplish this task, given her impressive track record. He needed to be careful, or she might add him to the list. "Yes...well, first we must find them, then we can decide what to do. I planned to attach a tracking device to his car so I could follow him at a safe distance."

Natalie studied the wall. She looked unimpressed. "This is a simple task. I'll do it for you."

"How do you plan to cross the wall?"

"I've climbed many walls much higher. Where's the tracking device you speak of?"

Ron opened the glove compartment and removed the device, explaining that it was magnetic and all she needed to do was place it in one of the wheel wells. She nodded, checked the street for onlookers, and opened the car door.

"One last thing," he said. "The car is a Lexus. It's probably in a garage behind the house."

Natalie stood by his car, rocking back and forth on her heels, like she was about to attempt the long jump at a track meet. Then she moved forward, crossing the street with a burst of speed that surprised him. She gathered herself and sprang as high as she could when close to the wall. She came down on it, almost at the top, grabbing the top bricks and pulling herself up without effort. Ron's mouth hung open in surprise. He had seen this done in movies, but always assumed hidden wires aided the jumper. Now he knew better.

Natalie straddled the wall, studying the terrain on the other side. She glanced at Ron, gave a thumbs up, and disappeared over the wall. He held his breath, expecting alarms and barking dogs, but nothing happened. He waited and hoped.

The wait stretched to an hour. An occasional car drove by, paying him no attention. It was a quiet night, with a lingering sense of peacefulness. His eyes grew heavy when he noticed movement in one tree near the wall. As a branch shook, a black shape jumped and landed on the wall. Natalie leaped down and moved, like a shadow, towards him. A white sedan turned the corner and raced toward her, the tires squealing on the pavement. In a flash, Ron recognized it as the car he saw at his office.

The car's headlights swept over Natalie as the driver screeched to a halt in the middle of the street. Two men armed with pistols stepped out of both car doors, took aim, and opened fire on her. She zig-zagged her way across the street, drawing her pistol from her belt, firing wildly as she ran. Ron bailed out of his car, and took cover behind it, looking for a clean shot. He watched as Natalie crossed the street, bullets flying around her. Either her assailants were terrible shots, or Allah was indeed protecting her.

She was within a few feet of Ron's position when a bullet spun her around. Lunging forward, she dropped to the ground behind his car. He opened fire to give her cover, hoping she was still alive. His first round shattered the passenger side window of the white car into a thousand pieces. That persuaded the men to stop the attack.

The sedan roared past, the passenger firing to give them cover. Ron dropped to the ground, seeking refuge behind his back wheel as bullets zipped through the air. The assailants disappeared, leaving behind a neighborhood of barking dogs and lights coming on in nearby houses.

Ron realized he was holding his breath and let out a whoosh of air. Natalie gripped her upper left arm with her right hand, a pained expression on her face. Blood dripped down her arm onto her clothing. "Where are you hit?" he asked.

"On my arm. I think he just grazed me."

There was no time to waste. "Come on, get in my car. We've got to get out of here. The police will be here any minute."

She hesitated a moment, then the distant sound of sirens convinced her of the wisdom of his plan. After holstering her pistol, she slid into his car. He put the pedal to the metal, heading for the freeway. A few blocks away, a police car flashed by them, with lights flashing and siren screaming.

He glanced over at Natalie, who appeared calm. "Listen, you're going to have to trust me. I'm heading home, where we'll be safe. I've got a first aid kit there with bandages and stuff to fix your arm if it's not too bad. We must avoid being seen and get some rest. Tomorrow, I'll drop you off wherever you want."

Turning her head, she gave him a penetrating look, then nodded. "You have proven yourself trustworthy, Ron Jackson. I'll go with you, but only for tonight."

He reached the 101freeway ramp and merged into the stream of cars, feeling the road vibrate beneath him. Surrounded by traffic, the tension eased, and his body relaxed. He took deep breaths to calm his mind.

"What happened over there?" he said.

"It was as you said. The car was in the garage. Someone had locked the door. It took time to pick the lock and check for alarms. Once inside, I placed the tracker where you told me, and then I locked the door and used the tree to climb the wall. Lights were on in the house, but no one noticed me."

"Good job, Natalie. I'm sure Zhao heard the shots, but he'll find nothing suspicious since you were gone by then. Okay, now tell me, who are the men in the white sedan?"

CHAPTER 37

She was quiet for so long that he didn't think she would answer the question. She turned to look at him. "I've made a powerful enemy since arriving here from Syria—someone who disapproves of my plan for vengeance. My death would dissuade others from defying him. That's all I can tell you."

Ron was not satisfied with her answer, but didn't press her for more information. She had just been shot, and it was not the right time to start an argument. The early morning ride on the 101 back to Ron's house in Carpinteria was uneventful, with no traffic or delays. The full moon illuminated the beach, visible a short distance away. Natalie dozed on the seat beside him while he mulled over her account of the men who tried to kill her. It complicated things. If she was a target, and he was helping her, he might become a target, too.

His worry increased when he thought about her attackers being Syrians, which meant ISIS. Being stalked by bloodthirsty jihadists was a dangerous scenario. And how did they locate Natalie at Zhao's house? The most likely answer was that they followed one of them. Given her exceptional abilities in surveillance, he deduced that he was the one who got followed. Anger boiled up inside him. This was the second time his surveillance skills failed him. He led them right to her. But he did not know she was even there.

After they arrived home, Ron sat at his dining room table, examining the gunshot wound on Natalie's upper arm. She had taken off her ninja outfit and was now attired in jeans and a t-shirt. It was the first time he had gotten a look at her without her outfit on, and he was impressed by how physically fit she was. There wasn't an ounce of fat anywhere on her body. Her face was attractive, with olive skin framed by thick black hair and those dark eyes that seemed to look into your soul.

"It doesn't look too bad," he said. "You're lucky those guys couldn't shoot straight. The bullet grazed you but didn't go through your arm. Instead of stitches, I can clean the wound and put a bandage on it so you won't have to visit the hospital. They have to report gunshot wounds to the police. You'll have a scar, but no lasting effects as long as it remains uninfected."

Natalie inspected the jagged edges of her wound. Blood trickled down her arm onto the towel it rested on. "This is of no consequence," she said. "Allah protects me. To locate the remaining cockroaches, we must continue to follow the plan. Once I have my vengeance, I'll deal with those who attacked me. This is of no concern to you."

"Natalie, it does concern me. Have you thought about how they located you? Most likely, they followed me or somehow tracked your cell phone. They know we're working together, so I'm in as much danger as you are. Tell me who they are, and I can help you find them."

"I don't know their names. They have no wish to kill you," she said stubbornly. "I'm the one who has defied them."

Ron was growing impatient. "How can you be sure of that? What have you done to defy them?"

Natalie shook her head and stayed silent. Ron stared at her for a few moments before shoving back his chair. In the bathroom, he found antiseptic cream, some alcohol, and a box of bandages. Thirty minutes later, he had cleaned and bandaged the wound.

He handed her a bottle of pills. "These are antibiotics the doctor gave me when I got sick a while ago. Take two daily and keep the bandage clean. Don't do anything strenuous with that arm until it heals."

She nodded. "Thank you for sheltering me in your home. I don't wish to put you in any danger. If we avoid being together, the men may follow you, but they won't find me. There will be no more shootouts. I have another cell phone that I've never used. This one," she held up her cell phone, "I'll throw away. The men can't track me if they don't know my number."

Ron placed the leftover bandages in the bathroom and walked back to her. "If we're to work together, we need to communicate. I cannot help you otherwise."

She grimaced and looked away. "Your old partner works for the police. If I give you my number, perhaps you'll share it with her, and *she* will track me. Remaining hidden is crucial for my plan to succeed. My life depends on stealth and surprise."

He had to admit it was a legitimate concern. Even though he didn't intend to share her number with anyone, she had no reason to trust him. That needed to be earned.

"Okay, we'll take this slow," he said. "Will you agree to contact me every day so we can talk? I may need your help, and you must know what progress is being made."

"Yes, that's acceptable," she said. "I'll call you every day."

With that settled, they slept for a few hours, rose early, and departed for Ventura by seven. Rush hour traffic slowed their progress to a crawl. The weather had flipped from the prior day, and now a strong, blustery wind rocked their car. A local TV meteorologist was forecasting rain for tomorrow, but Ron had seen this kind of wind before, and he believed the storm would bypass them out to sea.

An hour later, after they had fought the traffic, Natalie directed him to an alleyway near Zhao's house. She left the car, favoring her injured arm, and watched from the shadows as he drove away. When he glanced back in his rearview mirror, she was gone.

Ron drove back to the spot where he could watch Zhao's gate. The police officer who relieved him during the night was still there. He called Mary Ann. "Hey, I'm back on duty. Tell your guy to get some rest."

"What did you do last night?" Mary Ann said sharply.

She must have gotten a report on the gunfight at Zhao's. How much do I say? I can't tell her Natalie went over the wall.

"I guess you heard there was a minor commotion."

Her voice rose a notch. "A *minor* commotion? Ventura Police found forty-three shell casings on the street, right next to Zhao's house. Some were nine-millimeter, the same as your Glock. What a coincidence, huh? Maybe I should test your pistol and see if the casing marks match. Please tell me you weren't involved. Trouble seems to follow you everywhere."

Thinking fast, Ron improvised. "Uh...it wasn't my fault. Here's what happened. After being relieved, I was on my way home and realized my pistol was on the front seat. I pulled over and stowed it in the trunk, where it was legal to transport it."

"Really? I never knew you were such a law-abiding citizen. What happened next?"

"Natalie appeared out of thin air, catching me off guard. I think she followed me down there. She wanted information about the case. We were standing on the sidewalk talking when a car turned the corner. It stopped, and two guys jumped out with pistols and started shooting. We fired back, no Lone Ranger stuff, just self-defense, and they piled back into their car and took off. I couldn't allow Natalie to be questioned by the police. The FBI is looking for her. So, we took off," he finished weakly.

"Wow. That's quite a story. Once again, you cheated death," she said, "then departed the scene of a crime. Who were these guys shooting at you?"

"Natalie said they wanted to kill her for disobeying them. It had a connection to her time in Syria. She wouldn't say anything more. I just happened to be there when they attacked."

"Syria? That sounds like something separate from Teddy Bear."

"Yeah, that's what I think. She said she would deal with them after we find all the Teddy Bear cockroaches."

Mary Ann expelled a long breath. "I don't like this at all. She's holding back something that might be important to our national security. For five years, she lived among jihadists. Did they want her to do something to our country, and she double-crossed them?"

Ron saw movement ahead. The gate was opening. Just in time to rescue him from an awkward conversation.

"Hey, Zhao's on the move. I'll call you back when I determine where he's going."

CHAPTER 38

Ron reached into his glove compartment and removed his tracking monitor. He booted up the software, and a faint beep emitted from the speaker, indicating a successful connection with the device Natalie attached to Zhao's car. He grinned and relaxed, pleased that the device was working correctly. The monitor displayed a small blinking red dot moving away from Zhao's house, superimposed over a street map of the area.

He gave the Lexus a head start of several blocks before he began tailing it. Gusts of wind rocked his car, and it remained chilly outside.

Zhao took the reverse route he followed the day before, and within thirty minutes, he was back at his office. This time, his bodyguard stopped right in front of the lobby door. His passenger exited, slamming the car door behind him as he rushed inside.

Ron pulled into his surveillance post and called Mary Ann. "He went straight to work. He looked very nervous and practically ran into the building. I'm watching the parking lot now."

"All right, it's time to see if our plan will work. He seems ready to crack," she said. "Probably heard the shooting last night and assumed somebody was trying to kill him."

They spent the next ten minutes rehearsing their spiel. It had to be believable enough to panic Zhao into calling his boss. Ron would speak, because they felt male voices sounded more threatening than female. Mary Ann would listen and record the call.

With Hackman's phone, she called Ron back, then hit the conference button and dialed Zhao's cellphone. The phone rang only once before he answered.

"Where have you been?" Zhao hissed.

"Listen good, pal. I'm only going to say this once," said Ron. "Your friend Bob Hackman is our guest. He's been doing a lot of talking the last couple of days. We know all about you and Teddy Bear. That's a real moneymaker for you, ain't it? Selling kids to perverts. I'm sure the cops would love to have Hackman tell them about it. Then you could spend your life in lockup being Bubba's bitch. Experience life as a slave, like those kids you sold."

He paused, letting it sink in. "Despite my personal feelings about this, I'm a businessman, so I'm willing to give you a chance to avoid that fate. I want $500,000 in bitcoin. Then you get Hackman back, safe and sound, and never hear from us again. You've got two days to put it together. Otherwise, we dump Hackman off at the nearest police station along with a tape of everything he told us, and you spend the rest of your life in jail."

Ron cleared his throat. "Did you hear the shooting outside your house last night? That was us. We know where you live. Consider it a warning in case you try to run. We don't want any violence, do we? Oh, and don't try calling this number. It's going to be out of service after I hang up. I'll call you on another phone in two days to arrange the transfer, and you'd better have the money."

"W...who are you?" asked Zhao.

"We're entrepreneurs, just like you. Stop wasting time and get the money."

Mary Ann ended the call. Moments later, Ron's phone rang. "That was good," she said. "If I were him, I'd be shitting bricks right now. I've got the tap on his phone ready, so let's see if you motivated him to make some calls so we can find out who he works for."

She paused, then changed the subject. "Can you contact Natalie? She's a loose cannon, and we need to rein her in before she kills these people. Once that starts, she'd be a hunted woman forever. Whoever found her first would determine her fate: death or a lifetime in prison."

"I tried to get her number, but she refused to give it to me. She's aware of our partnership and doesn't trust me to keep it a secret from you. The only thing she agreed to do was to contact me daily to coordinate our efforts. I've got to tell you, though, she scares me. Her time in Syria honed her skills, turning her into a formidable assassin. If she thinks I crossed her, she'd probably kill me, too."

He paused for a breath. "There's one thing I don't understand. Those ISIS terrorists treat their women like shit. Why would they train Natalie for a mission instead of a man? What makes her different?"

"That's what I've been saying. She's hiding something. Nothing suggests she intends to harm us, but we can't trust her. What did she do that motivated someone to want her dead?"

"Natalie said the problem started in Syria," Ron pointed out. "It has to be connected to ISIS. That's been her entire life for the previous five years. Something significant must have happened for them to follow her to California."

"You've got to get her to trust you," Mary Ann said. "Then maybe she'll tell you the truth. I've got to go. Zhao's already making calls. Let me know if he leaves work. I'll be in touch."

With the tracking device placed on Zhao's car, Ron now had the luxury of getting a decent lunch with no fear he would disappear. After savoring a cheesesteak with fries, he had just returned to his surveillance post and was struggling to stay awake when his phone started ringing.

"Apologies for the delay," Mary Ann said. "Zhao called a guy, but they spoke in Mandarin, so nobody knew what they were saying. I spent hours finding a translator; then she had to transcribe the conversation. The person he called was Qi Wang, an analyst working at the Chinese consulate in Los Angeles. We think he's Zhao's boss by how he spoke to him."

"Holy shit, you mean the Chinese government might be behind Teddy Bear?" asked Ron.

"It's unlikely their government would stoop to getting involved in something as sordid as this. Exposure would damage their image. Wang is more likely a rogue employee who found a way to supplement his meager income."

"What did they discuss?" Ron asked.

"The focus was on mitigating the damage. $500,000 is a lot of money, and Wang was not eager to ask his partners for it. Instead, he wanted to lure you and me to a meeting and kill us. Zhao came unglued, warning that we knew where he lived and would kill him if we suspected anything. He reminded Wang that we had Hackman, who knew enough to destroy Uberlegen if he talked to the cops."

"He mentioned Uberlegen?" The Panamanian company that's tied to Teddy Bear?"

"Yes. I got the impression Wang cared little about what happened to Zhao, but he was worried about Uberlegen getting exposed. He agreed to call a council meeting to discuss the matter."

"That's perfect," said Ron. "It's what we wanted him to do. If we subpoena his call records, we can match them to the names of all the council members. Then we can arrest them all."

"Easier said than done," Mary Ann noted. "Teddy Bear is an international business. The council may comprise individuals living in different countries. Remember Franz Meyers, the money man the sheik paid? He was Austrian."

"Okay, but we can at least bust the ones in this country."

"We need the FBI for that. I've got no jurisdiction outside of California. Convicting them will require time and personnel to gather sufficient evidence. Before going too deep, let's see what Wang's call records reveal. I'll have all the information by tomorrow."

As the call ended, Ron dissected every word spoken by Mary Ann. He realized his ambitious goal of taking down the entire Teddy Bear criminal enterprise had been naïve. His bank account lacked sufficient funds to pursue the criminals outside the United States. Soon, he must find new clients to replenish his funds and let go of Teddy Bear. He slammed his hand against the steering wheel in frustration.

Would wiping out Teddy Bear's operations in California be enough vindication? We could turn over all our data to the feds and let them pursue the remaining criminals wherever they are. So far, the FBI has been slow to follow up on what they learned from the sheik. Would that change if they had names and evidence of criminal behavior?

He found no answers to his questions. Only after he did everything in his power to eliminate Teddy Bear would he know. Until then, the demons that tormented him would linger, clouding his mind and damaging his health.

As he continued watching the warehouse, the hours dragged by with agonizing slowness. He was getting hungry again. The odor of french fries permeated the car, and Ron remembered he had bagged some leftovers from lunch. They tasted good, even at room temperature.

Zhao did not leave the warehouse, even for lunch. *We spooked him,* thought Ron with satisfaction. The bodyguard ventured outside just as the sun was dipping below the horizon. After hustling his boss into the Lexus, they made a hasty getaway. He took a circuitous route back home, doubling back several times to determine if someone was following them. Ron was unfazed. There was no need to follow closely with the tracking device working.

They arrived at Zhao's home, the Lexus idling in the driveway while the gate opened. A new security guard, muscles rippling in his tight shirt, stood inside it, watching the approaching traffic on the street. He waited until the gate closed, then went back towards the house. Ron found a vantage point, parked, and exited his car to stretch his stiff legs. He was doing deep knee bends when his phone started ringing.

"We hit pay dirt," said Mary Ann. "Wang called four numbers, three of them within the United States. Of the three in the U.S., two were cellular, and one was a landline. One of the cell phones belongs to Baxter Pontreau, living in New Orleans. The other one belongs to Dominic Spironi, who's in Newark. The landline is associated with Custom Automotive, a business in Albuquerque, New Mexico. It's an auto repair company. He talked to Carlos Morales."

"And the international call?" asked Ron.

"It went to someone's cell phone in Austria. I'm checking with the local phone company there to get a name."

"Franz Meyers, the money man," he guessed.

"An excellent possibility. We know he's from Austria. With the information I gathered from the calls, I've been trying to establish the hierarchy of Teddy Bear. Wang was very respectful talking to Morales, so maybe he's the head guy at their headquarters in Albuquerque. He treated Pontreau and Spironi more like contemporaries. My guess is they set the company up kind of like the mafia, with Wang, Pontreau, and Spironi having territories and reporting to Morales. Maybe there are similar branches in other countries."

Ron whistled. "Damn. This is big time. I never expected Teddy Bear to have *territories*. What did they talk about?"

"Everybody ganged up on Wang. They wanted to know how Hackman became a target, but of course, he didn't know. So now Morales suspects there's a rat in Wang's organization, which makes him look even worse. The call to Austria was to verify the availability of funds, if needed. A conference call in an hour will decide the plan."

Mary Ann cleared her throat. "Here's the bad news. They're going to use Secure for the call. That app uses encryption, so I can't listen in."

"We've got their names and addresses. It doesn't matter if they pay the ransom or not."

"That's true. If they pay and then don't get Hackman back, they'll figure they were double-crossed, and we surrendered him to the cops. If they don't pay, they'll also assume we'll deliver him to the police. Either way, it'll put their business at risk. But it would be nice to understand their plans."

She paused a moment, gathering her thoughts. "Here's the thing. All of them will be searching for the means to safeguard themselves and preserve their business. I think they'll zero in on Zhao as the weak link. If he's dead, he can't implicate Wang, so the rest of the gang is safe, assuming Hackman didn't know them. They can then refuse to pay the ransom without fear of exposure."

"Zhao's probably thinking the same thing. I noticed he added a second security guard at his house."

"If they plan to kill him, they must move fast. The ransom demand deadline is in two days. If they refuse to pay, they'll assume we'll give Hackman to the cops, leading to an arrest warrant for Zhao within a day."

Ron disliked where this conversation was heading. "So now our mission is to keep this scumbag alive?"

"If he's convinced his boss is trying to kill him, the witness protection plan might look like an excellent alternative. With his testimony, we can nail Wang, Pontreau, Spironi, and Morales. Let the FBI and Interpol pursue the others."

Ron snorted. "The FBI isn't making this case a priority. What have they done since tricking the sheik into coming to New York? Interpol can't arrest anybody, they rely on local law enforcement for that. If these cockroaches are in unfriendly countries, we'll never get them. There's got to be another way."

CHAPTER 39

After following Zhao home, Ron sat in his car watching the gate as muffled sounds of the traffic outside competed with his glum thoughts. He sighed, depressed to be tasked with protecting Zhao while accepting that Teddy Bear was too big for him to take down. The demons were still there in his mind, whispering that he would never find the missing kids. Every time he took one step forward, another obstacle presented itself, taunting him that he was wasting his time.

Pounding the steering wheel, he tried to clear his mind. He couldn't give up now; he owed it to his sister and the seven other kids who had disappeared. However, working with Natalie and Mary Ann without betraying one of them was becoming difficult. He sensed that the time was coming when he would have to choose sides, something he didn't want to do. How could he choose between his old partner and someone who felt the same way he did about Teddy Bear?

The bright headlights of passing cars blinded his tired eyes, but he worried that if he shut them for even a moment, he'd drift off to sleep. Downing energy drinks all day had kept him going, but the caffeine was wearing off, leaving him exhausted. He had slept only a few hours last night before taking Natalie back to Ventura.

The ocean breeze brought a chill as soon as the sun had set, dropping the temperature by ten degrees. A weather front was curling down the coast from San Francisco, and the forecast predicted rain tomorrow. That was not good news. There was nothing worse than doing surveillance in the rain while freezing his ass off.

Mary Ann was busy expediting the paperwork to offer Zhao a spot in the witness protection plan. Before ending their earlier call, she assured Ron she would dispatch someone to relieve him. So far, that hadn't happened. With no action expected that night, he was eager to get home. His phone chimed.

"This is Natalie. I'm checking in with you, as we agreed."

He groaned inwardly. Too exhausted to match wits with her, he would keep his report short and vague. "It's been a very long day. I'm watching Zhao's house, waiting to be relieved. Then I'm going home to sleep."

"A good idea, Ron Jackson. Before you go, did your plan work?"

"We made the phone call. Afterward, he called up his boss, Qi Wang, to give him the bad news. By tapping his phone, we hope to uncover the identities of the other Teddy Bear members. This might take some time."

"That's a Chinese name. Is he in China?"

"No, the call went to a cell phone in Los Angeles."

"What did they say?"

He squirmed in his seat, caught between conflicting agendas. He needed Mary Ann's resources and was striving not to do something stupid that would lose her trust. If she found out he was feeding information to Natalie, that would end it. But Natalie operated outside of the law, and that had certain advantages. There was no bureaucracy involved. They could make decisions and take action immediately.

"They talked about whether they should pay the ransom," Ron said vaguely. "Wang decided he needed to consult other people in the organization before making a decision."

Natalie paused, seeming to think things through. "I don't think they'll pay. It would be easier for them to kill Zhao, thinking no one else knows about them."

Her ability, at age nineteen, to think things through impressed Ron. "That's my thinking, as well. Mary Ann has a plan to offer Zhao protection. In return, he'll have to testify against Teddy Bear."

"This is the American form of justice. Time-consuming and uncertain. It doesn't suit my purpose," she said.

There it was, out in the open. After five years of waiting, revenge consumed her thoughts. The bodies would accumulate, and their blood would be on his hands because he enabled it. He needed to convince Natalie that applying justice through the legal system was better than her method. The problem was that he wasn't sure he believed that anymore.

"I understand, but you're in America, and that's how we do things. If you kill people, you'll become a criminal yourself. It's better to be free and watch these cockroaches spend the rest of their lives in jail than to be in jail yourself. You're young, and you have a long life ahead. Trust me to see that justice is done."

"Trust you? You don't understand. Allah has shown me my path. In his mercy, he granted me the chance to seek revenge for the wrongs done to me. What happens after that is not important. When you have no family and were raised by jihadists, what hope is there for the future? My life will be short, so jail time is meaningless. American justice doesn't work for me."

Ron closed his eyes. Her words filled him with foreboding, as if she had already foreseen the future. He remembered the shootout from last night. *What was this path she talked about?*

She continued talking. "When I saved your life at the factory, you told me this was personal for you. I hoped that meant you would help me. Do you feel the same pain that I do? The need to fix something terrible so that others won't suffer?"

She seemed to know his secrets without him saying a word, an unexpected bond of suffering connecting them. "I do," he said. "God help me."

He couldn't help himself. His body ached, and his hands shook. He felt an overwhelming need to unburden himself to this woman who understood his pain. The story of his sister poured out like water through a breached dam. He held nothing back: the shame, the nightmares, the seven missing children, his overwhelming guilt.

***

In 1994, Ron was a junior in high school. A rising star on the football team, popular with the girls, invited to all the best parties. He believed he was well on his way to ascending to the top social rung at school while possessing uncanny maturity beyond his years. When he turned sixteen, he talked his parents into letting him get a car, critical to maintaining his status with the cool kids at school. As part of the deal, he agreed to pick up his younger sister from her junior high and give her a ride home after school. This he didn't always do. He had a life, after all, and his annoying sister's school was only a twenty-minute walk from their home.

He remembered it was a Friday, and he was looking forward to the weekend football game. While walking to his car after school, he stopped to flirt with a girl he wanted to date, a cheerleader he had noticed at the games. The sight of her smile and the scent of her intoxicating perfume made him forget about everything else. He tore himself away, but arrived late to pick up his sister, and found her school deserted. Tired of waiting, she must have walked home. He drove on, angry that he had wasted a trip to pick her up.

When he arrived home, his sister wasn't there. A frantic search turned up no clues. Somewhere between school and home, she vanished without a trace, leaving a devastating void in his life that echoed with unanswered questions.

His parents were careful never to blame him, claiming whoever took her was stalking her, just waiting for any opportunity when she was alone. This argument did not fool him. Everything would've been fine if he hadn't been late to pick his sister up from school. His selfishness had probably killed her. The authorities never found her body, and the thought of her possible survival as the prisoner of a child molester haunted him.

He withdrew from campus life, unable to endure the looks of pity he got from his fellow students. Everybody knew what happened. His grades declined, his social life was non-existent, and he started taking drugs to block out the guilt.

In a critical moment when he was contemplating suicide, his father stepped in and saved his life. "Become a cop," he counseled, "and make a difference in the world. You can protect the vulnerable. The kids need you."

The idea inspired him, giving him the will to continue. After graduating high school, he joined the Sheriff's Department in Santa Barbara and dedicated himself to becoming a detective. He rose through the ranks, achieving his goal, but never catching a case involving a child kidnapping.

He saw it as God's vengeance for his deeds. The nightmares that came never let him forget it. Desperate for relief, he believed that saving just one child might erase the guilt still simmering in his mind. He prayed to God to give him the chance year after year, and then it came.

It was a monumental case involving eight missing children, four of them babies no more than a year old. He failed to locate any of them.

He felt a profound sense of relief when he finished telling his story. He realized how foolish he had been to refuse therapy all these years.

"Fate has brought us together, Ron Jackson," Natalie said. "Don't you see that? We must remove these criminals from the earth. Whatever it takes."

"Yes," he said, sure of his decision. "Whatever it takes."

CHAPTER 40

"It's not a done deal yet," said Mary Ann the following morning. "The District Attorney is still mulling over offering witness protection. It's difficult because we're unsure how much he can help us. He might know nothing about the leadership of Teddy Bear."

"True," Ron said. "Wang or Morales might be a more suitable target for the offer." He was sitting in his car, parked down the street from Zhao's house, having just relieved the cop who had the night shift. An overcast sky marked seven am. Rain would be arriving soon. The noise of the morning traffic was picking up on the street.

Activating the hands-free speaker on his phone, he poured a cup of coffee from his thermos. He slept like a dead man last night, too tired to remove his clothes before collapsing onto the mattress. Telling Natalie his sister's story had been very cathartic, and he slept well, with no nightmares. He felt a twinge of guilt for not telling Mary Ann about it. However, revealing his deepening relationship with Natalie was unwise. It might make her doubt his loyalty, and he didn't need that complication.

"If Teddy Bear is going to hit him, today would be ideal," he said, "before they have to tell him the ransom won't be paid. If we can stop it from happening, Zhao might turn on them."

"The big conference call yesterday went on for two hours," she said. "If they hadn't encrypted the call, we'd know exactly what they plan. I wish I could give you some backup, but I'd have to bring in the locals. With all the paperwork involved, it would take days to set it up. If it looks like anything is going sideways, call me immediately."

"Will do. Let's hope he goes to work and nothing happens."

He settled in, waiting for the Lexus to appear. By ten o'clock, Zhao still hadn't left home. Something was wrong. A sense of unease washed over him, so he contacted Mary Ann.

"So far, our boy's been a no-show. He should've left for work hours ago. Perhaps he's afraid to venture beyond the safety of his home. Or maybe they hit him last night somehow, and he's lying on the floor dead. Wait...something's happening."

The gate across the driveway was opening. The muscular security guard walked out to the street, studying the traffic. Today, he wore a blue blazer over a golf shirt and jeans. There was a lump to the side of it. *That blazer's concealing a pistol.* Satisfied, the guard jogged behind the gate. A moment later, the Lexus appeared, making a quick right turn into traffic, and speeding past him.

"Zhao's on the move. He's taking a different route from yesterday and seems in a hurry. I'll follow."

He disconnected the call and made a U-turn when traffic allowed. The tracking device attached to the Lexus was working perfectly, so he kept his distance. Zhao headed toward the freeway, away from the warehouse.

A few minutes later, the Lexus headed south and merged onto the 101 freeway. Ron followed as his phone chimed.

"Where's he going?" said Natalie.

How is she so invisible following people? "I'm not sure," he answered. "My guess is he's making a run for it. He might have a safe house nearby."

"If he's anticipating trouble, others may be tracking him, too."

He hadn't thought of that, but she had a valid point. Zhao's boss might have ordered a hit, which meant his men might have been watching the house, waiting for an opportunity. "Don't worry, you put a tracker on his car. I don't need to keep him in sight to know where he is."

"I'll watch your back," she said. Then the phone went dead.

His eyes darted around the freeway, using his side and rearview mirrors to monitor the traffic. Everything looked normal. There was no one resembling Natalie driving a car anywhere near him. With a sigh carrying the weight of defeat, he acknowledged the truth. He would never spot her as she followed him. Even her car was stealthy.

The marker on his tracking software moved off the freeway up ahead at Ventura Road, then paralleled the Santa Clara riverbed for a while before turning south toward Oxnard. Ron knew where Zhao was going as he passed Gonzales Road ten minutes later. He sped up to close the gap with the Lexus. It made a right turn onto 5th and proceeded toward the airport.

Oxnard Airport was a small county-owned facility with a single runway and no commercial air service since 1990. Only small private planes and the occasional charter flight used it, making it a secluded spot.

The small terminal was a gathering place for the charter flights. A row of empty chairs shared space with a vending machine. A tall control tower stood beside it, and beyond that, rows of hangars for storing private planes.

The Lexus went past the terminal, turning right onto an access road leading to a gate. It stopped next to a keypad, and the driver's window rolled down. A hand emerged from inside the car and entered a code.

Ron pulled to the curb of the main road and watched as the gate swung open. To keep the car in sight, he needed help to get past the gate. He reached out to Mary Ann again. "Zhao is at Oxnard Airport. He's driving into the hangar area, but there's a security gate, and I don't have the code. I think he's planning to fly out of here."

"Shit. I wonder if he's a licensed pilot. Hang on, I'll call airport security and get the code for you."

He watched as the Lexus cleared the gate and drove toward the hangars. The gate jerked and began to close. He approached it cautiously, maintaining a comfortable gap between him and the Lexus. It made a left turn along a line of hangars and disappeared from view. Ron slammmed his foot on the gas pedal, shooting through the gate just before it rolled closed. Mary Ann came back on the call.

"Okay, the code is 4-1-9-2. I advised security not to allow Zhao to fly because we wanted to question him. Unfortunately, they don't have any officers at the airport to stop him. Security ordered the tower to delay him until a squad car arrives. If he tries to leave anyway, you could drive your car onto the runway, preventing him from taking off. Then get out and take cover somewhere. Do not engage. You have no authority to detain him, and I don't want anybody getting shot. Is that clear?"

"Got it. I'm through the gate. Zhao went down a row of hangars, and I've lost visual contact. I'm trying to find him now. Don't worry, he's not flying today. I'll call you when security gets here."

The dot on his tracking software stopped moving a short distance ahead. Ron parked his car and retrieved his pistol, its familiar weight providing a sense of security. He pressed his back against a weathered metal shed, blending into the shadows as he approached the drive down which the Lexus traveled. Glancing around the corner, he observed six hangars on each side of the drive. Then another driveway intersected, providing access to the runway. Beyond that, hangers continued.

The hangers offered ample space for smaller private airplanes. A large motorized door across the front folded into the ceiling when raised, to allow a plane to enter or exit. Some doors were open, revealing either a plane inside or an empty hangar. A smaller door offered convenient access when the larger one was closed. A few people were lounging about, socializing, laughing, and drinking coffee.

Ron spotted the Lexus parked near a hangar at the end of the row. The overhead door was up, revealing a gleaming white twin-engine plane. Its cargo hatch was open, and the two bodyguards were transferring suitcases from the car to the plane. Zhao was not visible.

His phone chirped, showing an incoming call from a restricted number, which meant Natalie.

"Two cars are approaching the hangar from the far driveway," she said. "Four men are in each car. They may be here to kill Zhao. Take cover before they arrive."

Ron sprinted down the driveway toward Zhao, planning to duck into an open hangar near him. He was a few steps away from it when two cars turned the corner and came to a screeching halt. Doors opened, and men with assault rifles piled out. The two surprised bodyguards dropped the suitcases and dove behind the Lexus as the assassins opened fire. Bullets tore through the body of the car, leaving shattered glass and bullet holes. The bodyguards hugged the wheels, which offered the most protection from incoming fire. Armed only with pistols, they faced insurmountable odds.

Ron reached the hangar across from Zhao's, took cover behind a large tool chest, and drew his pistol. Adrenalin rushed through his body, sharpening his senses. Time seemed to slow. He was out of breath from sprinting.

The assassins paid him no attention, probably assuming he was a civilian trying to hide. In seconds, all the locals disappeared into their hangars, leaving behind the reverberating sound of slamming doors. No doubt 9-1-1 calls were being made. The assassins were working against the clock to complete their task and escape before the police arrived.

They fanned out, firing in short bursts, trying to outflank the bodyguards. Unable to shoot back, the bodyguards huddled behind the car. The assassins moved toward Zhao's hangar as they scanned for potential threats. Ron noticed their body armor, which provided all the protection they needed.

A decision was required. He could hide behind the tool chest and let the two parties fight it out, or he could intervene and risk dying to save Zhao. Eight armed men with superior weapons and armor faced three poorly armed defenders. His best hope was to delay them long enough for the SWAT team to arrive. He drew in a long breath and peeked around the toolbox. The nearest assassin was about ten feet away. In a few seconds, he would outflank the bodyguards. If the bodyguards lost the cover of the car, they would die. He couldn't stand by while that happened.

He squeezed off three rounds from his Glock at the nearest assassin. Two of the rounds hit his armor and spun him around. The third was a lucky shot that caught him right between the eyes. As he fell, two other assassins stopped their advance and redirected their fire at Ron. He clung desperately to the back of the toolbox, feeling the vibrations as bullets pounded against it and zoomed past over his head. The box was heavy gauge steel and filled with tools, shielding him from the bullets. But it was being shot to pieces. He couldn't stay there much longer.

While searching for a new hiding place, he heard the unmistakable sound of another automatic weapon above him. He glanced upward, searching for the sound's origin, but saw only the hangar roof.

The barrage of bullets fired at him came to a sudden halt. A glance around the toolbox revealed two more assassins sprawled motionless in the driveway. The remaining five had regrouped and directed their fire at someone on the roof. The bodyguards saw an opportunity, stood up, and opened fire on their assailants, but their bullets couldn't penetrate the assailant's body armor. One assassin swept the car with his AK-47, and both bodyguards fell and didn't move.

The shooter above him emptied another magazine of bullets onto the assassins, this time from a different roof, and two more of them fell. The remaining three backed away, realizing the battle had turned against them. Ron emptied his pistol at them, to no effect. Another burst of fire, originating from the roof of a third hangar, felled one more assassin, causing the remaining two to retreat to their cars. The odor of burning rubber mixed with gunpowder lingered in the air as they raced away.

Ron looked at his watch. The entire battle took less than fifteen minutes, but it seemed like hours. He leaned against the toolbox, trying to slow his racing heart by taking deep breaths. Despite his efforts to calm himself down, his hands continued to shake.

He heard a noise and realized his phone was ringing. "Yes?" he said through a mouth so dry he could hardly talk.

"Are you all right, Ron Jackson?" Natalie said.

"I'm not hurt if that's your question. I don't know if my nerves will ever recover. Thank you for saving my life again."

"You were very foolish to risk your life protecting Zhao. I understand why, but part of me would have rejoiced if they'd killed him. I must go now. The police are coming."

His phone went dead.

The mention of Zhao made him realize he hadn't seen him during the battle. He gazed at the plane and observed movement in the cockpit. A moment later, an electric starter whined, and one propeller turned. *After all this, he thinks he can fly away?* Ron walked over to the hangar, loading a fresh magazine into his Glock. The second propeller began turning as he stepped under the plane and shot out every tire, making the plane immobile. Zhao wasn't going anywhere now.

CHAPTER 41

After determining he was involved in the shootout, SWAT whisked Ron off to the police station for questioning. Drew Kennedy, the Oxnard police detective who had the bad luck to catch the case, stared stonily at Ron while listening to him tell his story, or at least the part of it he was willing to tell. He had already taken Zhao's statement and was unhappy with the lack of details. Ron was proving to be no more helpful.

"As a licensed private detective," Ron stated, "I followed Zhao on behalf of a client I can't reveal. For what reason, I can't say. While I was observing him, eight men appeared and began shooting at him and me. I shot back in self-defense."

"Why were the men trying to kill you?" Kennedy said.

He shrugged. "I didn't know any of them."

It didn't help his case that several of the locals who were present reported that he was running *toward* the plane before the shooting started. Maybe the detective believed he had instigated the whole thing. This was counter-balanced by Zhao, who saw everything from the cockpit of his plane. According to him, Ron was a hero, valiantly defending him against a mob bent on his destruction. Why, he didn't know.

"Who was the shooter on the hanger roof?" Kennedy asked. "What happened to him?"

"I have no idea, said Ron, "but I suspect he worked for Zhao." He didn't mention the possibility the shooter was a woman.

Zhao didn't know either, but thought he worked with Ron. He testified that without the shooter's sudden appearance in the fight, the assassins would have succeeded in their plan to kill him.

There were so many spent rifle shells on the hanger roofs that only an automatic assault rifle could account for them—an AK-47, to be exact.

"You must know that it's illegal to own an automatic weapon in California or a magazine that holds over ten rounds," said Kennedy.

"Really?" said Ron. "I'm curious as to how every assassin had one."

Kennedy didn't find that amusing.

He had called Mary Ann just before an army of cops swarmed the airport, informing her he had stepped in it again and needed her help. She had little to say in reply. After all, she told him to tail Zhao. He hoped to God some serious back-channel discussion was happening between the police chiefs of Oxnard and Santa Barbara that would remove him as a suspect from what was shaping up to be the crime of the century in Oxnard. Otherwise, he might find himself implicated in a murder case that would keep him from focusing his full attention on the Teddy Bear investigation. The forensic evidence would prove that a bullet fired from his Glock claimed the life of one assassin.

A knock on the door interrupted Kennedy's interrogation. A man wearing a wrinkled gray suit with a loose blue tie around his neck stuck his head in and motioned for the detective to follow him into the hall. The door closed, leaving Ron alone in the interrogation room, which contained only two chairs and a table. The room had a strong odor of urine. He looked around, wondering if someone had peed in a corner. It said little about Oxnard's standards of cleanliness.

A muffled argument was going on in the hall, which stopped abruptly. The detective returned and sat in the chair across the desk from him. Tapping the tip of his pen against the table, he frowned at Ron.

"Well, pal, it looks like you've got some friends in high places who are vouching for you," he said, with a tinge of bitterness in his voice. "I think that story you just told me is a bunch of crap. This thing looks like a drug deal gone bad, but my gut tells me it's something else, and you know what that is. We'll work closely with the Santa Barbara Sheriff's Department on this. If a whiff of evidence says you're anything other than innocent, I'll be back in touch. You're free to go."

Ron thanked him for understanding his situation and beat a hasty retreat out the front door. A drizzle of rain was falling outside as he walked down the steps. Mary Ann leaned against the side of her car, wearing a windbreaker, and frowning at him. He grinned weakly and walked over.

"Thanks for getting me out of there. The detective didn't believe a word I said. I had no choice but to intervene. Eight of them faced off against two bodyguards. Zhao hid in his plane during the whole fight."

"Don't thank me. The chief made the call. I didn't have enough juice to do it. You can understand their reluctance to let you go," she said.

"I'm making friends everywhere. At least we saved Zhao's ass. He ought to be receptive to a deal at this point."

"That's why I'm here. This morning, the DA agreed to offer limited immunity. I'm going to pitch it to him now. He'd be a fool not to take it."

"What about the others? By now, they likely know that the hit failed. Do you think they'll try to leave the country?"

"Maybe, depending on what Zhao knows. They are all on no-fly lists. LAPD has agreed to tail Wang until we convince Zhao to testify against him. He works for the Chinese consulate but doesn't have diplomatic immunity. Therefore, they can pick him up anytime. The Chinese will make a stink about it until they find out what he's involved in, but we'll handle it."

She studied him. "Who was the person on the roof? Our little ninja?"

Ron hung his head. "Yeah, she followed me. I didn't know she was there until she started shooting. Saved my life and Zhao's. Just before the cops arrived, she disappeared."

"She killed six people with an AK-47. Where did she get that?"

"Uh...just for the record, I think I nailed one of them, so she killed five. Someone is supplying her with arms."

"How can someone enslaved in Syria for five years have connections to acquire weapons here? Where did she get the funds to pay for them? Someone must have arranged this before she returned. It's further proof that she has a hidden agenda and friends she's keeping quiet about. I need a meeting with her, or I may have to make her known to the Oxnard Police."

Ron spread his hands wide. "The only time I talk to her is when she calls me. I can't call her or trace her number because it's restricted. I don't know where she lives or what car she drives. She doesn't trust the police, or anybody else for that matter. But somebody wants her dead. I don't know if it's the people who gave her weapons, or somebody else."

"You've got to convince her we're her friends. If someone wants to do her harm, we can protect her. But if she insists on getting revenge her way, I'll issue a warrant for her arrest. Five people are dead. The Oxnard police want answers."

"I'll see what I can do," he said.

Mary Ann frowned at his answer. "I sense that you're not entirely on board with this. She's been there for you in life-threatening situations, but maybe your bond with her is becoming too strong and influencing your judgment. I'm wondering if I can rely on you."

He thought through an answer that would satisfy her, yet not reveal his alliance with Natalie. "Destroying Teddy Bear is the most important goal in my life right now. I want these guys arrested and sent to rot in prison. I think she feels the same way."

She gave him a hard stare. "Don't let guilt over past deeds cloud your judgment. We either do this correctly or not at all. I don't trust her, and neither should you."

Pushing herself off her car, she brushed past him and headed toward the steps to the police station.

Ron called Uber to catch a ride back to the airport and listened as the Indian driver, whose clothes smelled of curry, chatted away. It was late in the day, and the windshield wipers slapped back and forth as rain rolled onshore.

The driver dropped him off by the security gate that led to the airport hangers. After tapping in the code on the keypad, he waited for the gate to roll open. The rain came down harder, and he had no jacket, so his soaked clothes clung to his body as he ran to his car. Puddles of water formed on the driver's seat and floor mat as he drove home. He turned the heater on high, hoping it would help dry his clothes and make the trip more tolerable. All things considered, it was a fitting end to a miserable day.

Ron worried that his partnership with Mary Ann was coming apart. She had called him out at the police station, and he had evaded her questions. He had a long history with her and felt somewhat like a traitor in not telling her everything he was doing with Natalie. Was he letting his guilt influence his actions? Wasn't this a case where the result justified the means?

Perhaps he had been too quick to commit to working with Natalie. As Mary Ann had pointed out, there were still many unanswered questions. But their goals were so aligned he couldn't resist the opportunity. They were both seeking a way out of the hell they'd lived in for years.

Later that evening, Ron was organizing his bills, trying to make his money stretch a little further, when a call from Mary Ann interrupted him. "Good news. Zhao agreed to cooperate. He's enraged that Teddy Bear sent eight men to kill him, so now he wants to destroy them."

"What did he have to say?"

"For the past eight years, he's been in business with Teddy Bear. Wang recruited him. They have some family ties back in China. Hackman, his only employee, had the important role of vetting anyone who offered them a child. Once they agreed upon a price,

Hackman would arrange a meeting to pick up the child while Wang provided the money to pay off the other party. Then, they gave the child to Zhao, who would transport the kid to Albuquerque by plane. Once there, they transferred the child to an individual at a private landing strip outside the town."

"Morales, no doubt. Did he ID him?" asked Ron.

"No. He insisted that he had never laid eyes on him. The only guy he could identify was Wang. It makes sense. No reason for Morales to be there."

"So, we need Wang to tie this up in a nice big bow. How can I help?"

"I had a long talk with the LAPD today. The Chinese government will face embarrassment on an international scale when it's revealed that one of their consulate employees is involved in child slavery. If he's deported, there's a high likelihood the Chinese will put him on trial as a deterrent to others. Have you seen their trials? They take about two days. The court always finds the defendant guilty. There's no appeal. The government will take him out and shoot him. I heard they harvest body parts to sell on the black market."

"Hope I never need a kidney. Sounds to me like motivation to make a deal."

"The plan is to arrest him at work tomorrow to embarrass the Chinese government and pressure him to make a deal. It will be front-page news in media worldwide. I'm part of the LAPD strike force and will observe the interrogation. Until the court decides who has jurisdiction, Wang will live in a jail cell in Los Angeles."

"Suppose Wang disappears tonight like Zhao tried to do?" Ron said. "He's got to realize that Zhao will rat him out. Or perhaps the partners plan to kill him?"

"The LAPD agreed to sit on him tonight in case he gets any ideas. They'll follow him to work tomorrow before we do the bust."

"I hope this works, Mary Ann. Without him, we've got nothing on the other Teddy Bear bosses. Would it be okay for me to be there?"

Mary Ann cleared her throat. "This is an LAPD operation. I don't have the authority to invite civilians. Let's hope for the best. Tomorrow will be a critical day."

Ron felt anxious about not having a part in the plan. Until now, he had been involved in everything. *Was Mary Ann freezing him out, or was he being paranoid?*

CHAPTER 42

"They're going to arrest Wang today," said Ron. He yawned, reaching for a cup of coffee on the patio table in his backyard, where he worked out when time permitted. Rain during the night had left drops of water on the table. Today was cloudless; the sun was bright, and its warmth felt good on his skin.

"Do you think he'll be more afraid of the Chinese government than his partners?" Natalie said.

"We'll offer him a spot in the witness protection program, where his partners won't be able to find him."

"Who are these partners?"

He hesitated, knowing that crossing this line could lead to consequences he wanted to avoid. But he needed to continue earning her trust. Perhaps he could use this information as leverage to compel her to answer some questions. It might restore Mary Ann's trust in him.

"Our intelligence indicates three partners, all in the United States."

"What are their names?"

"Before I disclose that, there are some questions I want to ask you. Do you believe that I'm on your side? And that I'll protect you from the police?"

The phone line fell silent. "You've always told me the truth," she finally said. "Our goal is the same, but our methods are different. As for the police, how can you protect me? You don't work for them anymore."

"I can negotiate with them on your behalf. Advise you of what they're thinking. For example, the Oxnard police are investigating who killed the five assassins and why. Although we haven't disclosed your identity to them, Mary Ann has doubts about you. She believes you have a secret motive for being here. You indicated there are people from Syria who seek to kill you. Also, your skills are far beyond anything an enslaved girl would have. And where did you get that AK-47?"

After a moment of quiet, Natalie released a long, frustrated sigh. "All right, I'll tell you. I was more than a slave. Al-Tunisi sent me to training camps, where I learned the skills necessary to carry out my mission. The mission failed to gain every commander's acceptance, so some orchestrated my escape from Raqqa to tarnish al-Tunisi's image. I was happy for the opportunity to leave that hellhole and return home to my country. When he learned of my betrayal, al-Tunisi sent men to kill me in revenge. They were the ones who attacked us at Zhao's house."

"Tell me what your mission is," he said.

"I don't know. Someone was supposed to contact me."

Ron mulled this over in his mind. Some gaps remained in her story. "How did you get your weapons?"

"While living at the halfway house in Washington, a man approached me. His orders were to give me weapons so I could defend myself against men sent by al-Tunisi to kill me. The longer I stayed alive, the weaker it made him look. The strategy was to sow doubt among his followers about his leadership and encourage them to shift their allegiance to others. It's a common thing in Syria."

"Tell me about this man. Was he an American?"

"It's possible, but he spoke fluent Arabic. We met only once."

"What was his name? Can you describe him?" Ron asked, hoping for a new lead.

"I have his name, but first, tell me the names of the three men working for Teddy Bear," she insisted.

Ron hesitated. He didn't see how giving her the names would cause any disruption to the investigation. They were far away, likely to be arrested before Natalie could reach them. *But if she got there first?*

Whatever it takes, he reminded himself.

He gave her the names and locations of Spironi and Pontreau, while denying any knowledge of Morales' location. Albuquerque was only a day's drive away. Too close for his comfort.

In return, she gave him the name of her contact and a vague description. The meeting happened at night; he wore a hoodie, and the lighting was poor. She promised to call back that evening for an update on Wang.

He thought about Natalie's story while he waited for Mary Ann to call. It was a plausible explanation, answering most of the questions he had. But an uneasy feeling still nagged him. *Why was Natalie chosen? What made her unique?*

He could think of only one thing—she was an American citizen. Once the government confirmed that, it would mean guaranteed readmission into the United States. Could ISIS exploit this to send a terrorist into our country? By continuing to help her, was he becoming an accomplice to treason? Was her story a lie, crafted to gain time?

It lingered like a dark cloud in his thoughts. ISIS had trained her in stealth and weapons. Tailor-made for a covert operation aimed at assassination. Given the considerable time and money invested, lofty expectations were inevitable. *Had they really sent her here without knowledge of the target?*

He pounded the side of his head with his palm. Winston Churchill once described Russia as "a riddle wrapped in a mystery inside an enigma." It was a perfect description of Natalie. The more she revealed, the less he knew.

CHAPTER 43

The sun had slipped below the horizon, replaced by a rising moon illuminating a chilly night. Ron had just finished dinner, and the tangy odor of barbeque filled his house. He was on edge, wondering if LAPD had arrested Wang. As he was washing the dinner dishes, Mary Ann finally called.

"What a fiasco today was," she said. "It was lunchtime before the LAPD got their shit together, and we visited the consulate. When we asked to speak to Wang, they tried to stonewall us by saying he wasn't there. The LAPD had followed him that morning, so we knew otherwise. When we threatened to search the building, they suddenly remembered he was there. He came out, surrounded by a bunch of Chinese lawyers. We read him his rights and put the cuffs on him. The lawyers went berserk and started shouting about diplomatic immunity and such."

"What, they forgot he didn't have any?" said Ron as he dried his last dish and sat at the kitchen table to relax.

"After we pointed that out, they got on their cellphones and started talking Chinese, so we hustled him out the front door. You should have seen it. The media was outside waiting. We had to fight our way to the squad car. Slowly, of course. There were plenty of photo ops. I think Wang wet his pants. It's going to be featured on the news tonight."

He laughed, imagining what a circus it must have been. "Did he agree to cooperate when you got him to the station?"

"We couldn't get him to say anything. He requested a lawyer, so we stepped back. We've got him in protective custody. Tomorrow, we'll tell him Zhao has agreed to testify against him. Then, I will remind him of how the judicial system works in China. He doesn't have any good options, so I think he'll crack."

"I'm not so sure of that. It depends on who he's most afraid of. What about the three other bosses?"

"They're on the no-fly list, but we don't have enough evidence to arrest them yet. We need Wang for that."

"I talked with our ninja this morning," Ron said. He repeated what Natalie had told him.

"I'm not sure I believe all that," she said when he finished. "I can't see al-Tunisi not knowing she was leaving. She was a valuable asset, sure to be carefully watched. Isn't he the supreme commander in Raqqa?"

"Yeah, but I don't believe it holds the same significance as it would here. In ISIS, loyalties shift around from one leader to another. They lack the chain of command we have in our army. I have doubts about her story too, but for a different reason." He explained his theory of why ISIS chose Natalie.

"That makes sense," Mary Ann said. "But we lack any hard evidence to prove it."

"She shared the name of the individual who gave her the weapons. His name is Ahmed Nadeem. He is about 35 years old, has a medium build, and is clean-shaven. They met only once, in Virginia. Tracking him down would confirm her story. But it could be a phony name."

"If I were in his position, I wouldn't be stupid enough to give a stranger my real name. Anyway, there's insufficient information to determine where to search. I can check the name in NCIC for a match, but it's unlikely."

"I'm not going to hold my breath on that one," said Ron. He hesitated, carefully selecting his words. "Is there anyone left who's involved with Teddy Bear in California? What else can I do to help?"

"There's nothing more you can do," she said, her voice filled with resignation. "We've put the whole Teddy Bear operation in California out of business. That's as far as my jurisdiction extends. I've spoken to the FBI, and they've assured me they plan to apprehend the remaining scumbags once they have Wang's testimony.

"With him as the star witness, getting convictions should be no problem."

"I don't think this is their top priority," he said.

"Ron, you've dismantled a significant child slavery ring in California, and gotten closure on the Garcia case that's been haunting you for six years. Your sister would have been proud. Isn't that enough?"

Ron stood up, pacing around the kitchen, uneasy with her question. "I don't know if it's enough. There are still missing kids out there. If we knew where they were, maybe we could rescue them."

"The FBI will find them. It'll require time."

"That's the problem. Unless they act quickly, Teddy Bear will warn their clients that the FBI is coming after them. They'll hide or eliminate the children to ensure their silence."

"That's all speculation, Ron. Let it go."

"Will you still call me?" he pleaded. "Will you keep me posted on how things are progressing?"

"Of course. Take a break to relax and decompress. You and I have done a great service to humanity. Find a good psychologist to help you work it out."

After Mary Ann ended the call, he made himself a drink and went into the living room to sit in his easy chair, where he did his best thinking. He was being treated like a small child—praised for a good deed, then forgotten while the adults carried on. He was unhappy and confused. A decision was necessary.

Was he ready to say goodbye to the case? That was the first question he needed to answer. Had he done enough to forgive himself for his earlier failures in life? It was a troublesome question. He couldn't reach a definitive conclusion despite wrestling with it from every angle.

He saluted the moon outside his living room window and chugged half his drink. The familiar burn of the whiskey slid down his throat, the warmth spreading through his chest, comforting him. Tonight, it would be so easy to slip back into his old habits, drowning his insecurities in alcohol.

A few drinks with his friend Jack Daniels had a certain amount of merit. If he couldn't sleep and was off the investigation, he might as well enjoy himself. But before he could implement the plan, his phone chimed on the table next to his chair. He glanced at the display and frowned. It was a restricted number, and he remembered Natalie promised to call.

"Do you have any news on Wang?" she said.

"Did you watch the news tonight?" he replied.

"No, I don't watch the news. The reporters are all biased. They report only what they think their listeners want to hear."

"The police arrested Wang at work today, and all the media outlets were there. It was quite a show, from what I heard."

"Did he confess his crimes?"

"No, he demanded a lawyer, so the police can't question him until tomorrow. It appears that he's the last Teddy Bear employee to be found in California. I was told my services are no longer required."

"What about the remaining three men?"

"The FBI has the case. They've promised to investigate them. My old partner has no authority to arrest anyone outside of California."

"It'll take forever!" she shouted, full of anger. "The Syrians are relentless, and they have the resources to find me. I need to finish my business here and move on."

"To have enough time to plan your revenge on Teddy Bear," Ron advised, "you'll have to deal with the Syrians first. One person fighting two enemies at once is an impossible task."

Natalie snorted. "To kill a snake, you must cut off its head. The head is in Washington, D.C."

"Then that's where you must go."

"What about you, Ron Jackson? Are you content with your accomplishments?"

"I couldn't sleep thinking about this," he said. "Although we may have dismantled the Teddy Bear organization in California, it's a small part of the bigger picture. Plus, there are at least seven more children that were kidnapped under my watch. No one has seen any of them. I want to bring them home, where they can find peace and a sense of belonging."

"If you want to find the kids, force their abductors to reveal where they sent them," Natalie replied.

The glimmer of an idea formed in Ron's brain. Mary Ann had cut him loose, so he was free of any promises he made to her. Working with Natalie, they could continue to stalk the remaining three Teddy Bear bosses in the country and perhaps learn the names of others overseas.

He agreed with Natalie that the American form of justice was too slow. Going back to being a private eye and hoping the FBI pursued the bosses while the kidnapped children suffered was unacceptable to him. He and Natalie could do now what it would take the FBI years to accomplish. It would require compromise, but maybe they could each attain their goals.

"Perhaps we could work together," he said. "I can watch your back while you deal with the Syrians, and you watch mine when I confront Teddy Bear. But I won't help you murder anybody. There are ways to achieve revenge without killing. Take something they cherish from them."

"Maybe their daughter?" she said bitterly. "For six long years, I've endured unspeakable things that have tested the limits of my sanity. The pain they feel should be identical."

"Taking a thing they cherish can be worse for them than being dead. They must endure the loss for the rest of their lives," he said.

"Perhaps," she said. "But what if it requires killing that which they cherish? A wife or child? Isn't that the same thing?"

Ron sighed. "There must be a way to satisfy your thirst for revenge without killing someone. It may take time to determine what it is, but we can discover it together."

"Before I become your partner, Ron Jackson, you understand that if you ever betray me to the police, you will become my enemy."

"I'm no longer working with Mary Ann, so we'll be alone. But you'll have to trust me and not keep things from me."

They spent the next hour hashing out the ground rules and devising a game plan for their partnership. It was impossible to foresee the length of the mission or where it would take them, and he needed cash to live on. That meant he would have to sell his house, his only remaining asset besides his car. He was willing to do this to destroy Teddy Bear. Until he accomplished that, Natalie would take care of all the expenses. The enemies of al-Tunisi had supplied her with funds.

Ron estimated it would take a week to wrap up his affairs and put his house on the market. Natalie couldn't shake off the constant worry of being found by the Syrians. Despite his protests, she gave him only three days.

CHAPTER 44

With only three days to settle his affairs, Ron woke up the next morning planning to take everything worth keeping to his storage shed. Each item that he packed held a story that he wanted to preserve. There wasn't much. Some photo albums and keepsakes from his childhood. His first watch, given to him by his dad, when he was twelve. His wedding ring from a failed marriage. Clothes that he wasn't taking with him, but thought he might want later if he returned to California. It would all go to storage, along with his files from the office. His furniture held no value to him, so he opted to sell his house furnished. Later that day, a real estate agent would come to sign the listing.

A grin formed on his lips as he packed, illuminating his entire face. He felt laser-focused on what he had to do. He was all in, willing to make every effort to locate the missing children. Partnering with Natalie had been the correct choice, despite his doubt about why she was here. There would be no second-guessing that he failed to do enough.

A thick layer of fog hugged his home, preventing him from leaving. It gave everything a fuzzy look, and beyond twenty yards, all he could see was a blanket of gray. Without visual confirmation, it was impossible to tell from which direction sound came. Hearing a car, he could only guess which direction it would pass his house. Driving was impossible in that weather. On top of that, everything smelled damp.

By eleven o'clock, the sun had broken through, burning off the fog and allowing him to transport everything to storage. Mary Ann called just as he finished stacking the last boxes into his shed. The evening was approaching, and a clammy ocean breeze signaled more fog that night. He wiped some dirt off his brow and answered his phone.

"Thought I'd give you an update. Wang had his preliminary hearing today," she said. "He was bound over for trial, but his lawyer secured his release on bail. As a condition, he gave up his passport, but he's free for now."

"Did he agree to cooperate?"

"Unfortunately, no. I think he's planning on fleeing the country before he goes on trial. Then he won't have to give up anybody in Teddy Bear. Maybe he struck a deal with them, arranging his escape from America in return for his silence. From my perspective,

I have serious doubts about their willingness to let him live, but he might view it as his most prudent course of action."

"His testimony is crucial. Without it, our pursuit of Morales is at a standstill unless we can sway Pontreau or Spironi," Ron said, expressing his disappointment.

"We're not giving up on him yet. The FBI has Pontreau and Spironi in their sights. They're digging into their backgrounds, and it's just a matter of time until they find something. But right now, they've only got Zhao's story, with no collaboration."

Mary Ann continued her report. "Morales owns Custom Automotive, an auto repair shop in Albuquerque. He lives in a large house on three acres of land in Corrales, a suburb of Albuquerque. A background check turned up nothing. He's a pillar of the community, without even a traffic ticket to his name."

"Shit. Looks like we're stuck again."

"Patience is a virtue. What are you doing?"

"Ah...I'm going to visit an old friend of mine. I'll be available if you need help. Keep me informed, okay?"

"Will do, partner. Have a good time."

Natalie had shared her cellphone number with Ron as part of their new partnership. He called her to relay the news. As he expected, she was not happy.

"Wang is free, and the police have arrested no one else?" she said.

"That's it in a nutshell. They're looking into Pontreau and Spironi, but it takes time to build a case. One good thing, I know where Morales lives." He gave her the information Mary Ann shared.

"We must visit Wang or Morales. They are the ones who are closest to us," she stated. "We can make them tell us where the children are and allow me my revenge."

"Wang doesn't know where they are," he reminded her. "He's just the delivery boy for Morales. Getting him alone would also pose a considerable challenge. I'm sure he's expecting visitors."

"Then we must leave tomorrow before Morales disappears."

Ron grunted. "I have only two days to prepare now?"

"We must strike when the enemy isn't expecting us. It'll increase the odds of our success."

"All right," he said reluctantly. "You're the expert on that sort of thing. Let's do it."

Chapter 45

Parked along the side of a road skirting the edge of a mesa, Ron sat in his car pretending to be just another tourist taking in the panoramic view of the small town of Corrales below. It was an excellent vantage point from which to observe Morales' ranch. The early morning traffic was building, and there wasn't a cloud in the turquoise sky. The New Mexico air felt dry on his skin.

He focused his high-powered binoculars on the estate, noting every impressive detail. The main dwelling, a large, two-story adobe modern ranch house, occupied the front part of three acres of land, providing breathtaking views of the lush river valley. A brick driveway swept under a portico at the front door, then curved around the left side of the house to a free-standing six-car garage. A silver Lexus sat under the portico, but no people were outside. *How many children did he sell to afford this?*

The backyard was a summer paradise, containing a shimmering pool and jacuzzi with plenty of shaded patios. Behind the pool, a small guest house seemed as large as his Carpinteria home. The rest of the property consisted of fenced pastures containing grazing cows, goats, and horses. A large stable, built with steeples to mimic those seen in Kentucky, sat in the middle. A utility shed housed a tractor, farm implements, and a large riding lawnmower at the back of the property. It would be a long walk trying to infiltrate from the back of the property to the house.

A tall wall made of concrete blocks surrounded the estate. Privacy appeared to be important to the owner. It also eliminated any possibility of someone taking a shot at him in a drive-by shooting. Two electric gates provided access to the property. One guarded the driveway, and the other the stable, which was reached via a dirt road. Ron had seen them opened with a portable transmitter, or from inside the house. He took pictures of everything with his camera.

Earlier that day, he cruised by Garcia's auto repair shop to do the same thing. Custom Automotive was in an industrial zone close to the city center. It was a cheaply built concrete block building containing four bays with lifts. All four lifts held cars, and mechanics were busy working on them. Tucked into one corner of the building was a small office. Autos and pickup trucks filled the parking lot, some coated in thick dust, giving the impression of long-term neglect.

Natalie was on her own, somewhere near the house, studying the layout and trying to determine the easiest way to enter without being detected. He picked up his phone and pushed a button to speed dial her. Both were using brand-new burner phones, purchased just before leaving California. It was a precaution to minimize the possibility of someone following them from cell tower to cell tower.

"What do you think?" he said.

"I don't like it," she replied. "If someone triggers an alarm, it'll take too long to escape. His wife and two children may get in the way. We need a time and place to take him when he's alone."

"Humm…" he said.

They spent the night at a cheap motel on the outskirts of town. The next day, Ron accessed a website that listed local houses for rent and found a safe house that would serve as their headquarters while they were stalking Morales. Its condition was deplorable, with leaky pipes, mold, and a desperate need for a fresh coat of paint. The location, however, was excellent, in the backcountry of Corrales at the terminus of a dirt road. The owner accepted two months' rent in cash with no questions asked, pleased to find a renter for the long-vacant place.

They established a precise surveillance schedule to track Morales' every movement. Ron worked days, and Natalie took the night shifts. During the nighttime, she scouted Custom Automotive and identified where to cut the wires to the alarm system.

Very early in the morning, she made several trips to his estate, scaling the wall to scout the grounds, but never entering the house. Motion-activated floodlights provided the only exterior security.

Morales was an overweight, heavy-set man with a dark complexion. He had a full head of black wavey hair, streaked with gray, slicked back along his ears. Bushy eyebrows hung over a long, hooked nose. Ron kept meticulous notes on him from when he left home in the morning until he went to sleep. A pattern soon emerged.

During the week, his driver would pick him up at seven sharp and take him to work. The driver was a big guy with bulging muscles and a shaved head. He looked like a former wrestler. After dropping his boss off at Custom Automotive, he would disappear until lunchtime, when he returned to take the boss wherever he wanted to eat. Most days, it would be to a small Mexican restaurant across town, where he ate alone while his driver waited in the lobby. Occasionally, he would venture to a different place and have lunch with a friend.

After lunch, he would either return to the office or go home. There was no apparent pattern observed. It likely depended on how much work he needed to accomplish at the office. After work, the driver would take him home and disappear until the following morning. Weekends were unpredictable. Sometimes, Morales would stay home, and other times, he would take the family somewhere.

Once he arrived at work, he rarely left his office. He could see the parking lot through a window outfitted with security bars across it. Most of the time, he kept his door shut. Ron realized that no one in the bays could see him with the door shut, but there was no alternative entrance. The head mechanic dealt with the customers.

Morales had a wife and two children, ages twelve and ten. The school bus picked them up a short distance from the house at seven twenty every morning. The bus brought them home at three in the afternoon. His wife, Leticia, would often depart from the house around noon to meet a girlfriend for lunch or to shop. Usually, she returned before the kids got home, but a full-time housekeeper lived there too. Ron had never seen her leave the property except to walk the kids to the bus stop for school. Two ranch hands managed stable and yard work. Neither ever approached the house.

When they both believed further surveillance would be useless, they sat down to hash out a plan, a freshly brewed pot of coffee filling the air with its scent as they brainstormed.

Natalie ruled out trying to break into the house. "All the first-floor windows have bars on them. The only way to enter is through the front or back door. Both of them have security cameras monitoring visitors. Inside the house, they could have motion detectors that activate at night, possibly accompanied by panic alarms. To neutralize the alarms would require cutting the power to the entire house, which also might trigger an alarm. The wife and kids might get in the way. We don't have the staff or the time to grab him."

"His workplace is not an ideal place either," said Ron. "Too many workers around, and he's got that gorilla that drives him everywhere. We need to catch him when he's alone and vulnerable."

They chewed the fat a while longer, reviewing timelines, and a plan emerged. In an ideal scenario, a window of opportunity would occur when Morales would be at home alone, except for the housekeeper. This was when he was most vulnerable.

Two prerequisites were necessary for success. First, his wife needed to leave the house around noon, and then Morales needed to come home after lunch. They could tie up the housekeeper, force Morales into the car, and be gone in fifteen minutes. The challenge was gaining entrance to the property and getting the housekeeper to open the front door before he arrived.

They waited for the day when everything would align. A few days later, Leticia left to go shopping, leaving the housekeeper alone. Ron waited for Morales to finish lunch to see if he planned to go home. Natalie was in a stolen van on a side street near the house.

Natalie's phone rang. "It's a go," said Ron urgently.

Without saying a word, she hung up and drove the van to Morales' front gate. She pushed the intercom button on a post mounted next to the driveway and waited for the housekeeper to answer.

"Yes?" said a scratchy voice.

"Hi. I've got a package for Leticia Morales," said Natalie, trying to sound bored. "Special delivery. It requires a signature."

The housekeeper hesitated. "All right, drive to the front door."

The gate opened. She drove forward, stopped under the portico, and retrieved a large box from the back of the van. She held the box in front of her face to shield it from the security camera while walking toward the waiting housekeeper.

One step from the door, she hesitated. "Oh shoot. Would you hold this for a minute? I forgot the paperwork in the van." As the housekeeper accepted the box, a pistol materialized, aimed at her head.

"Quick now, back into the house. Do everything I say, and I won't harm you," Natalie said in a menacing voice. "Show me where the security panel is and the code to open the gate."

The housekeeper gulped and followed instructions, still holding the box. In just fifteen minutes, she was bound and gagged inside the hall closet. Natalie sprinted outside, leaped into the van, and maneuvered it around the corner, out of sight from the driveway. A few seconds later, she returned to the house and found a hiding spot near the front door.

She found herself holding her breath and said a mantra to calm down. The next thirty minutes were crucial. It was impossible to know how long Leticia planned to be gone. If she came home before her husband, it would ruin the plan.

Outside, she heard the squeal of brakes as a car stopped under the portico. A car door opened, and a conversation began. A quick burst of laughter followed the slamming of the door. The sound of the car driving away became fainter as someone inserted a key into the front door.

Natalie watched from her hiding place behind the living room couch as the door swung open. Morales wore a checkered western shirt and pressed jeans. A large silver buckle adorned his belt. On his feet were a shined pair of alligator boots.

He closed the front door and took several steps into the silent house. "Hello, anybody home?" he said. "Marisa, bring me a beer in my office." He strode down the hall past Natalie's hiding place. She rose silently and stalked after him. Closing the gap, she brought a sap down onto the back of his neck. He groaned, wobbled, and sank to his knees. A second blow caused him to fall over on his side, unconscious.

Natalie pulled him onto his stomach and handcuffed his hands behind him. Then she ran to the security panel and entered the code she had forced the housekeeper to share with her that opened the front gate. She opened the front door, removed a can of spray paint from her pocket, and hid her face while she sprayed paint over the security camera lens. With time getting short, she ran to retrieve her van. When she drove around the corner toward the portico, Ron was already there, his car idling at the curb. Together, they wrestled the still-unconscious Morales into the trunk of his car.

Natalie hurried back into the house, her voice muffled as she spoke through the hall closet door. "I've got your boss. If anybody calls the cops, you'll never see him again. Tell Leticia to stay by her phone for my call. I'll be watching her and the kids. If she tries anything, I'll be coming for her next."

She turned away, closing the front door with a soft click as she left. Nodding to Ron, she entered the van and drove down the driveway to the gate. He stayed close behind her when it swung open. They disappeared down the road.

Chapter 46

They drove to a secluded spot in a thinly populated area near Corrales. Ron removed two full jerry cans from the van and doused the interior, filling the air with the pungent smell of gasoline. He threw a lit match on the front seat and watched flames consume the van. The acrid odor of burning rubber filled the air. Satisfied that the fire would consume any DNA evidence, they fled the scene in his car.

Their next stop was the safe house. He was careful to stay under the speed limit getting there, and did nothing to draw attention. They both donned ski masks to hide their faces before opening the trunk. It proved unnecessary, as Morales remained in a deep, unconscious state. Together, they wrestled his limp body inside, tying him to a chair in a windowless room, which smelled like something had died behind the walls. Ron went to the kitchen, filled a glass with water, and returned.

"This will wake him up," he said, throwing the water on Morales' face.

With a groan, his eyes fluttered open, and he squinted at the two figures standing before him. Confusion crossed his face as he realized his hands were bound to the chair's arms. "Who are you?" he said.

"Who we are doesn't matter," replied Ron. "Look around. You are our guest in a place so secluded no one will find you. If you want to survive, your best chance is to cooperate and answer our questions. Answer truthfully, and we'll let you go. If you don't, it'll become excruciatingly painful for you before you die. My colleague," he pointed at Natalie, who was holding her AK-47 in her right hand, "would like nothing better than to kill you right now, so I suggest you cooperate."

"What do you want? Money? I can get that from my safe."

"I'm sure you can, but money isn't information. We are familiar with every detail about you, Morales. Tell us about Teddy Bear Fantasies."

Mentioning the name caused his eyes to grow large, and a look of surprise crossed his face. "Never heard of them. You've got the wrong guy. I run Custom Automotive, an auto repair shop. Have you got any aspirin? My head is killing me," he said defiantly.

Without a word, Natalie stepped forward and rammed the butt of her AK-47 into his stomach. Morales gagged, bent over double, and threw up on the floor. Spittle ran down his chin onto his shirt.

"Wrong answer," said Ron. "Like I said, we know everything about you, including that you're the head of the local organization. If you lie again, my colleague will help refresh your memory. Next time, it'll be more painful."

He continued. "Six years ago, your employee Zhao brought eight kids here. We want to know what happened to them. Let's start with Natalie Martinez. She was thirteen when you kidnapped her on May 21st, 2017."

Morales spit out the bile in his mouth and eyed Natalie, who had propped her rifle against the wall and now held a wicked-looking serrated hunting knife in her hand. "Okay, okay. Keep that psycho bitch away from me. Six years was a long time ago. How can I remember that far back?"

Natalie leaped forward, yanked his head upward, and, with a flick of the knife, made a shallow cut from his cheek to his jawline. Morales screamed and thrashed around. Blood flowed down his cheek onto his shirt. "You motherfucker, I'm gonna kill you."

She laughed and moved forward again, the knife gleaming in her hand.

"No more," he shouted as she reached him. "I'll tell you. Stay away from me."

She paused, hate filling her eyes. "Speak the truth, or your death will be more painful than you can imagine."

He was quiet for a moment, thinking back to that time. Since childhood, he had possessed an almost perfect memory. Now, it might save his life. "I sold her to Sheik Abdul-Wadid," he said. "He lives somewhere in Bahrain. We flew her out there, met him at some rural airstrip, and did the exchange. That's all I know."

"You can do better," said Ron. "Who flew the plane? Where did it come from? Who else was on it?"

"The guys who run the company sent a plane here to pick her up. I don't know the pilot's identity. It was none of my business. Bob Hackman flew to Bahrain with him and watched Natalie until we did the exchange. That's it; you've got to believe me."

Ron frowned. "Morales, let me make something very clear to you. We know more than you think about Teddy Bear. "We are asking some questions to which we already know the answers. They're tests to verify you're telling us the truth. If you lie, the punishment will be swift. You've just had a small preview of what may occur. She's highly skilled in her field and can keep you alive for days in intense pain. I'm sure you would rather avoid that. Think of your wife and kids. So, I'll ask you one last time: who else was on the plane?"

Morales looked terror stricken. Natalie inched closer to his face, the knife poised to strike. "Franz Meyers," he blurted out. "He was the only other person. I swear to God."

The interrogation went on into the night. Morales recalled every detail of where and to whom he sold three of the children. He swore that he knew nothing about the remaining four kids. Ron remembered that Angela Garcia gave those four babies to a woman, not her brother. That person could have sold the babies to someone else. Who that was would remain a mystery since the woman was dead.

Ron recorded all the information in a binder. He thought the buyers would be in the Middle East, but they were everywhere. It sickened him that the demand for kids outstripped Teddy Bear's ability to meet it.

Although Morales was willing to talk about the buyers, he dodged questions about Teddy Bear's management. He seemed more afraid of them than the consequences of not answering questions. Ron watched Natalie cut off several joints of some of his fingers. The blood and screams sickened him, forcing him to leave the room. *Whatever it takes, short of murder*, he reminded himself. It was the only way they had to learn who ran Teddy Bear and where they were.

Eventually, Natalie joined him in the living room and shared what she had learned. Teddy Bear was a multinational organization, and she knew the people who ran it, but they operated from countries in Europe. Men in India, Hungary, and Egypt bought the three children.

With Morales sobbing in his chair, the exhausted partners went outside to rest in two beat-up lawn chairs to consider their next move. Near midnight, the yard was pitch black except for the dim light from the house windows. The sky was clear, bursting with stars in the Milky Way winking back at them.

"Are you satisfied, Ron Jackson?" said Natalie.

He considered his answer. "Sharing this information with the police might save those three children. Finding the criminals who run Teddy Bear could be a problem, though," he said. "They're all in Belarus, Russia, or Serbia. Places where our law enforcement can't operate."

Natalie smiled. "I can go anywhere, without limitations. All I lack are the funds to pursue them."

"Do you think you can face them single-handedly? You're good, but you'll be in a strange country where you have no support and don't speak the language. The top people will expect trouble and be heavily protected when you arrive. It won't be as easy as it was taking Morales."

She shrugged. "It's Allah's will if I succeed. But first, I must deal with my enemies in Washington."

They both were silent for a while, each thinking ahead, trying to plan their next moves. The darkness of the night deepened, and the absence of any sounds other than the tree leaves rustling in a soft breeze was making Ron's eyelids heavy.

"Morales said he had money in his safe," Natalie said suddenly. "There may be enough to fund our needs. I'll get the combination from him."

She rose, silent as always, and disappeared into the house. In twenty minutes, she was back. "The safe is in his office at Custom

Automotive. He mentioned the sum of $100,000, which can be mine if I release him."

Ron gazed at her. "He has told us everything, and you have exacted your revenge. He is a beaten man, and you will have $100,000 of his money. Perhaps we should take the money, leave him here, and move on."

"I agree. It's time to move on to deal with those who wish to kill me in Washington," she said, her face a mask. "I should get the money now before someone alerts the police."

Ron marveled at her stamina. His brain was mushy, and he needed to sleep, not rob Custom Automotive. "All right. I'll stay here and keep an eye on Morales. Tomorrow, we can go to Washington."

She gave him a thin smile and walked to her car. In a moment, she was gone.

CHAPTER 47

R on woke with a start. Bright sunlight was streaming in a window, hitting him full in the face. The unfamiliar room disoriented him. He sat in an old stuffed easy chair, full of dust and holes in the fabric. His neck was sore, and his legs stiff. Silence filled the house. Birds chirped outside from a nearby tree.

He recalled Natalie leaving to retrieve the money from the safe. They were sitting outside on lawn chairs. After she left, mosquitos buzzed around his head, eventually driving him inside. He sat down in the easy chair to await her return. After that, he remembered nothing, so he must have fallen asleep. Judging from the sunlight pouring through the windows, it was mid-morning.

Rising, he did a few stretches, the tightness in his muscles dissipating. He craved a cup of coffee, but all the shelves in the kitchen were empty. He shuffled to the bathroom, splashed water over his face, and wondered what happened to Natalie. Perhaps she was interrogating their prisoner.

Wearing his mask, he entered the room where they held Morales captive. It was in darkness, illuminated only by weak light filtering in from the hall. Natalie wasn't there. In the gloom, he could see a shapeless mass on the chair. Guilt washed over him for neglecting to check on his prisoner during the night. He was probably hungry and dying of thirst.

Ron's fingers groped along the wall until he found the light switch. Light flooded the room. "Okay, it's time to wake up. This will—" He stopped, startled by what he saw. Morales slumped forward, his arms still tied to the chair. His chin rested on his chest, eyes closed. Blood soaked the front of his shirt, dripping down to the floor, where it had dried into a sticky mess.

Ron inched closer and bent down to study the body. The skin had a gray pallor, and the stench of decay and blood assaulted his senses. A jagged incision across Morales' throat had severed the jugular vein, causing a copious amount of blood loss. He was dead, but who had killed him? In a panic, he rushed through the living room, his heart pounding in his chest, and threw open the front door. Natalie and her car were nowhere to be found.

Angrily muttering to himself, he sprawled in the lawn chair and dialed Natalie's number. The phone rang, yet there was no answer. Enraged, he threw the phone across the yard and glumly considered his options.

He acknowledged the plan's brilliance. She had played him, in more ways than one. The agreement to seek vengeance without murder was mere talk. She manipulated him into leading her straight to Morales. Then she calmly walked out of the house after cutting his throat and made her escape while he fell asleep waiting for her to come back with the money.

She gambled that he wouldn't discover that Morales was dead for a while, and she won. By now, she had a seven or eight-hour head start should he try to follow her. He suspected she was passing through Colorado on her way to Washington, D.C., to cause more mayhem.

He felt like a fool. After she got what she needed from him, she discarded him like a piece of trash, leaving him alone to deal with a dead man. He realized now that the only acceptable form of revenge for her was death. She had no remorse for her actions.

Mary Ann had told him not to trust Natalie, and she was right. Once again, his relentless pursuit of the missing children had closed his eyes to reality. He wondered how much else of Natalie's story was a lie. Were there people in Washington trying to kill her? Or was this just a smokescreen to hide the real reason for the attack upon her at Zhao's house? Was she a terrorist on her way to carry out her mission for ISIS? Or was she making plans to kill the Syrians?

He was unsure of his next move. The logical thing to do would be to go back to California, share the information obtained from

Morales with Mary Ann, move back into his house, and rebuild his private detective business.

The plan didn't appeal to him. Teddy Bear was still in business, and three children needed rescuing. His faith in the FBI's ability to find them was nonexistent. Quitting the case would mean surrendering to the demons who would haunt him forever. That was not going to happen. Determination replaced the fog of uncertainty that plagued him.

Despite Natalie's deceitfulness, he still needed her if he was to have any hope of continuing. Both of them still wanted to destroy Teddy Bear. He sought the lost children, while she sought vengeance against those responsible. Why couldn't they do both? If she wanted to kill every soul who worked for Teddy Bear, he couldn't stop her, but would do everything in his power to persuade her otherwise. Self-defense was one thing, but he would not be a party to murder.

He believed she had left him to deal with the Syrians. His experience, gained from years as a cop, told him Natalie was overconfident in her ability to kill all of them. They had numbers and resources that she didn't. Eventually, they would track her down and kill her. He could help even the odds. She could help him by watching his back while he tracked the people who had the kids. She had skills he could never possess in that area and had proved it by saving his life twice in less than a month. But if he found out she was working with ISIS, he wouldn't hesitate to turn her over to the FBI.

Together, they had a chance to obtain both goals. Alone, they had none. He remembered how good he felt when he committed to doing whatever it took to find the children and destroy Teddy Bear.

His decision made, he found his cell phone and opened an app. After studying the screen, he grinned and shut it down. He stretched again and walked to his car. Before leaving New Mexico, he needed to dispose of a body, and he was going to need some gasoline.

CHAPTER 48

The safe sat exactly where Morales said it would be, tucked in a corner of his office with invoices stacked on top of it. Natalie wrinkled her nose in disgust at the smell of oil and solvents seeping in from the bays. She punched the combination on the safe's keypad and held her breath while turning the lever to draw back the bolts. If Morales lied to her about the combination, her plan would fall apart before it started. The lever turned in her hand, the bolts retracted, and the door opened. Inside, there was more cash than she had ever seen, neatly tied together in stacks with rubber bands. She took it all, shoveling it into a duffel bag she brought with her. In ten minutes, she was back in her car, speeding towards Interstate 25, north through Santa Fe, and into Colorado.

She made a quick stop at an all-night convenience store to fill her gas tank and load up on cans of energy drinks, hoping they would keep her alert throughout the night. Her top priority was to reach Washington as quickly as possible while maximizing the distance between herself and Ron so he couldn't find her when he discovered Morales was dead.

She felt no remorse for using Ron to find Morales. Allah had led her to him to assist in her endeavor, but now she had no further use for him. He had benefitted from their partnership. She helped him accomplish his goal of destroying part of Teddy Bear, so he should be content to go home and forget her. She didn't believe she owed him anything else. Her fight with ISIS was not his concern.

She had all the information she needed to exact her revenge. Ron had made it clear he disagreed with her methods, so it made sense to leave him behind when the chance arose. If he wished to pursue Teddy Bear without her, that was his decision.

Ever since the kidnapping of Morales, thoughts of returning to Washington had consumed her. Her time away from the influence of ISIS had bolstered her self-confidence and ability to make her own decisions. She no longer wanted any part in al-Tunisi's plan to bring jihad to America. Sending men to kill her ended that. Now, she needed to convince him that the price to kill her was too high.

When she remembered Morales' comment about money in his safe, she had an idea. She would use the money to return there, reestablish contact with Mustafa, and lure him to a meeting where she could capture him. With some persuasion, she would extract the names of his employees. She wanted to kill them all, to send a message to al-Tunisi.

The plan was appealing, but details that would make it viable were missing. Once she arrived in Washington, she could solve those problems. Allah would protect and guide her, but if he didn't, she had at least accomplished her revenge against those in Teddy Bear who orchestrated her abduction.

It was getting close to dawn, and the sky was glowing faintly orange in the East, when she realized the energy drinks she had been steadily downing were doing nothing but making her jittery. After being awake for over twenty-four hours, her tired body demanded rest.

She had passed the "Welcome to Colorado" sign an hour ago. Up ahead was the town of Walsenburg, its warm lights signaling a place to rest.

CHAPTER 49

Natalie had invested several weeks of hard work in establishing a new base of operations near Washington. She avoided the old safe house because it could be under surveillance. She had underestimated the ability of ISIS to find her in Santa Barbara, and she wasn't going to make that mistake again. Instead, she spent her days constantly on the move, hopping from one motel to another, never staying in one place for over two days. Her goal was to find an isolated house or warehouse for rent where she could operate without attracting unwanted attention from nosy neighbors. In early April, she found it.

The small cottage exuded a rustic charm in the countryside outside of Washington. It sat on an acre of fenced land, marked with "No Trespassing" signs on the fence posts. A mixture of maple, oak, and hickory trees filled a portion of the plot, and a family of gray squirrels lived in one of them. A small meadow behind the house attracted deer who jumped the fence to graze. Visitors accessed the house via a dirt road that snaked back through the woods, away from neighbors. The nearest one was over a mile away, across the access road. According to the real estate agent, they were city people who rarely visited.

The cottage's best feature was the basement, made with a solid flagstone foundation. It smelled of old wood and mold, which for some reason comforted her. Soundproofing only required covering the tiny windows so no one would hear the screams. Upstairs, there was a cozy kitchen, a spacious living room with a grand fireplace, a comfortable bedroom, and a bathroom.

It was a far better safe house than what Mohammad had provided her. It was another sign that Allah was with her, guiding her actions.

She focused on preparing for her guest. A local hardware store had all the rope and chain that she needed. Screws drilled into the basement floor anchored a wooden chair placed in the middle of the room. A table, which could hold any tools she might need, stood against the stone foundation wall. She cleaned and oiled all her guns and replenished the ammo she used in California. The nearest grocery store was forty minutes away. She planned to stay hidden at the house once she captured Mustafa, so she bought enough food for several weeks. Lastly, she purchased a five-year-old utility van that would be useful for her getaway.

After removing the license plates, she left her old car unlocked on a street in a bad part of Washington. Someone would strip it for parts in a matter of days. Nothing would remain but the steel frame. The car would cease to exist if anybody was looking for it.

With everything in order, she stood ready for the next challenge, luring Mustafa out into the open where she could spring her trap. All she had was his old phone number. He might have gotten rid of the phone since she left several months ago. But there was also the possibility he kept it in case she tried to reestablish contact.

She did not believe he would forgive her for disobeying his orders by going to California. He would attempt to lure her to a remote location with talk of reconciliation and then kill her. She needed him to come to her. If he answered her call, she would taunt him, play with his ego, and then manipulate him into meeting her at a place of her choosing.

The problem was, she didn't expect he would come alone. He knew how dangerous she was, and he would want favorable odds. If he brought men, it would give her a chance to kill them all, but the more men he brought with him, the less chance she had of surviving. She couldn't take on an army by herself.

It felt good being back in control, making her own decisions, sure of what needed to be done. The success of her endeavor relied on choosing the right location for their meeting, where she could use the terrain to negate her disadvantage in numbers. She needed room to maneuver without being seen, multiple lines of fire, and a quick means of escape if necessary. Somewhere secluded, where gunfire wouldn't draw anyone's attention.

It took another week to find it, ironically, by searching for abandoned places on the Internet. Christine was once a thriving mill town on the Patapsco River, northwest of Baltimore. By 1968, textile manufacturing became unprofitable, displacing ninety families after the mill closed. The abandoned town had deteriorated since then. Pictures online depicted the remnants of a bygone era, with crumbling walls and discarded machinery left to the elements. Trees, shrubs, and vines had reclaimed much of the area. A narrow dirt path that meandered alongside the river connected the ghost town to the main road. It was miles away from anything and rarely visited.

Intrigued, Natalie drove to the site, hoping it would fit her needs. The weather was marginal, with scattered dark clouds threatening either rain or snow soon. Parking at the trailhead, she followed the dirt trail for about a mile. Beams of sunlight cascaded down through the tall trees, creating irregular patterns of shadow which, with the proper camouflage, would make her invisible. To her right, a shallow river rushed past, creating a soothing gurgling sound. To her left, a bluff, covered in a carpet of dead leaves, rose twenty feet up from the trail. Anyone coming down the trail would be a sitting duck in a firefight.

The ruins of a white building with a two-story bell tower lay ahead. The closer to it she got, the clearer it became that it had once been a country church. Inside, it was a mere shell, the roof and the stairs to the tower having long ago collapsed. Around the back, she discovered a tree trunk blown over in a storm leaning against the church wall. The trunk extended to a gaping hole in the second-floor wall, which once contained a window. With curiosity and trepidation, she climbed the trunk and stuck her head through the hole. Part of the flooring remained, although it looked none too sturdy. She felt her way across it towards a gap that had once been the front window of the bell tower. The boards groaned as she walked on them, but held her weight. Being petite had its advantages.

The front window provided an excellent view of the trail, making this location a lookout and a first line of defense.

The area was quiet, disturbed only by chirping from a flock of birds deeper in the ruins. Stone foundations, covered in moss, poked out of the surrounding ground, providing cover should Mustafa force her to retreat. Water gushed over a small dam on the river, creating a five-foot waterfall. This would block anyone from wading in the river to outflank her. The path continued along the river, gaining elevation until it reached the top of the bluff.

The bluff ended at a ravine, its depths filled with a graveyard of old, rusted cars. It provided excellent cover from which she could hide and ambush her attackers. The path continued through the ravine, then climbed a hill crowned with more ruins. She made her way there, noting the advantageous hiding places as she walked.

The ruins atop the hill consisted of rubble where walls once stood by a weathered stone arch. Nearby, tombstones leaned precariously toward the ground, giving a clue to what had once been here. Their faint inscriptions dated back to the 1800s, indicating that it must have been the local cemetery.

Beyond this spot, the ruins faded into nothingness, leaving only small piles of stones scattered about. A dense, dark forest, its undergrowth overrun with tangled bushes and creeping vines, took its place. Retreating from here, she could travel to the main road through the forest, staying on the higher ground near the bluff.

She checked her phone to ensure cellular service was available and found a weak signal. Satisfied, she took a compass out of her pocket, oriented it towards the north, and struck off cross-country toward her car.

Back at her safe house, she analyzed the terrain, pinpointing dangerous areas. She had cover everywhere except for part of the path from the ravine to the cemetery. But the distance was minimal. Sprinting would expose her for about ten seconds.

She planned to pick off her attackers one at a time, retreating into the ruins and ambushing them as they attacked. Her advantage was knowing the terrain. Constantly moving and shooting from cover would help negate Mustafa's numerical advantage. But if he brought many men, they could flank and surround her, blocking her retreat.

She sighed and unrolled her prayer rug. Facing Mecca, she prayed to Allah to guide her. Tomorrow, she would start her preparations.

Chapter 50

Four days later, everything was ready to lure Mustafa to Christine. The weather cooperated, staying sunny and dry. Natalie had transported all her weapons and ammo there, setting up firing positions throughout the ruins and stacking stone blocks around them for protection. Each position was stocked with energy bars, filled canteens, and spare ammo. She marked a trail through the forest from the cemetery back to a hidden spot near the road where she would leave her van. A new burner phone sat in her pocket, which she would use only to call Mustafa. All that remained was to make contact.

She sat in her car in a supermarket parking lot, far away from her safe house, watching a mother scold two young children while wheeling a grocery cart toward her car. The sight made her think briefly about having children, but she quickly dismissed the thought. Her childhood had been a disaster. She didn't know how to be a mother.

She took a deep breath to settle her nerves and dialed Mustafa's number. If the call didn't go through, her plan would be useless, as she had no other means of contacting him. She waited with the phone to her ear, hoping for a connection and praying.

"Yes?" said the soft voice she would recognize anywhere.

"Mohammad Mustafa, I have returned," she said.

"Kaina al-Badawi," he said after a pause. "I didn't expect to hear from you again. You betrayed your faith and the trust I gave you."

"I betrayed your trust, but never my faith. Allah guided me on the task I undertook. Those who kidnapped and tortured me as a young girl needed to be punished. You traced me to California, where I went to complete this task. You tried to murder me when all you needed to do was be patient. Now I'm back, ready to resume the mission I was prepared for."

"You think it's that easy?" he hissed. "Why should I trust you now? How do I know you won't betray me again?"

"Because Allah has guided me back to you. I have dreams in which he talks to me."

He snorted. "Why would Allah talk to someone as insignificant as you?"

"I don't know why he has chosen me, a humble soldier, to carry out his will. I'm insignificant, yet in my dreams, he told me to come back, and I obeyed. Tell me my mission, and I'll carry it out."

"You don't tell me what to do, Kaina. Much has changed since you left. I need to consider your future."

"Do you refuse to follow Allah's wishes? The one betraying their faith is none other than you. Have the infidels corrupted your soul, or have you lost your courage? I'll give you one day to reconsider what I have said. If you refuse me, I will send word to al-Tunisi of your betrayal of the jihad. Then you will answer to him."

Mustafa laughed. "You are out of touch, Kaina; al-Tunisi has no power. Raqqa fell to the infidels months ago, and no one has heard from him since."

"He escaped Raqqa and is in hiding to make his enemies believe he is dead. Before I left Syria, he gave me instructions on how to contact him in case the Kurds captured Raqqa," she lied, attempting to make him angry. "I'll tell him of your treachery if you don't give me what I want. He has many loyal soldiers who will find you. You have one day."

Before he could reply, she ended the call. After taking the SIM card out of the phone, she drove back to the safe house, the silence in the car amplifying her racing thoughts. She was pleased with how the conversation had unfolded. Mustafa's arrogant sense of superiority was a weakness she could exploit. The disrespect she showed him, and the threat to contact al-Tunisi, should anger him to the point he would want to kill her at any cost. Using herself as bait, she would draw him to Christine.

The following day, a sharp knock on the front door of her safe house startled her. No one knew she was here. Could Mustafa have somehow found her? How was that possible?

Armed with a pistol, she exited through the back door. Sliding around the side of the house, she glanced at the front porch. A man stood there, silhouetted against the bright afternoon sun.

"Hello, Natalie," he said.

Surprised, Natalie stood frozen, her thoughts swirling in confusion. The man stood quietly, his hands spread away from his body, empty of weapons. She scanned the dirt access road but saw no vehicles. His car was likely parked along the main road, and he approached on foot without making a sound so as not to alert her.

The woods across the road could harbor many hostiles, but her keen senses saw no movement. If he had brought men with him, it was unlikely he would announce his presence, thus giving away the advantage of catching her off guard. She relaxed but hugged the house; the pistol gripped tightly in her right hand.

She had been so sure there was no way he could have followed her. It was another terrible miscalculation, which, under different circumstances, could have cost her life. "How did you find me?" she said, her voice barely above a whisper.

"It occurred to me that perhaps you might need my help some-time, and I wouldn't know where you were. I placed a tracking device on your car in Albuquerque so that I could find you. By the time you got rid of your old car, I already knew where you lived."

She considered his answer. It was a plausible explanation. He had used a tracker before with Zhao. "Are you alone?" she said.

"Yes. No one knows I'm here. Can we talk?"

She frowned, silently conveying disinterest in engaging in further conversation. Yet, here he was, so short of killing him, there was no alternative. "Come this way," she said.

He stepped off the front porch and walked past her, turning the corner toward the back door, then hesitated in front of it. "Opening this won't cause any explosions, will it?"

She smiled, imagining the unwanted attention an explosion would bring her. "No, you're safe." Nudging him out of the way, she opened the door herself.

They settled in two wooden chairs around the rustic pine kitchen table. Dappled sunlight filtered in through the kitchen window. Outside, a blue jay perched in a tree, calling its mate.

"Why're you here, Ron Jackson?" she said.

"That's a good question," he said. "A sane person would've returned to Carpinteria and forgotten you existed. You left me with a corpse and barely enough money to survive. But since you saved my life twice already, I felt an obligation to help. I assumed you were coming here to finish dealing with al-Tunisi. You're a very resourceful ninja, but you're only one person. You will die trying to do this alone."

She stiffened. "We accomplished your goals, didn't we? There was no reason to be partners anymore. That's why I left you in Albuquerque. This does not concern you. If my quest is righteous, Allah will guide and protect me. If not, I'll die. I've nothing to live for except to exact my revenge. I'm not afraid of death."

He rubbed his brow with his thumb and index finger. "Isn't it possible, Natalie, that Allah guided me here to help you? That he saw you needed help to accomplish your goal?"

Natalie sat back in her chair and studied him. "What do you know of Allah? You aren't a follower of Islam."

"True, I know nothing about Islam. But does that prevent Allah from using me to help one of his faithful?"

It was a premise impossible to prove or disprove. Who knew what Allah's plans were? Jackson, she admitted, could be of value to her. "Perhaps you're right," she said. "Allah sent me to you in California, and now he sent you to me. I will accept your offer. But there's not much time. Tomorrow is the day of reckoning."

"Tell me everything," he said.

Instead of telling him, she showed him. Together, they drove to Christine, and she walked him through the ruins, explaining her strategy. She pointed out the trail back to her car at the cemetery, and he shook his head.

"Fleeing through the woods will provide you with little cover. Mustafa will follow quickly and outflank you. He may also discover and disable your car before he attacks, so you would have no means to escape. Return to the ruins where you have cover and make a stand."

She thought for a moment, then nodded. What he said made sense. There was no honor in dying while running for your life. It would be a fight to the death.

CHAPTER 52

Mohammad Mustafa sat at a battered metal desk in a small office inside an old warehouse, staring at his cell phone. It was late morning on a beautiful, if chilly, day. Scattered clouds floated in the sky, but there was no wind, despite the forecast of rain.

Next to him, a man sat in front of many humming electronic devices plugged together with ethernet cables. He had an open line to a technician at the local cellular provider, who could trace the origin of an incoming call through their network. The tech was told this was a top-secret law enforcement operation designed to trace a terrorist threat targeting the United States. He was eager to be of service.

Outside the office, three identical black vans were parked next to each other inside the otherwise empty warehouse. The sides were windowless, with sliding doors and no identifying marks. Anyone checking their license plates would find them to be fake.

A knot of armed men wearing body armor stood nearby, talking among themselves. Most spoke Arabic, with an occasional word or two of English. Mustafa had ordered them to eliminate the target, a traitor to the jihad. They were also eager to help.

Mustafa's hands were damp with sweat. He had paced back and forth in the office all morning, snapping at anyone who entered. It took an all-night effort to gather his team in twenty-four hours, but he did it. The cost was immense, as always when urgency demands action. Unless Kaina called, he had spent a small fortune for nothing.

Her phone call two days ago had surprised him. As the months passed, he lost hope that she would ever call. Although he tracked her to California, she had proven adept at hiding. His men bungled the chance to kill her when she was with Jackson, and he never located her again.

He marveled at the unexpected turn of events. Instead of spending time and money to find her, she came to him in his backyard. Her mistake was her faith in Allah, naively thinking he would protect her. Mustafa didn't believe Allah nor any other god could do that when he sent his entire team to kill her. His task was to keep her talking on the phone long enough to trace her location. There would be no escape this time.

Something had changed her since their last contact. Her behavior towards him was quite different. She seemed confident in her abilities, no longer subservient to him. Her threat to contact al-Tunisi proved that. He worried she had tasted freedom from the ISIS dogma for too long and would no longer unquestioningly obey her orders. It confirmed his belief that she was a liability that needed to be eliminated.

He accepted this after much soul-searching. She had proved her worth to him when she eliminated the sheik with only a few days' notice. It was the ultimate test before the big mission, and she had impressed him with her creativity in planning the attack. Then everything fell apart.

As far as he knew, al-Tunisi was dead, although no one had found his body. It was likely that someone would find him buried under rubble in a bombed-out building in Raqqa. It didn't matter. There was always someone else waiting to take command when the opportunity arose. Someone he didn't know, who might believe everything Natalie told him. He had no intention of letting that happen.

He regretted the waste of a resource ISIS spent years training. Her American citizenship gave her a unique job qualification that would be impossible to replace. A revised plan would require years to become operational. Success had been so close, and it galled him that a nineteen-year-old girl ruined his brilliantly conceived plan.

Natalie had kept her plan for revenge well hidden. The humiliation of those who underestimated her and expected her blind obedience was a bitter lesson. He felt the sting more deeply than others since his idea led to the debacle. He was the one who convinced al-Tunisi that she could return to America and eliminate the mastermind behind the operation that obliterated al-Qaeda's caliphate. The plan had also included personal benefits that would have elevated him to a long-sought position of importance. That was now lost, too.

There was nothing left. No one had faith in him anymore. If he wanted to save face with ISIS, he needed to clean up the mess before Natalie caused more harm. He would find great pleasure in directing her painful death as an example to others who sought to defy him. If he could find her.

Mustafa's phone buzzed, interrupting his thoughts. He drew a deep breath, and let it ring three times before answering. "Yes?"

"What is your decision?" Natalie said.

He nodded to the tech sitting next to him. "Kaina, I was unprepared for your sudden reappearance. You gave me no warning that you were coming back. Yesterday, I reconsidered what you said and realized I was wrong to have doubted you. If Allah speaks to you, then you are his chosen one."

"I'm glad that you looked into your heart and Allah revealed the truth of my words. Tell me what my mission is."

Mustafa paused, stalling for time. The tech rolled his index finger around in a circle, indicating he didn't have the fix on her location yet. "Our mission, which was time sensitive, requires careful re-planning. When the opportunity presents itself, you will receive specific directions on how to proceed."

"Mohammad Mustafa," she said, "I'm no longer your servant. I've learned to think for myself. I don't believe in empty promises. If you want my help, you must tell me details about the mission."

"Very well," he said, his anger beginning to grow. "This is what I can tell you. The target is an individual within the CIA. A man responsible for planning attacks against the Caliphate. For security reasons, I cannot say his name over the phone. His death will honor you and strike a blow against the infidels."

"Praise be to Allah," she said. "This deserves my support. I seek no fame for myself, but my supplies are low. I used most of my ammunition in California, so it needs replenishment. Second, my AK-47 suffered damage beyond repair in a firefight, so I need a new one. Also, more money to survive while you re-plan the mission. Can you take care of these needs?"

The tech gave Mustafa a thumbs up, indicating he had the fix. "Yes, of course, Kaina. I will look into it immediately. Would you like me to provide a safe house for you in the meantime?" he asked hopefully.

"No, I've found a satisfactory location already. I will remain hidden until it's time to carry out the mission so no one can betray me. I'll contact you in two days to make arrangements to deliver my supplies."

"As you wish, Kaina. I have no desire to betray you," he said.

"Your words mean nothing. Do you think that I've forgotten that you sent men to assassinate me? Provide me with what you promised, or I will kill you myself."

Mustafa heard a click as the call ended. He slammed his fist on the table, causing the equipment to jump. "I'm going to kill that bitch." His angry eyes bored into the tech. "Where is she?"

Chapter 53

"Well done," Ron said, after listening to Natalie's conversation with Mustafa. "He'll be overconfident if he thinks you're out of ammo." Ron had timed the call, and as soon as it reached fifteen minutes, he slashed his hand across his throat to signal she should end it. In his experience, fifteen minutes was sufficient time to trace a call. Any longer might have made Mustafa suspicious.

"It will take Mustafa a few hours to travel here from Washington if he has a crew ready," he said. "If he needs to gather a crew, he might not show until tomorrow. And there are always the possibilities he was telling the truth and won't come after you, or couldn't trace your call."

Natalie gave a tight smile. "He'll come. My actions have undermined his standing and credibility with ISIS. He must eliminate me before they decide to eliminate him."

"Then I guess the key question is whether he'll come himself or send his goons. I'll call Mary Ann and pass on that tidbit of information he gave us about your mission. She can give it to the CIA, and maybe they can warn whoever it is you're supposed to kill."

"She'll want to know your source for the information," Natalie said.

"Humm...good point. I'll send her an email instead. Tell her I got it from a confidential source. She won't be able to ask questions."

Ron typed away on his phone and sent the message. Almost immediately, his phone vibrated, indicating an incoming email. His eyes flickered to the display, and a wide grin broke across his face. It was Mary Ann. The thought crossed his mind that this might be his last opportunity to speak with her. But now was not the time to get into an argument. He needed to concentrate on the coming battle.

His back was against a tall oak tree, the rough bark rubbing against his clothes. He and Natalie were sitting in the woods at the top of the bluff, near the white church in Christine. Dim sunlight seeped through the trees. A flock of starlings nesting nearby created quite a racket while ignoring the two humans below.

They planned to ambush Mustafa's men from concealed firing positions, hoping to eliminate a few of them. Then, they would fall back to their next positions and do the same thing again. They hoped that by the time they retreated to the cemetery, Mustafa's advantage in personnel would be eliminated, and they could capture or kill him. It was a plan with many unknowns, but it was the best they could do, considering the circumstances.

Ron was feeling the adrenaline rush of the upcoming fight. While he was confident in his ability to handle his weapons, he had never been in a situation such as this where men would be trying to kill him. Sweat poured down his neck, and his heart pounded. He wondered how many men Mustafa would bring.

Natalie sat nearby, wearing body armor that added weight and protection over her sleek black ninja outfit. Her AK-47 pressed against her leg as it lay on the ground. A belt around her waist held a holster containing a Glock 19 and many ammo pouches. She was busy adjusting the scope on her sniper rifle and appeared calm.

Ron, too, wore body armor over a camouflage jacket and pants. A pair of binoculars hung from his neck. Unlike his partner, he carried only two pistols—his Glock, and one that Natalie gave him. He tucked both guns into holsters hanging from his web belt. The mandatory three-day wait for a background check eliminated the opportunity to buy a rifle. That put him at a clear disadvantage in a firefight. The mercenaries who were coming would have rifles with superior range. They could stay beyond the range of his pistol and still blast away at him. However, he had some surprises in store that he was counting on to even the odds. Surprises that Mustafa's men would not be expecting.

His job was to defend the bluff, keeping Mustafa's men from outflanking Natalie, who would be defending the trail. The river would protect her other flank. Unfortunately, there was no one to guard *his* flank, so the best he could do was slow their advance while he retreated to avoid being surrounded. Hopefully, he'd eliminate a few of them.

By early afternoon, the weather deteriorated, and dark clouds rolled in. A stiff breeze was blowing, causing a chill in the air. Gloom enveloped the forest, limiting visibility. Ron was pleased. If Mustafa's men couldn't see him, they couldn't shoot him.

Every ten minutes, he opened an app on his phone to connect to a hidden camera in a tree alongside the road, which offered a real-time view of the trailhead. The tension grew as the trailhead remained empty. Two hours later, during another check, he sat up straight. "They're here."

Three black vans stopped in an open area near the trailhead. The side doors slid open, and men climbed out. The video feed was poor quality, making the men's faces blurry. Ron counted four in each van, plus a man who rode shotgun in one of them. He was tall, but thin. He took command, giving the men last-minute instructions. They all wore body armor and carried assault rifles. Each had an earplug in one ear and a mic to communicate among themselves.

Ron waved Natalie over to watch. "Could that be your guy?" he said, pointing to the tall man.

Natalie shrugged. "It's possible. I've never actually met him. I made up the description I gave you back in California. All I know is his name is Mohammad Mustafa."

Ron wanted to strangle her, but time was scarce. He took a deep breath as the men disappeared from view. "There are thirteen of them, counting the tall guy. If they spread out, I won't be able to hold the flank very long. When you hear the explosions, fall back."

Natalie nodded, then scrambled down the bluff. Ron watched as she climbed up the tree trunk into the bell tower of the white church, her TAC-50 sniper rifle strapped to her back. He faded back into the woods and tried to ignore his fear.

CHAPTER 54

Using his binoculars, Ron scanned the terrain before him, searching for any sign of movement. The thick vegetation made it difficult. He lay prone in a shallow trench, which he dug that morning in the hard ground to provide some protection against incoming fire. His camouflage clothing made him almost indistinguishable from the shrubbery surrounding him. Ahead was a low mound of rocks, placed to stop bullets fired at him in a head-on assault. The rock's protection was an illusion. Once Mustafa's men detected his position, they would try to move around him and he would have to retreat. It would be challenging to do that while staying hidden. To even the odds, he had surprises in store to slow the mercenaries' advance and take a few of them out of the fight.

He swept the area again, but saw no movement. They should have been here by now. Twenty minutes had gone by since the mercenaries arrived. Had they already flanked his position? If they had spread out deeper in the woods, they might already be behind him, closing in on Natalie. The battle would be over without him firing a shot. He was in a quandary: Should he retreat now or wait?

The wind had picked up, causing the tree limbs to creak and the leaves to dance, creating shifting shadows on the ground. Every branch that snapped, every rock that rattled away, caused him to jump. Dark clouds blocked the sun, making seeing anything in the woods difficult. He had decided to fall back when the crack of Natalie's sniper rifle reached him from the white church. The mercenaries on the trail began firing back, and then Natalie fired again. *With any luck, she's already killed a few of them.* Their body armor wouldn't stop the armor-piercing bullets she was using.

He swept the terrain with his binoculars for the third time, and was relieved to see men appearing in the woods. They charged straight ahead toward the sound of the gunfire, unworried about an ambush. He believed the mercenaries on the trail had radioed their position, ordering their comrades on the bluff to close in on her flank, thinking she was the only one there.

It was precisely what Ron hoped they would do. He waited until the mercenaries passed a tree he had marked, then picked up a remote transmitter and pressed the trigger. An explosion rocked the ground under two of the mercenaries, throwing their bodies into the air. The remaining men scattered and dove for cover, firing a few random shots, their bullets whizzing through the air over his head. He remained motionless, waiting for their next move. A moment later, one man leaped up and ran at an angle away from him, dodging through the trees. Ron's finger hovered over the trigger of his second transmitter. He pressed it, unleashing another explosion that reverberated through the ground and toppled the man. After a moment, he crawled away, dragging a mangled leg behind him.

Ron muttered a curse under his breath. He had triggered the explosion too soon, allowing the man to survive. His experience with C-4 was limited to a class he had taken at the Police Academy years ago when he contemplated joining the bomb squad. However, three mercenaries were no longer in the battle, which he saw as a positive beginning.

That was his final booby trap, so he needed to move. He crawled back thirty feet on his belly, then got to his feet and zig-zagged to his next position.

He darted behind a large fallen tree and listened. The forest was silent. There was no firing from Natalie's position, so he assumed she also fell back and her attackers hadn't found her new position yet. Mustafa's men now knew she wasn't alone. They would be more cautious, and the fight would become more intense.

***

Natalie kneeled behind the white church's second-floor window, watching the trail in front of her. She focused the telescopic sights on her sniper rifle and waited. She planned to engage Mustafa's men as far away from her position as possible to make use of the superior range and accuracy of her weapon. With luck, she could pick off a few of them before they were within range with their AK-47s. The tension in her body built as the minutes ticked by with no sign of them. Had Mustafa outsmarted her by sending all his men through the woods on the bluff above her? If so, why hadn't she heard any shots from Ron's position?

She spotted movement on the trail. The mercenaries were advancing cautiously, covering each other as they hop-scotched ahead. Anticipating their next move, she was ready when the next one moved up the trail. She fired once and watched through the scope as his head exploded. Having given away her position, the remaining mercenaries opened fire on the church. She fired two more times as they charged toward the church, killing one and wounding another in the leg.

As soon as she heard the blast from the first C-4 charge, she picked up her gear and fled down the tree trunk to her next position, a narrow slit in a rock wall she had built further down the trail. As she continued to peer through the slit, she detected movement inside the bottom floor of the church and realized she left just in time. These men were professionals, unfazed by blood. Death was a familiar presence to them, an accepted risk. Mustafa would have told them she was a traitor to the jihad, making them even more determined to kill her.

Leaves rustled in the breeze, but no one approached on the trail. *Was her flank in danger?*

Ron fired his pistol on the bluff above her, telling her he was still protecting her flank. Automatic rifle fire responded to it. In front of her, men laid down covering fire while one of them dashed forward to a pile of rocks. She waited for the next man to advance, then cut him down with a burst from her AK-47, fired through the slit. This revealed her location, and the remaining men concentrated their fire on the pile of rocks providing her cover.

With bullets whizzing around her, she abandoned the position, using a pile of rusted machinery as cover while she ran. Bullets whined off the machinery, and one smacked into her body armor. It staggered her, causing her to drop the sniper rifle she held in her left arm. She hesitated, then kept going without it, her heart pounding in her ears as she dived around a bend in the trail into the safety of the basement of a ruined house. The sniper rifle, while a superb weapon, fired too slowly to be effective in close combat, so she didn't think losing it would make much difference now.

The firing had stopped above her, indicating that Ron must have changed positions too. She wondered how many of Mustafa's men he had taken out. *Did he get a few with the booby traps?* His pistol's limited range made it unlikely he would get any more. She counted four casualties, leaving at most nine. *It's still not great odds.*

Her fingers traced the jagged edges of a bullet hole in her body armor near her left shoulder. Blood was absent, so the vest stopped the bullet. That meant the mercenaries weren't using armor-piercing rounds, a stroke of luck for her. That was the good news. The bad news was her shoulder hurt like hell, her left arm was stiffening up, and she'd lost her sniper rifle. But the battle was far from over.

***

Ron was loading bullets into the magazines of his Glock as fast as he could. He had fired thirty-five rounds at his attackers during his last stand, which emptied almost two magazines. The fire was ineffective, hitting no one because of the distance involved. Mustafa's men seemed to realize they were confronting only one defender, who didn't have a rifle. Therefore, they stayed out of pistol range, content to snipe away while trying to flank him. Even slowing them down was becoming difficult. He was breathing heavily, but thinking clearly.

He could smell the rain coming in the dark and windy woods. The mercenaries were out there, but not knowing where made him nervous. He peeked around the large boulder he hid behind, hoping to see something. A bullet whined off the rock just above his head, sending splinters into his scalp. They found him quickly this time. He shot his pistol at them blindly, then ran. A bullet, buzzing like a bee, passed by his ear. He changed direction, gasping for breath as he ran. Bullets began chewing up the tree trunks around him, ricocheting off rocks. Feeling like a sitting duck in the middle of a pond, he changed direction again.

Up ahead, between trees, he knew the bluff tailed into the ravine. The plan was to join forces with Natalie there, retreating through the junkyard of cars towards the cemetery. He hoped she wouldn't be late. His life depended on it.

Ron hung on, hiding behind a stone wall paralleling the end of the bluff. He had vaulted over it seconds before a round of bullets smacked into the stone behind him. His heart sank as he scanned the area and saw no sign of Natalie. It had been a while since he heard any gunfire from her position. He wondered if she was dead or captured. If so, Mustafa's men could flank him by coming up the trail, forcing him to flee into the junkyard to save himself.

The stone wall stretched into the distance, impossible for one man to guard. How long could he afford to stay there waiting for her? Any moment now, one of the mercenaries would breach the perimeter, forcing him back into the junkyard. He ran behind the wall, popping up to fire a few blind shots into the woods here and there before ducking down. As he rose to fire again, rifle fire erupted from the thick woodland in front of him, and a sharp pain shot up his right arm. Ducking back behind the wall, warm, sticky blood dripped through his fingers.

There was no more time to wait. If he didn't leave now, he would soon be dead. Cradling his right arm, he crawled behind the wall to where the trail disappeared into the chaotic junkyard maze. Startled by a noise from behind, he glanced over his shoulder. One of Mustafa's men stood there grinning, leveling his rifle at Ron's head.

"Say goodbye, you piece of shit," he said.

***

Natalie heard another burst of fire from the top of the bluff, closer this time. The wind was increasing as the storm approached, carrying the sound away. She remained in the ruined house's basement, awaiting the next attack, hoping to eliminate a few more mercenaries. It was a powerful position she could hold for a while against a frontal attack, but Ron was already retreating past her from the direction of the gunfire above.

In the ten minutes she had been there, her left shoulder became stiff and painful, making it difficult to raise her arm. She touched the angry purple bruise on her skin near her shoulder and winced in pain. She extracted two aspirins from a pouch hanging on her belt and swallowed them with some canteen water, hoping they would help. The AK-47 would be difficult to fire with only one arm.

Why hadn't Mustafa's men attacked? Were they content to wait, hoping the men on the bluff would flank her? They'd spot her in the open basement if they reached the bluff's edge and looked down. She had no protection from an attack there.

It was too risky to stay here any longer. She strapped her AK-47 over her right shoulder and left the basement. Her left arm dangled by her side as she climbed the trail toward the junkyard. She should regain contact with Ron at any moment if her timing was right. They could still win the battle.

The trail crested, and she could see the stone wall ahead. What she saw caused her to unsling her rifle and fire.

The burst of fire spun the mercenary around before he could pull the trigger. He fell to the ground and didn't move. Natalie struggled up the trail with her gear. Her eyes widened as she observed blood trickling down Ron's scalp and arm. He looked exhausted, and she wondered if she looked as bad.

"Make sure he's dead," she shouted as she ran toward him.

Ron put a round between the mercenary's eyes to make sure. Natalie raked the woods with her AK-47 to slow the advance. "Come on," she said. "We've got to move."

Together, they staggered into the forest of rusting cars, catching their breaths behind an old pickup truck missing its motor.

"What's wrong with your arm?" he said.

"Just sore. My vest caught a round near my shoulder. Let me look at *your* arm."

She ripped his sleeve up past the bleeding and examined it. "You're lucky. The shot just grazed the edge of your arm. Didn't hit bone or anything." She opened a pouch on her belt, removed a rolled bandage, and applied it to his arm. "Your bleeding is leaving a trail for them to follow. Do you think you can still shoot?"

Ron gave her a mournful look. "Do I have any choice?"

They could hear voices from behind the stone wall. Mustafa's men must have reunited and begun planning their next attack. They needed to reach the cemetery before time ran out. Moving deeper into the junkyard, they leapfrogged ahead of each other so one of them could always watch their rear. The occasional rattle of loose metal behind them was a clear sign they were being followed.

When they reached the end of the junkyard, they stopped to rest. Ahead of them was a quick dash over open ground to the crest of the hill, where the cemetery ruins would provide cover. Rain began to fall, restricting visibility and increasing their odds of survival.

"We need to reach the cemetery before they catch up with us," Ron said. "Right now, they won't have clear shots. If we wait, we're sitting ducks. Let's go together, catch them by surprise. Don't stop for anything. If I get shot, keep going."

Natalie nodded. "I'm ready, Ron Jackson."

CHAPTER 55

They sprinted up the hill, far enough apart that one burst of bullets couldn't hit them both. Icy rain was coming down harder now, the wind whipping it into their faces, making it difficult to see. The bare earth in front of them was slippery, slowing their progress.

Ron hadn't considered the impact rain could have on their ability to stay alive, but his only option was to run as fast as he could. The summit grew close when he heard a shout behind him. *Don't look back, keep going.* His legs were turning to rubber, and his arm ached. Out of the corner of his eye, he saw Natalie behind him; her face contorted with effort.

Scattered shots kicked up mud around them. Ron reached the summit and threw himself over the ridge, flat on his back, gasping for air. The crackle of gunfire continued behind him. He winced at the sound of a blood-curdling scream.

Natalie should have reached the summit, but she wasn't there. On his knees, he crawled forward to the crest and looked down. A few feet away, Natalie lay face down in the mud. A pool of blood was spreading out from her left thigh. Bullets continued to kick up the surrounding earth. Ron's heart raced as he grabbed his Glock, his left hand steadying his damaged right arm, and fired off rounds towards the source of the gunfire.

When the magazine was empty, he tossed the gun aside and crawled over the ridge, sliding down toward Natalie. He seized the AK-47 lying next to her and threw it over the crest of the hill. Grabbing her outstretched hand with his good left hand, he dragged her up the hill one agonizing foot at a time. As he reached the summit, a bullet smacked into his vest, knocking him and Natalie backward over the top, protected from the incoming fire.

He groaned. It hurt like somebody had smacked him with a steel pipe. But his vest had stopped the bullet. Next to him, Natalie coughed and spat out mud. Despite his pain, he had to help her. Without attention, she would bleed to death. He opened pouches on her belt until he found another bandage. With his knife, he cut a hole in her pant leg and examined her wound. A bullet hole in the back of her thigh oozed blood. There was no exit wound, so the bullet remained inside her. He bound the bandage tightly around the wound. Natalie moaned and opened her eyes.

"What happened?" she said.

"You got shot in the thigh before you made it to the top. I dragged you up here."

Ron crawled to the crest, peering down at the junkyard. No one was moving up the hill, so he turned to Natalie. "How many did you kill?"

"Five, counting the guy who almost killed you."

"I got three of them. That leaves five. We've got a chance if the last two booby traps work."

Natalie was quiet for a moment. "What about calling for help? Does your cellphone work?"

"You picked this place because it's so remote. It'll take hours to get a SWAT team here. We'll be dead by then." He swept his binoculars across the junkyard and saw movement. "They're moving right, trying to flank us. I'll place the rest of the C-4 charges at the crest of the hill over there. If they attack, it should stop them at the top. Can you defend here while I work?"

She crawled to the edge using her good right hand, dragging her left leg behind her, gritting her teeth at the pain. He handed her the AK-47. "Take an occasional shot so they'll think we're watching this side. Reload all your magazines. Once they rush us, there won't be time for that."

He retreated into the rubble of the cemetery and uncovered a hidden box containing the leftover C-4 explosives and detonators. Grabbing the box by its side handles, he carried it over to the side of the hill, his right arm screaming in pain. As he looked over the crest, he noticed a drastic change in the terrain. The valley floor rose towards the hill, and thick vegetation covered it until near the crest. Before going over the top, Mustafa's men faced a minimal risk of exposure. It seemed to be the logical place to attack.

Opening the box of explosives, he removed a small shovel carried by foot soldiers to dig foxholes. He carved out two areas beneath the ridge. He placed half the C-4 in each hole and attached the detonators. Then he covered the holes with rocks to divert the explosion's force toward the outer side of the hill. As he staggered back to Natalie, his heavy breathing condensed in the cold air.

"Mustafa's men are attacking us from the flank," he said. "They have cover close to the top of the hill there. I'll blast them with the C-4 as soon as they reach it. There are only five of them left. They may abandon their attack if I eliminate some of them."

Ron wiped wet hair out of his eyes as he looked down at her, a tiny figure huddled near the top of the hill in the rain, the ground turning into mud around her. Blood was already seeping through the bandage on her thigh. Her long black hair hung in strings along the sides of her head. Mud caked her face and hands.

"You can't move with that bullet in you, so this is our last stand," he said. "We either kill them, or they kill us."

"If that happens, we shall die with honor and meet Allah," she said. "Take my rifle. You'll need it when they come that way. I'll use my pistol to hold them off over here."

He nodded, took the rifle, squeezed her hand, and gave her his Glock so she would have more firepower. It occurred to him that this might be the last time he saw her alive. She gazed back at him, and he saw no fear in her eyes.

He returned to his position near the C-4 and scanned the area with his binoculars. Mustafa's men were already close to the top. He moved back from the crest to a firing position behind a crumbled tomb with a skull and crossbones chiseled on it, and waited.

To his right, a sudden burst of gunfire drew his attention. Natalie didn't return fire, so he figured it was a diversion designed to pull him toward that side of the hill.

Moments later, a hand reached over the summit near him, followed by the top of the head of a mercenary. Ron pressed himself against the tomb, trying to be invisible as the mercenary scanned the terrain. The head disappeared below the ridge. A small round item sailed over it toward him, producing a sharp metallic sound upon hitting a stone and bouncing away. He had time to realize that it was metal, then it exploded. Shrapnel sprayed the stone surrounding the tomb, but did him no harm. All he could hear was a ringing in his ears.

A grenade, he thought. *They've got grenades.* Peering over the top of the tomb, he spotted a mercenary halfway across the crest. He fumbled a detonator device from his pocket and pressed the trigger. The force of the explosion sent him tumbling backward. The base of his skull struck a fallen tombstone, jolting his senses. A sharp, shooting pain radiated down his back, leaving his legs numb. He watched the mercenary fly over him airborne, slamming into the ground near him. Smoke curled up from his clothes, and he didn't move.

Ron lay flat on his back, his thoughts muddled. He needed to do something. *What was it? The second detonator!* He patted his pockets with his good hand until he found it. He didn't know if the enemy was anywhere near the C-4 charge, but it was the only defense he had left, so he pressed the trigger.

The C-4 exploded, throwing debris in the air, followed by a pressure wave that passed over him. No bodies flew by him this time. He lay there for a while, his breaths shallow and labored, waiting for the end. Fatigue seeped through him, making each moment a struggle to stay awake. His eyes closed, and everything faded to black.

CHAPTER 56

A faint voice called out his name. *Leave me alone. I'm already dead.* The voice persisted, and someone shook his shoulders. *It's time to meet God.* Ron squinted through one eye. A stranger in combat fatigues, covered by a rain parka, looked down at him. *Why would God be wearing combat fatigues?*

"Get me a stretcher over here! He's alive," said the voice.

I'm alive? He opened his other eye and looked around. He was lying on the ground in the cemetery. Two men, dressed like the voice, approached with a stretcher. Orders were being shouted, but he couldn't see anyone else. A vicious headache pounded his head. Freezing rain pelted his face and clothes. He winced as he tried to move his swollen right arm and saw blood seeping through the bandage. On the plus side, he could hear again, and his legs were no longer numb.

The voice gazed at him. "Who are you?" Ron said.

"Eric Masters. I'm a medic with the FBI's Rapid Deployment Force. Are you Ron Jackson?"

"That's right."

"You're safe now, Mr. Jackson. We're going to get you to a hospital."

Two men lifted Ron onto the stretcher. As they lifted him, he waved his good left hand. "Wait, my partner is here, a woman dressed like a ninja. Is she alive?"

Eric nodded. "Yes, across the hill. She was being overrun until we arrived. They broke off the fight and fled. Other than a nasty bullet wound in her leg, she's okay. We gave her a pint of blood to keep her going until we get her to the hospital."

"How did the FBI get here?"

"Mary Ann McDonald called us from California. She gave us your cellphone number and indicated that you could be in trouble with some terrorists. She talked to the right people, so we tracked your signal here. We had a chopper available, so we got here pretty quick."

Ron grinned. "Mary Ann's my old partner from years ago when I was on the force. I passed that info to her just before they attacked us."

Eric raised an eyebrow but asked no more questions. "Share the details with the boss at the hospital," he said.

Eric nodded, and four soldiers, each manning an edge of the stretcher, began moving down the trail toward the junkyard. Daylight had disappeared in the driving rain, making it difficult to see ahead, even with the light from the rescuer's headlamps. Every time one of them stumbled, the stretcher would jerk, making Ron's headache worse. His right arm was on fire, and he felt an overwhelming exhaustion, a release of the stress he had felt all day.

Ron spotted Natalie on another stretcher a few steps ahead of him, her face illuminated by flashes of lightning. Her eyes were closed, and she appeared to be asleep or unconscious. There were no other stretchers, leading him to assume they were the only survivors.

Eventually, they reached the clearing where Mustafa parked his vans. It was a beehive of activity. Floodlights illuminated the entire area, chasing away the darkness. A medivac helicopter sat in the middle of the road, its rotors motionless just a short distance away. Heavily armed men, all in camouflage, milled around. A few of them were searching Mustafa's vans.

The soldiers carefully placed the two stretchers underneath an easy-up canopy that protected them from the rain. A man wearing a yellow rain slicker jumped out of the helicopter and hurried towards them.

Ron turned his head toward Natalie. She was very pale under the dirt that caked her face. A bag of IV fluid fed into her arm. Her eyes looked vacant. He had the impression she was in shock.

"Hey, how you doing?" he said.

Her eyes focused on him. "You fought well today, Ron Jackson. We killed many of Mustafa's men. Did he die?"

"I don't know. There'll be people waiting to talk to us at the hospital. They will know."

The man from the helicopter arrived. "I'm Doctor Lee. I'll be with you on the ride to the hospital. Let's get you two on board so we can leave."

CHAPTER 57

The following day, a stocky man wearing a rumpled, dark blue suit a shade away from purple knocked on the door to his room at Baltimore Sacred Care Hospital and entered. Ron judged him to be in his early fifties, and his haggard appearance hinted that he had been up all night. His eyes were bloodshot, with dark bags under them, accentuated by the scruffy stubble that covered his cheeks. His hair was uncombed, sticking up in different directions. A ketchup stain appeared on his shirt where attempts to clean it with water had failed.

The smell of disinfectant hung in the air. Morning sunlight streamed in through a window that overlooked cars moving in and out of the parking lot. Beyond that, a greenbelt separated the lot from a busy road. Everything outside glistened from the rain that fell the previous night. In the distance, planes circled in a turquoise blue sky, preparing to land at Baltimore/Washington International Airport.

The previous evening, nurses unloaded him from the medivac chopper and rushed him down to the emergency room. Doctors cleaned the dirt off his injured right arm, sutured it up, and administered a hefty dose of antibiotics. Despite his wish to leave the hospital, his doctors insisted that he spend the night, concerned about the potential for a concussion. Painkillers dulled the pounding in his head, allowing him to sleep. In the morning, the back of his head was too tender to touch, but his headache was gone.

The man's gaze darted around the room, taking in everything and verifying they were alone. After closing the door, he pulled a chair over to Ron's bed, sat down, and yawned. Reaching inside his jacket, he removed a billfold and flashed his credentials.

"Jack Fineman, FBI Special Agent in charge of this case. Thanks to you, the last twenty-four hours have been hell around here. Dead people everywhere, a terrorist plot to kill a CIA man, and you and Natalie making a last stand in a ghost town, blowing up everything in sight. If you're up to it, I'd like to ask you some questions before I catch up on my sleep."

Ron looked him in the eye. "Have they briefed you on who Natalie Martinez is?"

"Yes," he said with a nod. "The CIA shared their files with us. It's an amazing story. If the media ever gets ahold of it, they'll make a movie about her life. Kidnapped, sold into slavery, then rescued and freed to come home to America, where she exacts her revenge, or something else. There's a lot of discussion as to what her intentions were."

Fineman yawned again, then continued. "Mary Ann McDonald enlightened us on how you got involved in this. I understand you were present when we interviewed Sheik Abdul-Wadid. But that was a child slavery case, which got mixed up with this terrorist plot. It seems you and your friend Natalie are involved in both. Explain why you two fought it out in Christine with a band of mercenaries."

Ron spent the next hour explaining to Fineman how they shut down Teddy Bear's California operation. He omitted to mention the trip to Albuquerque and would warn Natalie to do likewise. Nobody needed to know about that.

"Did Natalie ever give you any reason to suspect she might be working with ISIS?" Fineman asked.

Ron gave a heavy sigh. "She was with them for five years, so I was suspicious of her motives when I first met her. But if she was working for them, why would they have tried to kill her, twice? She came back here to confront them."

"Where did she get all her weapons? That sniper rifle and the C-4 she had are military, not available to the public."

"She told me a rival of al-Tunisi supplied all of it to her to defend herself against Mustafa, who was working for al-Tunisi. Natalie disowned al-Tunisi when she got here, and the longer she stayed alive, the weaker he looked in Syria."

Doubt showed on Fineman's face. "The AK-47 makes sense, but a sniper rifle is for assassination, and the C-4 is to blow stuff up, not for protection. However, she destroyed a terrorist organization right in our backyard, which could cause a significant amount of embarrassment to certain individuals if publicized, so…"

He moved on to another question. "Did either of you ever meet Mohammad Mustafa?"

"No," said Ron.

"Let me show you some pictures. Tell me if you recognize anybody." He opened his briefcase and took out four photos, spreading them on the bed.

Ron studied them. "I've never seen any of these guys before. Are they part of the group that attacked us?"

Fineman nodded. "Yes, they were the survivors. We picked them up when they tried to flee to their vans at the trailhead. Nobody's talking, so we don't know if Mustafa is part of this group." He paused, acting like he wanted to add something else, but changed his mind.

Ron shrugged. "I know thirteen of them came in the vans, and a tall, thin guy gave the orders."

The agent's interest picked up. "How do you know this?"

"We had a spy camera at the trailhead and saw them arrive." An idea popped into his mind. "Natalie talked to the guy on the phone. If you can record those four guys talking, she might pick out which one is Mustafa."

"Worth a try," he said, getting up to leave. "For your information, we discovered nine bodies at Christine. We have four mercenaries in custody, so we have apprehended all of them."

A short time later, a nurse entered his room to check his vital signs and shared that Natalie's surgery went well. She was resting comfortably in a room nearby. Hearing she was okay was a relief to him. Ron needed to talk to her now. If Fineman doubted Natalie's intentions in returning to America, he would be back to interview her after obtaining recordings of the four prisoner's voices.

Ron waited for half an hour after Fineman left, just in case he forgot to ask something, and came back. He thought about visiting Natalie's room to chat. However, the nursing staff would notice that and mention it to the FBI, who would wonder what they discussed. Instead, he called the hospital operator from the phone on his bedside table and asked to be connected to Natalie's room. She answered after a few rings.

"How are you feeling?" he said.

"The doctors told me I lost a lot of blood. Had you not bandaged the wound tightly, I would have bled to death before the medics arrived. I owe you my life. "Thanks be to Allah that he brought you to me."

"You saved my life three times this month, so I'm glad I could reciprocate. Are you alone?"

"Yes."

Ron made himself more comfortable in his bed. He waited as a doctor walked past his open door, carrying a clipboard while talking to a nurse. "Okay, listen to me. Jack Fineman, an FBI agent, came to my room today and interviewed me. He'll be coming to see you next. He has questions about how you got your weapons. I told him you got them from Ahmed Nadeem to protect yourself, like you told me. He has doubts because the sniper rifle and the C-4 are not weapons intended for self-defense. Also, they're military, not available to civilians. Could you please provide him a good explanation for why Ahmed supplied these weapons? Fineman thinks ISIS gave them to you, which will raise questions about what your true motives were."

Natalie remained silent for a moment. "I'll do my best, Ron Jackson. It's a complicated situation. Allah will guide me."

"Listen to me. This is very serious," he said. "The FBI could detain you as a terrorist. Lock you up and throw away the key. Don't you want to apprehend the individuals in charge of Teddy Bear to complete your revenge? Didn't we pledge to do whatever it takes to make that happen? I can't do it without your help."

"That's true," she said. "My mission isn't yet complete. Allah has protected me so far. He sees the righteousness in what I do. I'll think of something to explain the weapons."

Ron felt relieved. "That's better—one more thing. You were never in Albuquerque. Don't even mention it. You drove here from California after the police arrested the Teddy Bear people. If the FBI connects you to Morales, they will charge you with murder."

CHAPTER 58

"Hi, Natalie," Fineman said. "I hope you're feeling better this morning. The doctor told me you'll be fully recovered once the wound heals. If you don't mind, I must ask about your involvement with Mustafa. This is a complicated case, and I want to understand everything correctly." She was resting in her hospital bed when Fineman, along with a woman he introduced as Special Agent Amy Haus, dropped by to speak with her.

Natalie's room was close to the nursing station, so she could hear the staff sharing gossip and jokes when her door was open. Outside her window, it was a sunny day, and the ground was dry after absorbing all the rain from two days ago. She watched a pigeon walk back and forth on the windowsill.

Natalie steeled herself for the interrogation. She felt weak and her leg throbbed. After talking the previous morning with Ron, she had spent the rest of the day rehearsing her story. She needed to get it right so they would believe her. For the next hour, she gave Fineman her statement, corroborating everything Ron had told him yesterday. Then, the questioning turned to her weapons.

"Natalie, I need to ask a few more questions," Fineman said. "Then I'll get out of your hair, and you can rest. There's some confusion concerning how you acquired your weapons. You didn't bring them to America, yet you had a good arsenal at Christine. Can you clarify that for me? How did you get the weapons?"

She told him how Ahmed Nadeem, a rival to al-Tunisi, supplied them to her for self-defense.

The FBI agent pursed his lips and scratched his head. "See, here's the problem with that. I don't know of anyone who would use a sniper rifle or C-4 explosives for self-defense. Those weapons are for things like assassinations. Was Nadeem expecting you to assassinate someone?"

She took a deep breath and launched into her explanation. "No, he gave me what he had in inventory. As a low-level courier, he did as he was told and delivered whatever was available. He knew nothing about the difference between a sniper rifle and an AK-47. He surprised me by giving me so many weapons, especially the C-4, which I didn't know how to use, but refusing them would have insulted him. In hindsight, it saved our lives at Christine."

Fineman leaned forward in his chair. "Who did he work for?"

"That's difficult to say. In Raqqa, men are loyal to their tribe, and some tribal chiefs didn't like al-Tunisi. They helped me escape to make him look weak, but I never knew who gave the order. They arranged it that way so that even under torture, I wouldn't be able to betray them. Nadeem told me only that the weapons were from my friends in Syria."

The FBI agents exchanged glances. Haus shrugged her shoulders. "Okay, let's move on," she said. "Did you ever speak to Mustafa?"

When she nodded yes, Haus removed a pocket mini cassette recorder from her briefcase and placed it on the end table next to her bed. "We are trying to identify if he is one of the four surviving terrorists. Listen to these four voices. Tell me if you recognize any of them."

Natalie eyed her, but said nothing.

She inserted the first microcassette into the player and pushed the play button. A man was talking to an interrogator. His voice was not familiar. The agent repeated the routine with two other cassettes and received identical responses. She inserted the last cassette and pushed play.

Natalie's face lit up. "That's him."

"Who is it?"

"Mohammad Mustafa."

Fineman shot a glance at Haus. "Thank you, Natalie. We suspected he was our man, but we had no proof until now. You and Ron have broken up a very dangerous terrorist cell within the government. You have our gratitude."

Without further explanation, the agents packed up the cassette player, shook hands with her, and left. She felt triumphant, knowing Mustafa and his men were caught. ISIS sent all their available men to attack her, and now they were dead or in jail. Allah had protected her once again. Despite her relief, she remembered Ron's statement, and her eyes flashed with determination. Their work wasn't finished; it was entering a new phase. She was looking forward to it.

CHAPTER 59

Several weeks later, the prisoner sat in a steel chair bolted to the floor in an interrogation room in the Federal Correctional Institution Cumberland. Cold metal handcuffs bit into his wrists. A chain looped from the cuffs to an eyebolt, which was welded to the table. He was tall, thin, and pale, like he had spent too little time in the sun lately. Encased in slippers, his feet were chained together. He wore an orange jumpsuit, the same one all prisoners wore. His back was ramrod straight, and there was an aura of arrogance on his face.

The room was stark, painted an off-white, now yellowish with age. It contained no windows. A flickering fluorescent light in the ceiling was the sole source of illumination. The room smelled of mold because of poor ventilation. A small camera near the corner of the ceiling observed the prisoner. Soundproofing made the room so quiet that the prisoner only heard his heartbeat. Outside, the afternoon sky grew dark, hinting at another storm that might deliver rain that night.

The door clicked open. A man entered and sat in the chair opposite the prisoner. Max Brodine was head of the Directorate of Operations, working out of CIA headquarters in Langley, Virginia. His job was to analyze intelligence acquired by human resources and try to make sense of it. He possessed a broad-shouldered frame, large hands, and a booming laugh that reverberated down the hall. His physique had served him well as a running back at the University of Alabama in the 90s. But today, his face was a mask of fury. The man sitting across from him was his second in command.

Max was working at the White House as a liaison to the President when an opening arose at the CIA. The President believed it would be an excellent fit for him, and no one argued with the President. Therefore, despite having no experience in that line of work, he accepted the job. Now, he wished he had turned it down.

"Winston Vanderhogen, or should I call you Mohammad Mustafa?" he began.

The prisoner grimaced but refused to look at him.

"How did it ever come to this, Winston? A blue-blooded family tree, three generations of wealthy, respected lawyers, and you, a graduate of Yale. Second in command of the Directorate, my most trusted deputy. What could possibly have motivated you to betray your country to ISIS?"

"Why do you care, Max?" he snarled.

"It's eating at me, son. Why would you want to join ISIS?"

Winston looked up, hatred burning in his eyes. "Betray my country? That's not what I was doing. I was saving it from you, you incompetent hick. For twenty-seven years, I've worked my ass off for the CIA. I *earned* my position. The only reason you got *your* job was because you were kissing the President's ass."

He pointed his handcuffed hands at Max. "I know more about covert operations than you ever will. Operations were strictly by the book until your arrival. Then, you introduced shortcuts. The intelligence we're getting now is terrible. Nobody in other countries trusts the CIA. Once, a job here brought great pride. Now, the best agents are retiring in droves. You've ruined the morale. Soon, something big will slip through the cracks, like the World Trade Center disaster. Americans will die, and the media will hold the CIA responsible. I didn't want that on my conscience."

He paused to regain his composure, his hands trembling. "With you gone, I could have rebuilt the CIA. With what I know about ISIS, I could have destroyed them. Had my plan succeeded, I'd have been as famous as Allen Dulles.

He glared at his interrogator. "I was just days away from executing the plan. You would have died a hero, the government would have blamed ISIS, and nobody would have guessed I was involved with it. During a crisis, the President would want an experienced person to lead the Directorate, which would have been me. But because that bitch Natalie Martinez didn't do her job, I'll never be able to save the CIA."

Max sat back in his chair, stunned by what he heard. "You're delusional, Winston. The most important thing in your life is stroking your ego, not saving your country. You're going to rot in prison for the rest of your life. Think about that. I hope your family can find the strength to forgive you."

Shaking his head in disgust, he got up and left, slamming the door behind him. Winston bowed his head and cried.

ABOUT THE AUTHOR

Michael Preston lives in Southern California with his wife Pat and their boxer Hope. When he is not writing, he enjoys making piles of sawdust out in his wood shop. He also loves a good game of poker with the members of his poker club. He and Pat have explored the world, observing how others live. A recent trip to Egypt to see the pyramids and temples was amazing.

This is the second book in a planned trilogy about the private investigator Ron Jackson. To be notified of new releases, please send a request to prestonauthor@gmail.com to be added to his email list. As a gift, he will send you a short story that he wrote. He will not share your email address, and you can unsubscribe anytime.

ALSO BY

Ron Jackson Series

Ticket To Paradise

Available through Amazon

https://www.amazon.com/Ticket-Paradise-Michael-Preston/d

p/1509243690